West Country Jubilee

West Country Jubilee

by

Irene Tester

SEDGMOOR

BOOKS

Miracle at Hunters Head

Jubilee

Number 49

British Library Cataloguing in Publication Data
A catalogue record for this book is available from the British
Library

ISBN 0-9544647-0-2

Typeset by Amolibros, Milverton, Somerset
This book production has been managed by Amolibros
Printed and bound by T J International Ltd, Padstow, Cornwall, UK

About the author

Irene Tester, nonagenarian, is an Oxford history graduate of 1931, and a member of the Society of Friends, at one time serving on their national Finance Committee. Her career was in teaching and then organising, at different levels, under the Somerset County Education Committee. She has been active in education, politics (Labour), and voluntary organisations. She was Mayor of Bridgwater in 1971/72 and now spends her retirement years in a small Devon village, where writing fiction, after a lifetime of preparing reports, has finally tempted her.

The Miracle

at Hunters Head

Chapter One

The gallant butcher's boy

Was it a miracle that saved Hunters Head? It would be more correct to say that it was a whole series of miracles.

It all started with the unlikely figure of Andy Hawkins, who was driving the butcher's van far too fast up the dilapidated approach to Hunters Head. Andy was not the butcher, nor indeed the first assistant. He was the second assistant, at a much lower level in the structure, having graduated from being 'the butcher's boy'. He was driving the van with a commendable efficiency, at a higher speed than anyone else would have contemplated up that awkward drive. He was bringing the usual weekend order, but on the Friday evening instead of the Saturday morning, because of the number of bed and breakfasts that August had produced. His mind was neither on the meat nor on the customer, nor indeed on the beauty of that particularly lovely stretch of a famed Devon village. He was reflecting on the charms of one particularly lovely Maisie, and whether she would or wouldn't meet him later on, and if she did meet him, would she... or would she not? His mind dwelt on a variety of pleasurable possibilities, and it was indeed little short of a miracle that he was able to halt the van as he swung round the corner and came upon the owner of Hunters Head, Uncle Silas, on his knees in the middle of the drive. He appeared to be investigating something, though praying might have been more appropriate.

The van screeched to a halt, a shoulder of pork sliding swiftly forward and precipitating itself against the back of the driver's seat.

'Mr Silas,' expostulated Andy, 'now didn't ee 'ear me coming?' What on earth, he thought to himself, could the old boy have been doing not to hear the van coming? He felt a wave of compassion for the 'poor old geezer' and got out to propel him into the passenger seat.

'I... er... I was... oh, it's Mr Hawkins,' quavered Mr Silas. 'Do you know, I believe I've been having a bit of trouble with my hearing aid, and it... ho, ho,' he chuckled happily away, quite oblivious to all that might have happened. 'It isn't aiding me to hear, not aiding me one little bit. And now,' he exclaimed, as he became aware that Andy was manoeuvring him politely into the van, 'well, now *you* are being my aid, and I believe going to take me right up to the door. Now I call that kind of you, Mr Hawkins, I really do. Proper kind, we say here in Devon. You're being a real aid.'

Uncle Silas had been an artist, a painter of country scenes. He might have explained that he thought his hearing aid had fallen out, and that, when he got down on his knees to investigate, he had been struck by the colouring of some of the stones. He might have, had he not switched his mind to enjoying being a passenger in the butcher's van. It was not for Uncle Silas to be wasting time offering explanations for something that was over, when there was some new experience to be enjoyed. Andy, still not knowing why Mr Silas had been down on his knees in the drive, drove the rest of the short distance warily. It wasn't so much that he had narrowly escaped running somebody down. At his speed of driving, in that sort of country, that was an everyday occurrence. He had a background of poaching, or 'exchanging' things, and buying and selling expeditiously, which had impressed on his youthful mind the importance of noticing anything unusual. So something was troubling his mind, he was not sure what, Uncle Silas was obviously unharmed. But something was wrong, he was sure something was wrong. What was it?

He suddenly realised. Yes, that was it. Why was Mr Silas's hearing aid not working? Why was Mr Silas, the well loved and well looked after, being allowed to have trouble with his vital hearing aid? His niece, Miss Jane, always turned him out for his daily adventures, such as walking to the village post office, or calling at The Hunters Arms, absolutely immaculate, brushed and cared for. And the hearing aid was as carefully tended. So something must have gone wrong. Clearly, something was amiss.

By this time they had reached the front steps. Miss Jane was at the door. Mr Silas sat on, smiling and unperturbed, while Andy was unconsciously getting ready to face up to whatever the mishap was that he was sure had occurred.

'I've brought Mr Silas along,' he explained, quite unnecessarily. 'I picked him up on the drive. Will you have the meat here? Or shall I take it straight down to the kitchen for you, while Mr Silas gets out?'

Miss Jane looked at him a bit vaguely and said that it was kind of him. Mr Silas still sat in the passenger seat, enjoying this unexpected position, and wondering why those stones had been that blue colour. Andy did not know whether to unload the meat, or to help Mr Silas out. It seemed to him too that Miss Jane was not giving him as much lead as might have been expected. She wasn't even answering his question properly, so he turned to his passenger.

'Mr Silas,' he said. Then he remembered that he must shout. 'Mr Silas, time to get out. You're home. Home. We're here.'

It would have been easier to yell get out, but one could hardly do that to the old gentleman. He turned to Miss Jane to explain about the hearing aid not working. He was embarrassed to find himself shouting at her too, as if she was deaf, and even more embarrassed when he saw tears come to her eyes as she started to turn away.

Whatever the mishap or disaster might turn out to be, the immediate steps were to get Mr Silas out and to unload the meat. Actually, a great deal sorted itself out in the next half-hour. There was the explanation... meat on a Friday night because of the extra holiday trade for the guesthouses during August... then the other four residents of Hunters Head being out, having gone to the Summer Stars Seaside Show at Ferrington. Then there was getting a warm drink for Mr Silas, and taking it upstairs for him because he'd decided he wanted to look up something about stones in that interesting book that Jane had brought him from the library van... and putting a light to the log fire in the hall, because of course Andy must sit down and have a hot drink too, after carrying all that meat down to the fridge... even if, thought Andy, it was not 'all that', considering there were six in the household. Finally, there they were, Mr Silas having pottered away up to his room at the top of the house, and Andy and Miss Jane sitting companionably together in front of the fire, while Andy started to explain. 'But you see, there he was, on his knees in the middle of the drive. He said he hadn't *heard* me, and I couldn't understand how you'd let his hearing aid run down.'

The next few minutes were earth-shattering, more for Miss Jane than for Andy. He had not intended his simple statement to be a reproof, but Miss Jane started to sob.

'Oh dear,' she wailed. 'Oh dear, it's all more than I can cope with. I don't know what on earth we're going to do. I... I *forgot* about the new battery for his hearing aid. It's... it's the expense. No, I don't mean the battery; I know that's free. It's... it's absolutely everything. I've only kept this place going at all by having in these other people.' Miss Jane waved a hand vaguely in the direction of the upstairs bedrooms, whose tenants were even now sitting happily in the stalls at the distant Ferrington Summer Stars Seaside Show. 'I've just managed so far. Only just. And now (sob) I had to give Ed the sack today. I just can't afford a gardener, even a part-time one. And I don't know how I shall manage without. Oh dear, I... I don't even know how I'm going to pay for the meat you have just brought. I don't know how I'm going to manage. Uncle has always lived at Hunters Head. It's his home.'

Miss Jane, having now broken some of life's strictest rules, that is, not to give up, and not to talk about money outside the family, fairly burst into tears. She put her head down and wept. Andy (who was known to his mates, and not without reason, as Randy Andy) promptly put his arm round her.

Perhaps it was living alone with a widowed mother, or having had to survive a large number of emergencies, but whatever it was, he thought he had learnt some of the facts about women that had escaped the notice of his mates. The basic facts were that women were unreasonable and that they liked crying. And if one enjoyed their company, as Andy assuredly did, one had to put up with these facts. He had learnt that it was unwise to argue or to explain; one just said 'there, there' respectfully or even tenderly, and sort of put an arm round them, again respectfully or even tenderly, until it was all over. He looked speculatively at Miss Jane, whom he had always thought of as... well, a lady, and years older than himself. She was properly taking on, crying away there, shoulders bent and heaving. He kept the protective arm round her. 'There, there,' he said, 'now don't take on so. There, there, dear me, dear me.'

'Dear me' was a good line. It changed easily into 'dear one' if the situation demanded it.

'There, there, Miss Jane. There, there, my dear.'

It doesn't sound very romantic, but to Miss Jane, aged thirty-five, practical, over-burdened, and just having acknowledged a secret that was wearing her down, the kindly words were manna. She blurted out that it was silly of her, she knew, but it was their home. She wept anew.

'There now.' Andy's voice was warm; his arm round her tightened, and with his free hand he produced a large handkerchief. 'Here, your little hanky's no good for this. You have mine.' He absent-mindedly whisked hers away, and pushed it into his pocket. 'What a time you have had.' In his own short life, there had been financial troubles in plenty, and he knew only too well what losing one's own home meant. Poor things. Could Jane (he had stopped thinking of her as Miss Jane) sell something or swap something? Most of the expedients though that had enabled the Hawkins family to survive were not, he realised, open to people like Jane. He continued to proffer sympathy.

'I'm sure we'll be able to think of something. Of course you want to stay here, of course you do.' There was a pause. Jane stopped weeping so bitterly. Andy went on. 'Why don't you have more people staying here? It's a big house, and you've got just the four?' Jane nodded, and they counted up together, as if she and Andy did not know the answer perfectly well already. 'Just the four,' he was saying. 'Mr and Mrs Hetherington, and Mrs Arbuthnot.' He stopped himself from saying *that* Mrs Arbuthnot, but they both knew what he meant. 'And the woman who's her companion, the one with the funny name.' Jane, who had stopped crying, added, 'Miss Spinks.'

Andy groped for words to express a very clear idea. 'Yes, Miss Spinks. You ought to have some of the... the more *refined* people here, say a bit like Miss Spinks, people who mightn't want to stay at The Hunters Arms.'

Jane was feeling brighter. All the same, she shook her head. She said, 'Hunters Head looks big, and it's lovely, but it isn't what you'd call a convenient house, and there

9

aren't any more proper rooms. There is only one bathroom... and you've no idea how long Caroline Hetherington takes in it. Not everyone wants to walk up and down stairs. And then the kitchen is one floor down from here, and we have to lug everything up to the dining room. It's because it was built on a slope.' Miss Jane, of course, was right. Hunters Head was a lovely house to look at, or to live in, but whoever built it had not been concerned with saving trouble for the domestic staff.

Andy very sensibly fell back on comfort and philosophy. 'Now look, my dear, you're a real example to everyone here. You'll manage somehow, I'd lay twenty to one. You always have done, and you always will. You're a wonder.'

Jane stopped sniffing. It was a comfort to have the problem acknowledged. Andy's philosophy of 'there, there' was quite a help. So too were his expressions of admiration.

They sat on, Jane leaning back very comfortably against Andy's stalwart form. Andy had by now accustomed himself to the new situation, and found that he was beginning to enjoy it. Jane was really rather attractive. It seemed to him that a very pleasant dalliance, and in the warm too, was increasingly possible. The car was not due back from Ferrington yet, and nothing was likely to arouse Mr Silas from his investigation of why the stones were blue. The prospect was much more inviting than hanging round a windy square waiting for a problematic Maisie.

To his lasting credit, and indeed his immediate surprise, he found himself getting up and saying, 'Well, Miss Jane, I must be off now. Going to meet Maisie. Look, there's one thing I can do for you.' He went over to the table, took the bill, and receipted it. 'There you are. A present from the butcher's boy. To wish you the very best of luck.'

He seized her hand, kissed it, and swaggered out. It was a consciously gallant and picturesque exit.

So there were two miracles already: the saving of Uncle Silas, and the paying of Miss Jane's butcher's bill. Or were the miracles really Andy's generous forbearance from an available pleasure, or the awakening of a certain undefined hopefulness in Jane?

Chapter Two

That morning

Andy departed, and didn't get home till very very late. The four people who had been to the summer show duly returned, had their evening drinks and retired contentedly to their beds, unaware that any miracle had taken place. Uncle Silas slept well, as usual. Jane slept better than she had been doing of late.

Of all, it was Andy who woke first. This was in response to a spirited summons from his mother. 'Andy! Andy! Get up. It's Saturday and you've got an extra round to do.'

Andy jumped out of bed, sniffed appreciatively at the smell of frying bacon (the butcher's best), and cantered down the stairs. My, what a fine day. How happy his mother looked. Probably glad to have bacon to fry. He too was in a happy mood, and kissed his mother before sitting down, which made her wonder if something was up. Theirs was not a very elegant cottage, but Andy could understand how Miss Jane felt about keeping on Hunters Head. It was home to her, even if you wouldn't want a great place like that yourself. That bacon smelt good, and there would be steak for tea.

'Ma,' said Andy. 'They're pretty hard-up at Hunters Head. I was wondering – do you think they could do with having more people there, more paying guests like?'

Mrs Hawkins had 'done a day' occasionally at Hunters Head, and she thought of the layout. There were the top two, north-facing rooms, where Uncle had once had his studio, and where Jane and he now slept; the first floor (south-facing) had the two master bedrooms, each with a small dressing room, one of which was now a bathroom, and this floor was the one occupied by the four 'guests'. The *small* dressing room was of course the companion's. Then dining rooms and a lovely hall on the ground floor, and down again to the kitchen quarters, with a kitchen and more oddments.

Ma replied much as Jane had. The place was not exactly convenient. And in any case they did not want their *home* turned into a guesthouse.

Andy said that this was what Maisie had said when he asked her. This was a piece of information that Ma registered with interest. If Andy was talking this seriously to Maisie? Well, she was a lot better than some of the floosies he'd been out with.

Andy dismissed any further thoughts about Hunters Head; he had done what he could, and was now looking forward to the evening with Maisie.

At Hunters Head, Uncle Silas was waking up and looking out of the window at what he could see of his silver birch waving in the light morning breeze. Actually it was not his silver birch, as it was the other side of the wall separating Hunters Head from the castle. Therefore it belonged to Lord Pomeroy. But Uncle always thought of it as his. What a nice month September is, he thought. It *was* September, wasn't it? And should he get up and have a little walk outside or should he wait for his early morning cup of tea? Unable to decide which pleasant prospect to go for, he went to sleep again.

Jane had slept excellently. Acknowledging her problem had helped her, as acknowledging the existence of a problem usually does. Just for a minute, on this lovely August morning, with the sun shining, she felt mysteriously secure. Perhaps prayers had been answered and things were going to be all right. Enveloped in this comforting thought, it took her a little while to become aware that just at the minute something was not all right. There were sounds of alarm and distress where there should not have been. In fact, at Hunters Head something was up.

'Oh dear,' she muttered, 'oh… get my dressing gown… on to the landing… whatever can have happened?'

By the time she had got down to the Hetheringtons' bedroom on the first floor, it seemed that quite a crowd was there. There was poor Mr Hetherington lying on the floor, and his wife ('silly young Caroline' in Jane's mind) on the verge of hysterics, while the sense of crowding came from the unexpected presence of 'that Mrs Arbuthnot', her figure enhanced by the quilted scarlet dressing gown she was wearing. These indeed were the ones whose presence paid to keep Hunters Head afloat. Of all of them, Mrs Arbuthnot was the largest, the most determined, the most thoroughly self-centred, and the one with the loudest voice.

The loudest voice was taking charge.

'It's all right. Poor Mr Leslie has just had a fall, hasn't he?'

Mr Leslie coughed agreement.

'Caroline, stop making that noise, and give me an eiderdown and a pillow. Miss Jane, put that pillow under his head. I can't bend down. Feeling better, Mr Leslie?' This seemed to be a command rather than a question. 'A hot water bottle now, and a nice warm drink.'

Jane headed thankfully for the kitchen, obeying the unspoken command to take Caroline too. What an awakening. Everything had seemed so nice last night, when everyone returned and went to bed. And now. The best bedrooms and the good payers. Jane put such thoughts away and hurried on to the kitchen. A castle cat obligingly moved off the stove.

Jane filled the hot water bottle, and produced the first cup of tea, then took up both to the Hetheringtons' room, on the first floor. The room already looked... well, more orderly somehow. Ah yes! the bedside table ready, the bed tidied.

'Miss Jane, my dear, you'll have to give him his drink.' The loud voice continued, 'It's all right, he just had a fall. And now I think we'll have a cup of tea too.' Jane obediently went down again to the kitchen, where Caroline was sitting nursing the cat... not unconscious of what a pretty picture they made.

More cups of tea. One for Caroline. Two to take up for Jane and Mrs Arbuthnot. The two women drank in unexpected camaraderie, Jane sitting in the best chair. Mrs Arbuthnot was sitting on the bed, clearly contemplating what was to be done next; it was what the silent films, beloved of Uncle Silas, would have entitled 'The Next Step'.

There was a deprecating cough from Mr Leslie. 'Excuse me, but I don't think Caroline likes anyone sitting in her chair.' Jane sprang up guiltily; though it did occur to her that Caroline might have been more likely to object to Mrs Arbuthnot's sitting on the connubial bed.

'I think we shall send for the doctor,' said the commanding voice, 'and someone to help lift Mr Leslie.' This reminded Jane that Ed had been given notice, and no one else could be expected. Would Caroline help? The voice said no, but perhaps Miss Jane?

Mr Leslie had now become fully aware that there were women in his bedroom. He corrected himself. Ladies, properly covered, and everything absolutely in order. He himself had no special objection to two such pre-eminently nice women – ladies – but he felt that Caroline might not like it. And if they intended staying, as it appeared that they did, until he could be got up off the floor, then he must get up off the floor. He stirred, and found to his surprise that he could move quite easily.

'What about your legs?' questioned the commanding voice. 'Miss Jane, turn back the eiderdown so that we can have a look.'

To his great embarrassment he had to demonstrate, by wagging each leg in turn, that they were not broken. Then, with a helpful arm from that Miss Jane (funny her being in his bedroom) he wavered up and back into bed. He was glad to promise Mrs Arbuthnot that he would stay there, certainly till his breakfast was brought up, not that he felt he wanted much. Within a couple of minutes, he was asleep.

'Mrs Arbuthnot,' squeaked Jane, 'whatever happened?'

'Well, he fell out of bed,' boomed Mrs Arbuthnot in a sort of muffled roar. 'Dreaming, probably. Perhaps he wanted to get away from that Caroline. Ha, ha.'

Jane looked at Mrs Arbuthnot, seen in a slightly different light from her usual staid propriety.

'He'll be all right now,' went on Mrs Arbuthnot. 'Presently a little warm bread and milk. Old-fashioned, aren't we? And a glass of port is very stimulating.'

Jane felt doubts about both, but was not going to argue with one so indubitably in charge of the situation. 'And your breakfast?' she asked, to which she received the quite devastating answer that 'the rest of us', that was Mrs Arbuthnot, and Mrs Arbuthnot's companion, and Caroline, and presumably Uncle Silas, would come down to breakfast, 'to save carrying up the trays'. This was the first intimation that anyone had had that Mrs Arbuthnot knew that trays did not just levitate up and down stairs.

Jane withdrew to dress, slipping quickly upstairs. It was, she had realised, the kind of morning for slipping quickly from one place to another. She must slip downstairs again, then up again, tea for Uncle, get dressed, slip down again to the kitchen, get breakfast. But on the way she stopped and looked out towards the moor. A miracle of a morning. The morning sun lighting up a golden Hound Tor, throwing the valley into accentuated darkness.

And there had been miracles inside too. The miracle

of Mrs Arbuthnot appearing as ministering angel. And the even greater miracle that she could make an even slightly ribald joke.

Jane went on up and got dressed.

Chapter Three

Breakfast below stairs

The inhabitants of Hunters Head, with the exception of the stricken Mr Leslie Hetherington, assembled for their breakfast in the kitchen. This was a room hitherto unknown to Mrs Arbuthnot, to young Caroline and to Miss Spinks. It was Miss Spinks who held the office of companion to Mrs Arbuthnot, and one thought of her, if one thought of her at all, as Mrs Arbuthnot's companion. She was one who'd be described as spare rather than thin. She wore clothes, good clothes, of indeterminate hue, which had lasted well and gave promise of going on lasting for a long time yet. The slight tinge of pink in her cheeks that morning surprised Jane.

Caroline had gracefully accepted banishment from her room when it had been suggested that she might find it difficult to look after an ailing husband. 'Oooh,' she had averred, 'I simply can't bear illness. You see, I'm much too sensitive, and I just faint if I see blood.' Jane omitted to say that whatever the matter was with Mr Leslie, at least he was not bleeding. Nor had she noticed that Caroline was particularly sensitive.

Mrs Arbuthnot automatically took charge. 'Caroline, go and sit down. And shoo that cat out.' The last instruction was unnecessary, the castle cat having taken one look at Mrs Arbuthnot and left of its own accord. 'Mr Silas, you will sit here.' As Mr Silas had not yet put on his hearing aid, this had to be repeated. 'Mr Silas, here please. And Miss Spinks, kindly help Miss Jane to pass over that fried bacon.' Jane's household took its unaccustomed seats. It was not only the seats that were unaccustomed, but also what they had for breakfast. Up till then, there had been trays and special menus for all. One had a lightly boiled egg (the white just set, please, but I don't like it runny), and some liked scrambled egg. Most had drunk tea, but the Hetheringtons had always had coffee – black for Caroline, and white, with *hot* but not boiling milk for Mr Leslie. Expensive cereals. The toast had had to be different for each, and Uncle Silas always had porridge, a little bit thicker when the first frosts came. This day, cowed by Mrs Arbuthnot, they all ate fried bread and the butcher's second-best bacon, and drank tea. There was little conversation. What there was, was mostly of the 'would you please pass the butter?' kind of remark, as they unhappily manoeuvred their way round the elbows of unaccustomed neighbours, and scraped their chair legs as they leant forward to reach for mustard or marmalade.

Presently Mrs Arbuthnot remarked that as soon as breakfast was over (those who had thought of asking for a second cup hastily decided otherwise), she would be telephoning to Dr Lazenby. 'No, Miss Jane, even if it is a little early yet, I think it is necessary. Please get me the number.'

Miss Jane felt that it was too early to phone, but dutifully obeyed. She was becoming convinced that if she had not already had a telephone in the kitchen, one would have mysteriously appeared there for Mrs Arbuthnot. All the same, it was early. She dialled, and prepared to speak a little apologetically.

'Thank you, Miss Jane,' said Mrs Arbuthnot, taking the phone from her. 'Is that Dr Lazenby? Yes, thank *you*. I am now quite aware that it is not Dr Lazenby speaking. I assume that you're answering from his surgery or from his bedroom, and that I am therefore addressing Mrs Lazenby.' (Oh dear, thought Jane.) 'Now, Mrs Lazenby, if you will please attend, this is an important message for your husband. This is Mrs Arbuthnot of Hunters Head speaking, and I want Dr Lazenby here at once... at once. No, it is not for me. I am perfectly well. I am speaking on behalf of Miss Marner, and we have a serious accident on our hands. It is Mr Leslie Hetherington. Yes please, at once.'

She replaced the phone and turned pleasantly to Jane. 'There you are, Miss Jane. Dr Lazenby will soon be here. He's coming straightaway.'

Mr Silas looked round and smiled on everyone. As he had only just switched on his hearing aid, he had not heard the original explanation of why they were all having breakfast together in the kitchen. Life was indeed full of pleasant surprises. 'What a lovely morning,' he was saying, 'and how happy we all are.'

Jane reflected that perhaps Uncle's sight was beginning to go as well as his hearing.

'Jane, my dear,' he carolled on. 'You're looking... rosier I think than of late. Isn't she, Mrs Arbuthnot?'

Mrs Arbuthnot somewhat icily remarked that it was not Miss Jane's state of health but Mr Leslie's that was of concern to them.

Mr Hetherington not well? Mr Silas was sorry, very sorry, if it appeared that Mr Hetherington was not well. 'And on such a beautiful morning, what a pity. Jane dear, ought we not to do something, call in the doctor, or take his temperature, or something, if Mr Hetherington isn't well?'

The resulting explanations, and the clearing up of the breakfast things, and indeed the dispersal of the guests from the kitchen, took the short time that elapsed before Dr Lazenby's car could be heard coming up the drive.

Mrs Arbuthnot puffed her way up the flight of stairs that connected the kitchen to the hall, in time to confront Dr Lazenby as he entered. Jane was thinking that the last time he had been summoned, he had diagnosed indigestion, and she couldn't dismiss the uncharitable hope that Mr Leslie would turn out to be at least a little bit ill. Mrs Arbuthnot took over.

'I will go with Dr Lazenby, Miss Jane. I think I have had more experience of nursing the sick than you have. Good morning, Dr Lazenby.'

The doctor's eye rested professionally on Mrs Arbuthnot's bulky figure. 'Gently now. You've been hurrying. You must take it gently if you're going upstairs.' He looked sternly at her. 'All right. You can come up the next flight too, but gently. You must count up to five, and wait, for each step. See... one, two, three, four, five, and *wait*. One more, and two, and three, and four, and five, then wait, and then one....'

In fact, it was quite a merry little party (one-two-three-four-five and wait, one-two...) that reached the first floor. Jane, now firmly cast as junior assistant to Mrs Arbuthnot, went up behind them. She hesitated about going into the bedroom. She felt she must wait outside until summoned. She noticed that Caroline was showing no inclination to be involved.

The consultation went on inside the bedroom, and presently the door opened slightly. She could hear the doctor's voice. 'Well,' he was saying to Mrs Arbuthnot, 'you seem to understand the situation. Were you at one time a nurse?'

No, not exactly,' came the reply, 'but I did have a very considerable experience with the late Mr Arbuthnot, who was ill for a number of years, before mercifully he was taken.'

For a moment Jane wondered where the last Mr Arbuthnot had been taken to, and whether he might not have been glad, just a little bit glad, to escape from his masterful wife. She put the uncharitable thought away from her. Why was she having so many uncharitable thoughts this morning? It must have been the worry. And her mind went back to how to go on managing at Hunters Head. How not to let Uncle know that the princely amount he had been giving her ('and an extra ten shillings for yourself, Janey,' for he still thought in terms of 'old' money) was now utterly inadequate. How to manage the grounds of Hunters Head now that she had had to dismiss Ed. How to keep going for the demanding Mrs Arbuthnot and the ladylike Miss Spinks, who also had very little money. And that clever Mr Leslie and his silly young wife. All of them so much more settled and happy since they had come to live at Hunters Head. It had seemed like a miracle when Uncle had for some unaccountable reason accepted 'guests, Janey'. What had then been a miraculous amount of money was now miraculously small. And no central heating. Wood to be cut and brought in. Cheap when one had had the labour. Vegetables from the garden... cheap again, if one could pay for a gardener. Having guests had been hard work but it had enabled Jane and Uncle to remain in this beautiful, beloved home. And now, as a last straw, someone to be nursed. Or worse was the chill thought that perhaps Mr Hetherington and his money would have to go away, and one could hardly put anyone else in with Caroline.

A cheerful Mrs Arbuthnot emerged from the Hetheringtons' bedroom. 'It's going to be quite all right, Miss Jane. Doctor says complete bed rest for a couple of days, and on Monday he'll send us Mrs Miller on the district. I shall see to the room now, and Miss Jane will see you out, Dr Lazenby. Thank you for coming so quickly. Oh... and Miss Jane, perhaps you will pop on down to the kitchen then and prepare me a little light soup for Mr Leslie. Goodbye, Dr Lazenby. Yes, we shall be able to manage over the weekend, quite well.'

Miss Jane accompanied a somewhat amused Dr Lazenby down to the hall. At least it had been something more serious than indigestion if Mr Hetherington was to stay in bed for two days. Dr Lazenby paused a moment to have a few words. 'Nothing much to worry about. Could have been much worse, but he'll need looking after now. You'll find that Mrs Arbuthnot's going to be a tower of strength to you. You'll have to keep an eye on her though... she's much too stout, and she's not as young as she was when she looked after Mr Arbuthnot... as she said, before he was taken.'

Dr Lazenby grinned and departed. Miss Jane sped down to soup-making in the kitchen, unsure whether it was a miracle or a catastrophe that she was witnessing. Or both?

She found herself, as so often, totting up in terms of cash. The tea had been cheaper than coffee and milk, but bacon was dearer than the eggs would have been. The bread though cost less than cereals. There had been less electricity used, and it had been much less trouble for her for everyone to have breakfast in the kitchen rather than in three different bedrooms. Altogether, something had been saved. She felt apologetic about grudging any of them anything, but there just wasn't the money. She noticed that someone had washed up the breakfast things and attributed this action to the worthy Miss Spinks.

According to Jane's accounting, a little money had been saved. She did not take much notice of what might in the long run prove more important... that others in the house might be prepared to do more. As Andy would have said, women are rather like that, a bit short on taking a long view of things.

Chapter Four

Comrade Arbuthnot

The household started to slip into its new routine, and the new pattern worked surprisingly well. All breakfasts, following that fateful morning, were served in the kitchen 'to save trays'. Midday dinner was still in the dining room, and then everyone helped in carrying things up and back to the kitchen 'to save Miss Jane'. Everyone helped, at least everyone but Uncle, who usually forgot about it until tea time. Someone, and presumably this *was* Uncle Silas, as it could hardly have been anyone else, daily brought in a selection from the surprisingly large amount of vegetables that Ed had got ready before he left. What a pity Ed had had to be dispensed with; he had done even more than Miss Jane had realised. Jane herself, of course, continued to do a large amount of cleaning and cooking, without anyone noticing it as in any way remarkable.

The four paying guests were still on the first floor; what had once been a dressing room was now the one and only bathroom, so often occupied for so long by Caroline, not that it seemed to matter much to anyone else. A professional proprietor of a guesthouse could have told them that the whole place was really quite unsuitable for guests anyway, what with not enough bathrooms and too many stairs, and too much space wasted, but Miss Jane had to make do with what she had. She had never intended to run a guesthouse anyway. Mrs Arbuthnot was spending more time looking after Mr Hetherington than his own wife did. Mr Leslie was, if not better, then at least 'a lot better'. Funny, the English language, thought Jane, why was it that someone who was 'a lot better' was not as well as someone who was 'better'? The fact that Mr Leslie was at least 'a lot better' was in no small measure due to the ministrations of Mrs Arbuthnot, who toiled up and down the stairs carrying nourishing drinks and jigsaw puzzles, while young Caroline spent happy hours in front of the television set in the dining room, exclaiming how wonderful everybody was. It was also discovered that it was Caroline who had washed up on 'that morning'. She had shared flats long enough, in what appeared to have been a previous existence, to have learnt some of the simpler arts of running a house, and certainly the quickest way of doing anything herself when all else had failed.

The household tended to date things as having happened before or after 'that morning', meaning the occasion of Mr Leslie's sudden illness. About a fortnight or so after 'that morning' Miss Jane was in the kitchen getting ready the mid-morning drink, as well of course as having an eye on the pastry, the potatoes and the preparations for a cheese soufflé.

'Elevenses,' she called out, and set off up the stairs from the kitchen with the tray. She had counted everyone up. Miss Spinks was out; it was quite remarkable how often she was out these days. She never used to be. And if one asked her where she had been, she never seemed to have much to tell. 'Just a stroll through the castle grounds,' she would say. Uncle Silas was out – nothing unusual in that, it was Thursday – so he would have gone to the post office and would now be in the village talking to someone. Caroline, to judge from the reverberations of the eleven a.m. programme, was in the dining room. Miss Jane took the drinks up to the hall, one black coffee (for Caroline), two white coffees (for herself and Mrs Arbuthnot), and Mr Leslie's special hot chocolate ('so much more nourishing for a convalescent, but only use *half* milk', had been the order). Mrs Arbuthnot took the tray, with her own coffee and Mr Leslie's hot chocolate, and made for the stairs.

Things started to happen unexpectedly at Hunters Head after 'that morning'. Mrs Arbuthnot now slipped on the bottom step. Jane was just in time to make what would have been a creditable rugby tackle and save the tray, the drinks, and indeed Mrs Arbuthnot. She flung her arm round the massive figure. It was then that the next miracle occurred. Quite suddenly, she felt a wave of affection for that unlovely woman. Up till then, she had viewed Mrs Arbuthnot as a determined and upright woman, one to attract respect, trepidation and even admiration, but hardly affection. Suddenly Miss Jane saw her as someone else who had troubles. For Mrs Arbuthnot too, Hunters Head had become a haven, and perhaps she too was realising that the present situation was precarious. Jane longed to comfort this unhappy figure.

'Now, Mrs Arbuthnot,' she said, 'you sit down and have your coffee here in the hall. I'll slip up with Mr Leslie's.' It seemed to Jane that the situation was oddly like a previous one, and she grinned at the memory of herself sobbing in the arms of the butcher's boy. Dear Andy. And now here was a weary Mrs Arbuthnot, also worrying, and she, Jane, must do the comforting. Mrs Arbuthnot was fast ceasing to be the dragon who demanded the best rooms in the house. She was, after all, a managing sort of woman, but she was really concerned about Mr Leslie, whom she judged to be so poorly looked after by a frivolous young wife.

Jane took up Mr Leslie's hot chocolate, and came back to have her own drink. She looked at Mrs Arbuthnot with a new friendliness. 'You've been having a time. You know, Mrs Arbuthnot, although you and Dr Lazenby make a joke of these stairs, you oughtn't really to keep going up and down like you have been doing.'

At the mention of Dr Lazenby, Mrs Arbuthnot gave a little smile. 'Oh yes, one-two-three-four-five and wait. You know, Miss Jane, he reminds me of the old country doctor who was supposed to have told his patient to put a piece of wood twelve inches high, the number of the apostles, to keep his window open at night. And what he really meant was that the man was to *have* the window open at night.'

Jane too smiled. 'Yes,' she said, 'only I always heard that it was *eleven* inches, after the *good* apostles. I suppose you'd have to make do with two inches in our village, for the vicar and the Methodist minister.'

'Well, yes, or *three* inches if you count Father Kennedy, because quite a lot go to the Catholic church in Yeohampton.'

'Or *four* if you count the Salvation Army, where the Hawkinses used to go.'

The two women continued to drink their coffee together in a very amicable silence.

'Pretty flowers,' remarked Mrs Arbuthnot, looking at a vase of autumn flowers and grasses. Jane looked at them too, but in some surprise, not having put them there herself. Miracles might happen, but she did not believe that flowers picked themselves and came indoors and popped into a suitable vase, which they had providentially filled with water. It must have been Uncle.

Mrs Arbuthnot put down her cup and spoke with sudden determination. 'Miss Jane, I'm finding the stairs a difficulty, I must admit. And Mr Leslie is going to need waiting on for some time now. I've been thinking... do you think it would be better if he and Caroline were down on the ground floor? We have most of our meals in the kitchen now, and we don't really use the dining room. It would save carrying things up to the second floor, trays and cups and things for Mr Leslie.'

Jane agreed. She herself had often juggled the rooms round in her own mind, though for a different reason. She had been trying to fit in one more, or even two extra guests. Mrs Arbuthnot, relaxing in the warmth of being looked on as a companion-in-arms instead of a dragon, was working out the possibilities and was well on the way to altering the household's sleeping arrangements. 'Mr Leslie and their big bed in the dining room, with his desk and all his papers and things, and Caroline's music (if you can call it that) and tapes and so on in the little 'annexe'. You know, I think he'd be better on his own.' This was a polite euphemism for 'without Caroline', and Jane was very far from agreeing.

With great temerity, Jane brought out a further idea. The suggestions made so far were all right, but Mrs Arbuthnot too ought not to be using the stairs too much. And if *she* could have her bedroom on the ground floor, it would be better still. There was the little room, once a breakfast-room, and now supposed to be Jane's 'study'. Not that Jane now had time to study anything but the cost of next day's dinner. Perhaps Mrs Arbuthnot could temporarily manage with that? Though of course it was not as nice as the room she was accustomed to. Mrs Arbuthnot agreed. She had actually thought of this herself, and only an unaccustomed reserve had held her back from mentioning it outright.

The same things were occurring to the two women as they mentally reviewed the available accommodation. Hunters Head had been built at times when owners had money, and domestic servants were legion. The domestic staff had lived downstairs, in what was now Miss Jane's kitchen and in all the odd pantries, sculleries, conservatories, et ceteras that led off the kitchen and merged into potting sheds and the garden. At the top of the stairs that led from the kitchen up to the hall had been the sacred green baize door, now part of a cloakroom wall in the village hall, then effectively keeping all sound of the 'downstairs' from the ears of the 'family', who presumably were not robust enough to stand up to the sounds of daily life below.

31

Miss Jane's study had once been 'the breakfast-room'. And if everyone was now going to have meals in the kitchen, and the only thing Jane had time to study was how to make ends meet, then it would do very nicely for Mrs Arbuthnot 'to save the stairs'. Jane felt a bit sorry that one had to do so much to save something, the money or the expense or the trays or now the stairs, but it would certainly be sensible to have three of the household all on the ground floor. She had never remotely envisaged that Mrs Arbuthnot would agree to this. Both women then gave a sudden thought to Miss Spinks.

'It will be no problem for my companion to have her room still on the first floor,' said Mrs Arbuthnot. 'Miss Spinks is a very healthy person and has no trouble with her legs.'

So that was Miss Spinks settled. At least her legs did not have to be saved. She would have the choice of the three rooms on the first floor. If she had not been Miss Spinks, one might have imagined her spreading her things out, but being Miss Spinks, one knew that she would modestly keep her own little room. That left Miss Jane and Uncle Silas with bedrooms up on the second floor, where one-time domestics had slept, when they had scurried past the family rooms at the end of the day up to the 'attics'. Probably they had been too tired to admire the magnificent views that obtained, which was indeed one reason for Uncle remaining up there. Uncle had had his studio there, in a cold well lit north-facing room. They had even gone to the extravagance of having a WC installed as well as a sink. Jane knew that Uncle now used his studio as little as she used her so-called study. It was a good thought that he had retained his appreciation of beauty even if he no longer painted it.

So that was that. Everything had now been settled, in theory. It only remained to carry it out in practice. Men at this stage would have repaired to The Hunters Arms to share a convivial pint. Jane did the nearest equivalent, and went and fetched second cups of coffee, for herself and her fellow-conspirator.

Caroline, thought Mrs Arbuthnot, might enjoy making the 'annexe' into a... 'a sort of *boudoir*... with that pretty dressing table. And Mr Hetherington's things could go... there, or no... perhaps in that other corner'. Jane was convinced that Caroline would agree to anything that provided her with television and a place for her records and her tapes and so on. And then her mind turned to the vase of flowers. Was it Uncle who had brought them in? She thought of Andy, and smiled. Help from Andy would have been more likely to take the form of half a pound of sausages. Then... yes, probably Uncle Silas. Uncle had such unexpected ideas about helping, and this might be one of the ones that had worked. She pictured him bringing them in as a surprise for her, and mousing about downstairs in one of the old conservatories and finding this particular vase. Lucky he had found one without knocking the rest over. On second thoughts, perhaps he *had* knocked the rest over, and it was just that she hadn't had time to go down there.

'He might have done,' she said aloud and chuckled. Mrs Arbuthnot, not a mind reader at the best of times, looked at Miss Jane in some surprise. 'Who, dear? Might have done what?'

The surprise was now Miss Jane's, at being called 'dear' by Mrs Arbuthnot. She caught her hand impulsively and bent over and kissed her. The alliance was complete.

Chapter Five

Vacating the first floor

A kind of Indian summer ensued at Hunters Head. The idea of the proposed move was expounded to all concerned, and all concerned were happy to concur. Alterations from the original plan had to be made of course, and Jane's idea of managing the move unaided was wildly out and in the end she had to have paid help. But all the same, it seemed to usher in a brief period of euphoria. Andy would probably have explained it by pointing out that another thing about women was that they positively enjoyed moving the furniture about; he remembered how pleased his mother had always been when she had succeeded in rearranging the two armchairs, settee and a table, which was at one time all that they had. (His mother, being older and more experienced than Andy, would probably have restrained herself from pointing out that the only thing that prevented Andy from acting in precisely the same way with the inside of the van was that it did not belong to him.) Perhaps Jane was also enjoying having an ally on this domestic occasion. Certainly it brought in a pleasant period for all concerned, even if it would have been more realistic to realise that the new arrangement of people/rooms was not going to make much long-term financial difference.

Uncle withdrew from participating in moving things. He had had such a pleasant walk round the village that morning, and was now ready to go up to his room for a read and perhaps a snooze. Mr Hetherington obviously could not help. That left the women. Mrs Arbuthnot made a good chief, but the Indians were a bit thin on the ground. Miss Spinks carried Mrs Arbuthnot's things from the big bedroom where they were to the little ex-breakfast-room, carrying each article with a dedicated steadiness that somehow reminded Miss Jane of a bygone cartoon of a procession of people extinguishing a fire with water carried in teacups; time was not going to matter. Caroline carried with great speed and a belief that a good shove helps. It was true that on the whole it was 'things' that had to be carried, for some of the furniture belonged in the rooms rather than to the occupiers. At a crucial stage in the proceedings, Jane was called to a lengthy conversation on the telephone. It started with asking her if she could possibly do the flowers for the church next week instead of the week after, and it ended with the suggestion that if she was moving furniture, the best firm to do it was that very good but expensive firm in Roxton. 'It's worth it, my dear,' she was assured. When she disengaged herself, she found that her troops (or perhaps Mrs Arbuthnot's troops) were mutinying about beds. Two single beds, large, had been right for Mrs Arbuthnot and Miss Spinks and could be moved, but for Caroline and Mr Hetherington the double bed from the first floor must come down. There was also Mr Hetherington's own desk, which, even with its drawers out, looked larger than Jane had remembered. She admitted defeat. Paid help must be produced.

It was not finding help in the village that was going to be the problem, merely the paying for it. There were strong middle-aged women who could be glad of a little extra money (except the ones who had gone on the mid-week bus to Yeohampton). Some families had student sons whose holiday jobs had ended early. Andy could always find someone ready to do a job in exchange for ready money.

She phoned the grocer first. She explained the situation. His son Michael she knew had not yet gone back to university. She wondered if he would be free to do a few hours' work. Could he come and help move furniture?

Yes, certainly, Miss Jane. Michael was out on the round but he would soon have finished, and would then come up to Hunters Head. He would be glad of an extra job, for everything cost so much these days. Miss Jane could not have agreed more.

Michael duly arrived. He was an amiable young man and also, perhaps more important, he was strong. He moved furniture willingly and efficiently. He was polite to the older women. He complimented Miss Jane on 'real' coffee. He most affably assisted Mr Hetherington down to the ground floor, and expressed a genuine admiration for some of his books. He accepted the fee from Miss Jane and gave her back the pound, which he said was 'over the rate'.

'I say, thanks very much,' he said. 'Jolly nice of you. I'd like to come and give you a hand in the garden – I see you need it with a big garden like this – but I've got to get down to some work now. I'll be back at university by the end of the month, and there won't be much time in the Christmas vac to do any swatting. Three of us are planning to do Tripoli then; it's all right there out of season, though it's not much there in the summer.'

To Miss Jane, Torquay would have been a dazzling prospect. Not in fact that Michael was any more likely to be in Tripoli than say Twickenham or Texas at Christmas. But what it was to be young and carefree. To think that one might go to Tripoli, 'all right out of season of course', and probably follow that up with Sumatra in the summer. Oh well. Jane reflected that her wildest dreams were limited to finding a volunteer gardener, or the money to employ Ed again.

She accompanied Michael to the front door and waved him a cheery goodbye. Then she turned to producing for everyone a very belated cup of tea, and some of those 'nice crunchy biscuits, Miss Jane... I know I ought not to as I'm slimming.'

Everyone, surprisingly, seemed pleased with the move round. Mrs Arbuthnot was happy in the new room. The double bed was in the former dining room, and this turned out to be where Mr Hetherington would also have his desk and his papers, while Caroline fluttered round in the smaller annexe and cooed ecstatically over the wallpaper. 'Oooh... what pretty paper... oooh, those dear little rosebuds... isn't it all *sweet*?'

The point of the exercise actually had not been just to

give Caroline pretty wallpaper, but to have more people sleeping on the ground floor to save carrying trays upstairs. Miss Jane noted that, conversationally speaking, among the things now being saved were Mrs Arbuthnot's legs. The move had been a good one. Mrs Arbuthnot mellowed. The Hetheringtons' double bed was in what had previously been the 'commodious dining room', which also gave ample space for Mr Hetherington's large desk. There was room for all Mr Hetherington's books and papers, not that he was one to spread things about. Mr Hetherington prospered. Caroline now spent her days in what had once been a kind of 'serving-room' to the dining room. She enjoyed the proximity of the television set as well as her tapes and the pretty wallpaper. Miss Spinks, as Mrs Arbuthnot had said, was pretty healthy, so there was no need to 'save her legs' and move her down from the first floor, leaving her the choice of three bedrooms. This therefore left the 'hall' still as the convenient space for people coming from the front door. Even Miss Spinks seemed to be a little more sprightly. Perhaps, thought Jane, Miss Spinks was enjoying a kind of renaissance now that she was free of the constant company of Mrs Arbuthnot. It was not that Miss Spinks neglected any of her duties. She looked after Mrs Arbuthnot's clothes, posted any letters, took books to and from the library van, and always asked if there was anything she could do before going off to... . Miss Jane wondered with a bit more interest what it was that Miss Spinks did when she went out. Sit and read? Find a quiet corner and have a little doze? Needlework? One would have expected Miss Spinks to produce acres of those crochet squares, but although she was an excellent needlewoman, her ability, she confessed, was purely utilitarian. 'I can do quite a good mend, my dear, and alter things, but I quite fail to see the point of all that embroidery. Even petit point,' she added, with a sedate smile at her own little joke. Jane in any case had more to worry about than where Miss Spinks went when she went out. The electricity bill would soon be due.

Mrs Arbuthnot's organising ability found scope as she rearranged her things to fit the smaller room that had been Jane's study – smaller and still very pleasant, and indeed, now that you had meals 'downstairs' in the kitchen quarters, more convenient.

Chapter Six

Arrival of the enchanted Americans

Uncle was passing some especially pleasant autumn days. He was unaware of the anxieties of the women, for he belonged to a generation that had felt that running the household was entirely a woman's work, and that it was not up to a man in any way to interfere. It was a nice autumn. What made it particularly interesting was that he had discovered an elderly visitor at The Hunters Arms who enjoyed a game of crib. So Uncle would come home and give his listeners a blow-by-blow account of each exciting finish. 'You see, Janey, we each wanted three to get out, and it was his first take, and then I got four, counting the one for thirty-one.' It was true that Uncle enjoyed his games of crib. It was also true that he enjoyed winning, and Jane always listened when he came home, glad when his step sounded that of the victor.

Still in September, she was setting the table one day for their combined lunch/dinner meal and heard him arrive in the hall. It was all right... it sounded as if he had won. He was trotting happily in, humming a tune. The tune was, in fact, the current number two in the charts, which had been floating out of Caroline's room, to be picked up by all within earshot. 'Hello, Miss Caroline,' Uncle Silas called out, and then had a little chuckle to himself as he remembered that he had *not* remembered to call her 'Mrs Hetherington'. Funny, she looked more like a Miss Caroline. He thought to himself why the name Mrs Hetherington should conjure up one picture, and Miss Caroline something entirely different. Perhaps it was the shoes; that may have been it... the shoes. Ah, yes, and now he must remember that he had a message for Miss Jane, from his friends at The Hunters Arms. A message for Janey, and he mustn't forget; he happily dropped his raincoat in the wrong place and sat down.

'Did you win again?' asked Jane.

'Yes, yes, I did. I mean, no. Or did we... yes, we were just finishing and there was this message for you. That's right. I've got this message for you. And then I did win, though it was not my first take.'

Uncle smiled contentedly. He had won, and he had remembered that he had something to tell Janey. And now, what was for dinner? Breast of lamb? With his niece's specially made stuffing, from the herbs in the garden. How very nice. He went to call the others, and this time he remembered to address Miss Caroline as Mrs Hetherington. He hummed away as he congratulated himself on all the things he was not forgetting.

He went downstairs and took his place at the table. Jane decided not to pursue the question of what the message had actually been, or at least not till after the meal had been served. Most of Uncle's messages lacked, should one say, a time element? It could have been to tell her that Mr Smith was wearing a *red* carnation and not a pink one. Or had she noticed the failure of the gladioli that were always in the garden on the left of The Hunters Arms? Or had she seen the fabulous and apparently eternal crop of anemones in the garden on the right and did she think it was because they were heavily manured, and would she like to have some, et cetera, et cetera.

It was a good job, reflected Jane, that no one wanted a second helping of potatoes, as they were running a bit short. Ed's supply of potatoes seemed to have been a bit scanty. The second course, still referred to as 'afters' by the older people, was rhubarb crumble, with the last of the rhubarb, and with the top of the milk masquerading as cream.

Uncle Silas suddenly remembered his message. He laid down his spoon and fork, and looked around with the air of a headmaster who is going to announce a half holiday.

'The message, Janey,' he said. 'I've just remembered it.' Everyone listened attentively. 'The Hunters Arms is full up, so they said they wondered if you could take some visitors, now that our first floor is empty.

For a moment, Jane wondered how 'they' knew that the first floor was empty. But, of course, this is the kind of thing that one's village unerringly knows. Michael, who had moved the double bed, could have told his brother, and his brother was in The Hunters Arms' first darts team. Or Dr Lazenby after his last visit could have told his receptionist, and his receptionist was aunt to Andy's Maisie, and Maisie told et cetera, et cetera. There were plenty of ways for the details of the rearrangement to have been reported in The Hunters Arms.

A sudden thought struck Miss Jane. The first floor was not empty. When Mrs Arbuthnot went to the ground floor, Miss Spinks had stayed on the first floor. Jane began to wonder if she had imagined Miss Spinks, but no, there she sat, eating rhubarb crumble with every sign of appreciation and looking quite pink-cheeked.

'Uncle,' said Janey, 'the first floor isn't empty.'

Uncle considered this piece of information. Jane was usually right on matters like this. On the other hand, this was also the kind of thing, he had discovered, that the bar of The Hunters Arms was right about. He shrugged his shoulders. He had delivered the message; it was not for him to work out what this might or might not entail.

Before Miss Spinks could confirm whether she was indeed sleeping in a room on the first floor (and if she wasn't, then where on earth...?), there was the noise of a car driving up to the front door.

Needless to say, this was a car bearing the special visitors from The Hunters Arms. Jane went out to meet them, ready to explain why they would not be able to stay. Quite apart from Miss Spinks and where she was sleeping, one could hardly have the place turned into a bed and breakfast. It had been kind of The Hunters Arms to think of it, but it was really not a possibility, let alone the miraculous solution to all her troubles.

The car drew to a halt. For some reason, Jane felt that it was somehow a cheerful car. Perhaps it was the colour, or the way the luggage was piled in, or the Dartmoor pixie surmounting the trailer (£2.20 reduced for the end of the season at the River Café), or, more probably, the exuberant waving of the passengers in the car.

The driver emerged. No, thought Jane to herself, he did not emerge, he shot out.

'Say, let me introduce myself,' he was saying. 'You must be Miss Jane.' He seized her hand and shook it, and gazed at her with admiration, rather, she felt, as if she had been the Eiffel Tower, or someone who had just been given a national award for conspicuous bravery. 'Folks,' he said, and turned to his equally radiant and admiring passengers. 'Here is Miss Jane. We sure are real glad to make her acquaintance.'

Jane by now was feeling distinctly bewildered. That they were Americans was obvious. She would hardly have been more surprised if they had been little green men from Mars. But why, and how...?

The friendly stranger went on. 'Now, you must be wondering who we are. My name is Jackson, Robert F Jackson, operator in real estate, from Nashville, Tennessee, and this is my wife, Barbara. And these are our friends, our great friends, David J and Eleanor Cartwright. Great folks are David and Eleanor.' He transferred his admiring gaze from Jane to his great friends, and then back to Jane. 'You must be wondering how we came to be here. You must be surprised, but you see, Miss Jane, you are really kind of famous. Your uncle, Mr Marner, has been telling us all about your village and your lovely house, and about you too. We've been staying at The Hunters Arms, you see, and now they can't have us any longer. Don't mistake me, it's not their fault. We only booked in for a couple of nights. We usually only stay anywhere the couple of nights, don't we, folks?' He looked at his passengers, who asserted with enthusiasm that yes, they usually only stayed a couple of nights anywhere.

'But your village,' went on Mr Jackson, waving his arms round, 'your village, and the views over these lovely hills, and your old castle, and... and the ravens, and just about everything. We were on our way from Tintagel, and were making for Glastonbury, weren't we, folks?' Folks agreed. They had been on the regular American sight-seeing run, Plymouth, Tintagel, and Glastonbury, after which it would be Stratford-on-Avon.

Robert Jackson's wife Barbara then took up the tale. With great gusto she went on to explain, 'Then I guess it was all my little old fault. I was reading the map for Robert, and I missed the turning. So that was how we found ourselves in your lovely village. And we're real glad we did.'

It was easy enough to laugh at American phrases and ways, but their appreciation of one's village did warm one's heart. Jane at once liked these friendly people and wished that they could have stayed. Not that it was any good. Miss Spinks had still to be occupying one of the bedrooms on the first floor, whatever The Hunters Arms thought. Jane thought with regret of the sum of money that had come unbidden into her mind, which she might have charged if she had been able to take in anyone.

'Oh, dear,' she said. 'I have really not got enough room.' The Americans looked disappointed, and her mind ranged over the possibilities. 'But do come in and have a look,' she added. 'And then we will all have coffee, and Uncle

Silas and I will try to think of somewhere else in the village that you would like.'

The party proceeded indoors. Perhaps 'swept in' would have been more accurate, except that that might have implied that the Americans were invaders and unwelcome. They exclaimed with pleasure at nearly everything. They admired the rustic side gate ('say, did you ever see anything like this back home, Barb?'), a belated delphinium, and, once more, the sunlight striking the grey walls of the castle. 'That's a real smart place for a castle; guess the chap who built it had an eye for a view.' Jane refrained from pointing out that most castles had been built so as to have an early view of approaching enemies. This particular one was fairly modern, and might have been influenced more by scenic factors.

The Americans enthused over the hall, and especially over 'a real old-fashioned open fire, with logs that look like real wood'. Jane thought of what logs were likely to cost in the coming winter. The party obediently followed her up the stairs. The large room was eminently suitable, and untenanted. They would be delighted to have it. They followed her into the other rooms and these too, to Jane's surprise, appeared to be empty. Funny, no sign of Miss Spinks's clothes. Jane sidled up to the bed, and put in a tentative hand. No sheets either. Then what had Miss Spinks done with the clean sheets she had been given two days previously? Even if miracles were becoming frequent occurrences at Hunters Head, Jane's wildest imagination could hardly conjure up a picture of Miss Spinks slipping down to the post office with a clandestine parcel of sheets to post away to some distant relative.

'My dear Miss Jane, these rooms are just perfect. Aren't they?'

Warmth and friendliness engulfed the whole party. The rooms were free. The view was superb. The Americans were delighted at the prospect of staying in the village, which had so caught their imagination. And finally, the figure they had in mind for paying was far in excess of anything that Jane had dared to hope for, even though this could be, she assumed, reckoning in dollars and not pounds. In no time at all, it seemed, these warm-hearted people had everything arranged about staying. One could almost have said that they had commandeered Hunters Head, if one had not felt cheered by contact with such exuberantly friendly people.

'Miss Jane, we're all fixed up, and right now we'll be off, won't we, folks, for an afternoon jaunt? Can't waste a lovely afternoon like this staying indoors.'

Folks agreed. And would Miss Jane like to come too? Or dear Mr Marner? Or indeed any of the others? Mrs Arbuthnot replied that thank you, *she* had responsibilities (oh dear, again thought Jane) and would Caroline mind if she, Mrs Arbuthnot, had a little lie down while Caroline took in her husband's coffee? Uncle smiled blandly at everybody, having turned off his hearing aid, and retired up to his room. Jane thanked the new guests, and waved them goodbye, promising them a real Devon supper at eight o'clock. The visitors drove off, with enthusiastic promises of returning by eight.

This left Jane with the opportunity of asking Miss Spinks... well actually, now that the moment had come, it was difficult to phrase it. If one said, 'What have you done with the sheets I gave you?' or, 'Miss Spinks, where have you been sleeping?' it might suggest, quite erroneously, that one suspected something improper. Jane put the question as tactfully as she could. 'Oh, by the way, Miss Spinks, I was just wondering about your room. I mean, well I mean, were you comfortable, and are you, I mean, are you all right?'

Miss Spinks's demeanour immediately reminded Miss Jane of a rabbit finding itself confronted by a stoat. It was quite astonishing. But the rabbit was brave.

'Miss Jane, I do hope that you will excuse the action I have taken. I know that I should have consulted you. I am sleeping... out there.' Miss Spinks pointed dramatically. Actually 'out there' did not, as it first seemed, indicate the under gardens of the castle, but meant the vague assemblage of unused sculleries, pantries, potting sheds and the like, which, along with the kitchen, occupied the bottom floor of Hunters Head. Time had indeed been when these had all been in use, and Jane knew there had been a time when Hunters Head boasted a full-time housekeeper-cook and a parlour-maid, as well as having a gardener in every day. There had been occasions when as a small child she had had glimpses of that hidden land 'the downstairs'. Little had she then realised how well she was to get to know at least the kitchen.

Miss Spinks now led the astonished Miss Jane down the kitchen stairs, through the kitchen, and out along the passage, explaining as she went. 'You see, Miss Jane, I am finding it very refreshing to go out early in the morning. And now that I am not needed so much by dear Mrs Arbuthnot, I habitually go out before breakfast. I go by the back door, here, so as not to disturb the household. Also, and I do hope that you will excuse the liberty I have taken, but I have in a way moved down here. I found what I think must have been a butler's pantry. And it seemed so convenient, to the back door, and so on, that when we moved round, I brought my things down here. I have been using it as if it were by own room.'

She opened the door of the one-time 'butler's pantry'. She had turned it, miraculously indeed, into what anyone would be glad to refer to as 'my own room'. An old settee had been metamorphosed into a bed, there were curtains up, and on the window sill stood several competently arranged vases of flowers and grasses. The erstwhile sink was doing duty as a washbasin. Miss Jane gazed with admiration, not to mention amazement. 'Miss Spinks, how beautiful,' she said, though wondering if it would not have been more accurate to say 'how surprising' and 'how resourceful.' Of course Miss Spinks might stay down here.

So these early morning walks were the cause of Miss Spinks's reddening cheeks. Jane had never before thought of Miss Spinks as being eccentric. She had to admit to herself that it was providential that Miss Spinks's eccentricity had broken out in time to leave an extra room on the first floor ready for the well-off American guests. On second thoughts, she had also to admit that *she* would have preferred a common sink or washbasin to herself rather than a more genteel one that was in a bathroom shared with Caroline. Perhaps Miss Spinks was just being sensible. Miss Spinks went on: 'I have also been tidying up some of the old herb beds that are near the back door. You may have seen what I have brought upstairs.'

So that was the explanation of the prettily arranged vases, and the offerings of bunches of different herbs. 'How helpful you have been, my dear Miss Spinks,' said Jane. 'And I imagine that it is also you who have been bringing in all those vegetables that Ed left for us. It has saved me so much trouble. At one time I thought it was Uncle! I am very grateful to you, I can tell you. You must let me know if there is anything else I can provide for you down here.'

The interview ended. Miss Jane retired to the kitchen, to prepare the special Devon supper and be grateful for Miss Spinks's contributions to it. She was content at having solved the mystery of where Miss Spinks was sleeping, and also the other mystery of the bringing in of the vegetables. It was odd though that in some indescribable way Miss Spinks's demeanour as they parted had then reminded her of a rabbit that sees the stoat going away again.

Her thoughts turned to the next meal. Oh dear, how often one's thoughts had to turn to the next meal. She put them resolutely out of her mind, and went into the garden. What a beautiful position. She looked over to the west, where the grey stone of the castle was outlined against a vivid sky. Away to the north, cars still darted along the main road, like... like a line of little hurrying beetles. Overhead there were two buzzards, no four... it must have been a family that had not yet separated. They were wheeling and floating high in the sky. What was it Uncle had once said? 'If it looks like a moth and mews like a kitten, and is up in the sky, then it's a buzzard.' What a beautiful afternoon. A few yellow leaves already on the oak trees. And the spindle-berry in the castle grounds, showing red and orange. What beauty. And even if the next meal needed thinking about, it was splendid that one had the wherewithal with which to produce the next meal.

Chapter Seven

Oasis in time

It was with great pleasure that everyone looked back afterwards on the visit of the Americans. To a household that contained a number of people with secret worries, the American guests were most refreshing. They had such great confidence in everything undertaken. A play in an outdoor theatre at the far end of the Cornish coast? How splendid; they must run down there for the evening. It appeared that folks had two cars between them, so there were always invitations to accompany them on these 'little outings'. There was an interesting production at Stratford-on-Avon? They had intended to visit Stratford-on-Avon, but now they felt they must return to their beloved Hunters Head for the night, so they would drive up for the day and come back after the evening performance.

Miss Jane had been brought up in a family that had only recently come to terms with motorcars instead of horses as a means of transport and she would have felt daring in dashing off even to Plymouth for an evening. The Americans appeared to have mastered time and distances. It was only a visit to York that seemed to justify an overnight stay (and that because they had dashed up to see 'the wall' as well). Jane also thought to herself that if one had the money it might make one a bit more daring. She put this thought from her. It was not only the supreme confidence of the Americans that livened everything up. They were basically kind people, who had this heart-warming appreciation of the village and its surroundings.

'Mr Silas, we've been down to the river, as you said. But you never told us about that second bridge, over the little stream. Say, did you know that the people there had employed the same chap who had repaired the big bridge to build the little one, in that grey stone?

'Miss Jane, we walked right up to the big pool. Does all the other side belong to the lord of the castle? And do you think it was His Lordship who was on the other side of the bridge telling that other man what to do with a fallen tree?'

Miss Jane thought it was more likely to have been the bailiff, but if the Americans came with her to church the next Sunday, she rather thought that it would be Lord Pomeroy whose turn it was to read the lesson. The Americans were enthralled. 'Say, folks, we don't have anyone like that reading the lessons back home. We'll have to tell our minister all about this.'

Their enthusiasm was not confined to the old and the grand. They liked the flowers down by the river... 'those funny seeds that pop'... and they were full of admiration for the birds... 'a dear little black and white one, darting

54

away only a foot or two above the water'. They were impressed with people's manners, and rightly so. So many things to tell them 'back home'.

Uncle Silas came into the hall. He was sorry that the American friends would not be stopping longer, and he wished that they were in now, and he wondered if dear Janey would have enough time to play a game of crib with him. She was a good player, he thought to himself, as she whisked through the house setting things to rights, but she needed more practice in order to become what he would call a really good player. He considered the situation. He would tell Janey about that last game he had had – no, not the last one, the one before the last, when his opponent had got twenty-nine. Twenty-nine, Janey. It would be nice to have a game now. Jane ought to have time too to enjoy a game instead of working all the time.

The cloud caused by the absence of his friends passed, like the autumn mist down by the river when the sun came up. 'Janey,' he called, 'I've just thought of something.'

Jane looked at him wonderingly. He was years older than she, and he still had this ability to radiate enthusiasm. She wondered what the 'something' would be that had caught his imagination. Mint in flowerpots in the bathroom? A picnic down by the river? Everyone to go to early morning Communion, or to Evensong next week at the cathedral? Or to accept the offer of a beehive? She pushed aside the thought of all that she had to do, and sat down beside him to listen.

'Janey, dear, I know I am not always observant. But now with these extra people (and very pleasant people, I must say) you have had a lot to do. You're beginning to look a bit tired. I've been thinking, Jane, that it might be a good idea if we had some paid help, permanently. Also I heard that Ed would be willing to come again to do the garden. I think you should arrange this.'

Jane, accustomed as she was to the impracticability of some of Uncle's ideas, found this one particularly hard to bear. The dream of having permanent help! Paid help! A daily. Anyone. For even two hours every day. She gulped, threw her arms round Uncle and kissed him. How could he be so unpractical? How could he think that they could afford it? Where was the money to come from? Didn't he know that... no, obviously he didn't.

Then Andy arrived at Hunters Head, as he often did. Andy was a little less carefree than he had been a month ago. He was finding that he really liked Maisie a lot. His sudden upsurge of tenderness for Miss Jane that evening seemed to have made him more selective in his attitude to the girls of the district – they were more than long legs and pert smiles and he would have liked Maisie to take him a bit more seriously.

He drove carefully nowadays, half expecting Uncle Silas to materialise within a few feet of the bonnet. He drove round to the bottom door, noticing how much tidier the lower garden looked. That bit, he supposed, was what they called a herb garden. Not that he believed in messing about with all that picking when you could get a packet of 'Grandma Made It' stuffing from his employer. He wondered what some of the herbs were. Pretty they looked, with all those different greens and bluish sort of colours.

He took in the meat and was startled to find his Maisie (what a hope – *his* Maisie) installed in the kitchen. It did not occur to him that it was his own stories of Hunters Head and indeed of Miss Jane that had impelled her to come and have a look, and formally to do some regular work there. Maisie was clearly in a position of authority. Even if the contemporary young woman does not toss her head, the effect was the same.

'Put the meat down there.' (As if he didn't already know where Jane liked the meat put.) '*And* wipe your shoes. And here are yesterday's scraps.'

She handed him the equivalent of an American 'doggy bag'. It looked as if the interview was going to be all too quickly over, but Miss Jane arrived and then there was coffee. And then Mr Silas came down and was delighted to be offered a lift down to the village. Andy relaxed. He wondered if Mr Silas would again be giving him a five pence piece as a 'tip'. ('Here's a shilling for you, young man, you're so kind.') Rum old bird, Andy reflected, and they must still be finding it pretty hard going.

Presently the telephone rang. 'Yes, this is Hunters Head. This is Miss Jane speaking. Who? Oh, Mr Jackson, you're back.' (Thoughts of how to turn a light supper into a substantial meal in the time.) And you're staying to a meal at the seaside?' (Thank goodness.) 'No, yes, no... oh, I see, you'd like to come back with both cars and take us all to the theatre, at the seaside, to the *Autumn Dream Nights*, as a farewell treat? (Would everyone want to go?) 'But, Mr Jackson, how very kind. I will ask the others. And we'll be ready, yes, by seven o'clock.' The call ended.

'The others' were of two minds. Caroline and Mr Silas thought the whole idea absolutely delightful and Jane set to work to persuade Mrs Arbuthnot to go, promising to look after Mr Hetherington herself. By the time Mr Robert E Jackson, and his great friend David Cartwright, and the cars, had arrived, the party had sorted itself out. Mrs Arbuthnot, after several changes of mind, had decided she and Miss Spinks *would* go. Mr Silas was in great good humour, and was recalling with pleasure that the first time he had seen *A Midsummer Night's Dream* (apart of course from school productions) had been at the Old Vic, and he had been sitting in the pit. Caroline said that she had once played Titania, presumably not at the Old Vic, and added that Bottom had been a real good-looker. Miss Jane gave up trying to explain that it was *Autumn Dream Nights*, and not Shakespeare's *Midsummer Night's Dream* that they were going to see. The cars arrived, and the expedition departed, leaving Jane to look after Mr Hetherington and to ponder on the financial situation. It was a good time that they had had with the American visitors. That bunch of roses in the hall looked nice; Miss Spinks must have looked hard to find those special ones.

The party arrived home late. It seemed like a gloomy foreboding to Jane that the expedition appeared not to have been successful, in spite of the good nature of their hosts. Miss Spinks said that she thought it had been, well, almost a bit vulgar, but how kind it was of Mr Jackson to think of taking them, and now would everyone excuse her if she retired to her room? Mrs Arbuthnot said that she didn't know what things were coming to, really she didn't, and snorted off to her room without even enquiring how Mr Hetherington had been. Mr Silas remarked a little sadly that the text had been changed so much that it was not at all as he remembered it; he had, he said, rather looked forward to it; ah well, but of course, he added courteously, the journey there and back had been very very nice. Would they mind if he went straight up to his room? Caroline said that it had been *gorgeous*, burst into tears, and fled up to the bathroom.

Jane turned in surprise to Mr Jackson. Robert, and everyone else, explained. This was what had happened. Caroline had joined in all the jolly choruses, and to such an extent that she had had a few moments of glory with the spotlights turned on her, so perhaps things were looking a bit dull after that.

'We were real sorry, ma'am,' went on Mr Jackson, 'that you weren't able to come along too. And I'm sure you would have had the spotlights on you too. Wouldn't she?'

The Jacksons and the Cartwrights were cheerful, friendly and appreciative. 'Miss Jane, we'd sure have had you up on that stage, along with Caroline Hetherington, now wouldn't we?' All concurred. 'What we were really sorry about was that your uncle did not enjoy it much. Mrs Arbuthnot didn't enjoy it, but there are a lot of things that she doesn't enjoy, but Mr Silas is such a one for entering into anything. He really participates.'

Their appreciation of her uncle, and the whole atmosphere of sharing and good cheer made Jane realise all too clearly that the next day was going to be a sad one. They chatted on, happily, over Miss Jane's 'real' coffee and 'some of those special homemade scones'. All promised that they would write, and that they must keep in touch, until they came again.

Mr Robert Jackson and party finally retired. Jane climbed the stairs unhappily. She noticed that the clouds, very suitably, seemed to promise rain. The Americans leaving. Worse, members of the household on edge. Worst, Uncle upset... she wondered if she could have prevented his going on the wretched outing. Caroline unsettled. Mrs Arbuthnot annoyed. Was this the end of the miracle?

Chapter Eight

Burglar Spinks

Jane did not believe in what she felt were 'conjuring trick' miracles. Trays did not go upstairs on their own. The miracle had been when Mrs Arbuthnot stopped demanding food upstairs. Nor had the delightfully arranged flowers flown of themselves into vases, but had been brought in, unlikely though that had seemed, by Miss Spinks.

Jane slept well after the day's tribulations. The number of times that she had gone up and down stairs, with trays and without, ensured her fitness, and, worry or no worry, gave her the ability to drop off to sleep as soon as head touched pillow. So she had, as usual, slept well, and was ready to get up, and was feeling a little bit more ready to face up to the troubles ahead... not too far ahead either. The real problem of course was the money. To be able to keep Maisie on. Uncle's suggestion of paid help! She needed some help all right, though probably it ought to be someone to replace the departed gardener rather than an extra pair of hands indoors. The vegetables prepared by the erstwhile Ed must be nearing their end. She reflected on her uncle's complete lack of comprehension, but smiled as she thought of his quite artless good nature.

The church clock sounded, reminding her that Uncle Silas's artless good nature would soon need to be stimulated by an early morning cup of tea. So she got up, dressed quickly, and went down to the kitchen. She opened up the Aga, put the kettle on, welcomed a castle cat, and looked out of the window. In spite of last evening's clouds, it was now a fine morning. The early sunshine showed up some bright red gladioli, still flowering in the castle gardens. The whole valley looked fresh and sparkling, as if newly made by a beneficent creator. Even the usual sounds seemed quiet. What a rare morning.

The silence of the whole valley, or at least of that part of it that belonged to the castle and Hunters Head, was suddenly and rudely shattered. There was a clash of two discordant voices. There was a man's voice, Devonshire, booming, discomfited. Then there was the cool and very inimical voice of Miss Spinks. Miss Spinks was addressing the unhappy Devon bellow.

The man with the bellow clearly felt that he had right on his side, but it was the thin articulate voice of Miss Spinks that was winning. Jane listened. She could hardly help listening, and she listened with growing amazement.

'Mr Stanley,' Miss Spinks was saying, 'I am perfectly well aware of what I am doing. I have taken a few carrots, and some onions, and just a few, a very few if I may say so, potatoes. And if you, as His Lordship's gardener, or

His Lordship, grudge them to our Miss Jane and the master, then you should be heartily ashamed of yourselves. Heartily,' she repeated, as if that was the end of it.

'But, ma'am,' protested Mr Stanley, 'they belong to us, I mean to His Lordship.' Mr Stanley's voice sounded uncomfortable. He was uncomfortable. It wasn't right to have to argue with a lady... nor was it right, surely, for someone he regarded as a lady, to be dodging into the castle gardens and taking vegetables... this was *stealing*, and stealing wasn't right. Mr Stanley felt extremely uncomfortable.

Miss Spinks continued undaunted. 'Mr Stanley, on our side of the fence we have a quantity of parsley, and marjoram, and lemon thyme, all, if I may say so, of better quality than yours. Do you think that our Miss Jane or Mr Silas would begrudge you any? Come along, Mr Stanley, I ask you to come in and to help yourself.' She used the word 'ask', but the tone implied 'command'.

The gardener, cowed and bemused, and still muttering to himself that it was 'not right, not right at all', followed Miss Spinks through the convenient connecting gate, helped himself to parsley, and withdrew in bewilderment. It was of course true what the lady had said, about the castle not missing the few things that she had helped herself to. But all the same, it wasn't right; he really didn't know what things were coming to. She did ought to have asked, and then His Lordship could have said yes or no. A lady. Coming in when no one was usually about, and taking their vegetables. He tried in his mind to avoid the word stealing.

Jane stood at the window quite dumbfounded. She could

not help feeling a twinge of admiration for the effrontery of Miss Spinks (Miss Spinks of all people), who had not only been caught red-handed (or ginger-handed when carrots were involved?) stealing the vegetables, but had then dragooned the worthy Mr Stanley into coming in and taking parsley that he did not particularly want, in return. So that had been the reason, Jane suddenly realised, for all those early morning walks of Miss Spinks's. This was not the first time she had purloined the vegetables (purloined sounded a little bit less incriminating than 'stealing') from the castle gardens. She must have been doing this for weeks. Jane was horrified to find that she was wondering if there would be any runner beans left, as the castle's runner beans were (a) very good, and (b) usually lasted longer into the autumn than anyone else's in the village.

Miss Spinks came in with her little hoard of vegetables, to be greeted by an incoherent Miss Jane.

'Dear Miss Spinks, this is wonderful of you, but you know, we mustn't....'

'Yes, dear, I am sure you're right,' was the reply, in Miss Spinks's usual quiet almost timid tone of voice. Even in that moment, Jane noticed that the odd 'frightened rabbit' look had vanished. 'Miss Jane, I didn't know what to do to help... well, to help you and... well, all of us. I have known... I mean I have come to realise because of course I could not know... I have realised that you were finding finances somewhat strained. I do like walking early in the morning, and then, on the morning after poor Mr Leslie was so unfortunately taken ill, I caught sight of the carrots in Lord Pomeroy's garden, far more than they were going to need at the castle, or indeed for Mr Stanley's household. There was a little pile of them. So I just slipped in and took a small quantity. I should not have dreamed of doing so if there had not been plenty.'

'But, Miss Spinks,' said Jane. 'That was... that was *ages* ago. You mean you've been doing it *ever* since then? Ed had not left a whole lot of... well... everything we've been having since. You mean it all came from the castle?'

'Yes, all of it,' came the reply. 'You see, it was not difficult. Provided I got up early, and if I may say so that has never been a difficulty for me, there was no one about. His Lordship has always permitted residents of Hunters Head to take the short cut through the castle grounds (which is indeed a much appreciated privilege) so no one would have suspected me of doing anything wrong by being there. Actually...' the voice faltered a little, 'although I was always very careful, I did encounter Lord Pomeroy this week. I was a little bit later than usual, and I had just taken four onions, the large ones. I had heard you say something about onion sauce, and I knew we were rather low. Well, I only just had time to put the onions into a large bag that I carry with me, and His Lordship made a little joke about my bag and always being prepared; after which he went and cut some roses for me, as he said he did not want me to go away empty-handed. I felt that I was doing wrong in deceiving him, because of course you could not say I was going empty-handed when I had the four large onions. Those roses that are in the hall now were from Lord Pomeroy.'

Miss Jane looked at the upright figure in front of her with a rather more discerning eye. She tried to imagine the scene in the garden... Lord Pomeroy, pleasant and serene as ever, presenting Miss Spinks with the roses, for which she genteelly thanked him while concealing the onions that she had just annexed from his kitchen garden.

'Now,' concluded Miss Spinks, 'I find that the excitement has made me a little bit fatigued. I would be glad if in the circumstances I might have my breakfast straightaway. Then I shall wash and change, and then I will go and see Lady Pomeroy.'

Jane felt that she had suddenly lost the train of thought. 'Go and see Lady Pomeroy?' she repeated.

'Why, yes, Miss Jane. I shall go up to the castle to find out when it will be convenient for me to see Lady Pomeroy – to make my apologies.' (Jane understood now; in an earlier world, ladies talked to ladies, and wives could repeat things to their husbands but ladies did not talk to gentlemen about matters of delicacy. Money and theft were matters of delicacy.)

Miss Spinks looked different now. She was not being threatened, she was acknowledging defeat. The rabbit knew that it could not escape from the stoat. She went on. 'I do know how difficult it has been for you to keep Hunters Head going. I was trying to help. When you asked Ed to leave, I knew you would find it hard to keep going. And then when the American guests came in, dropping like manna almost from a beneficent heaven, we were able to manage, with having all the vegetables free. I should of course be saying that it was you, dear Miss Jane, who managed. But I don't see how you can go on managing much longer.'

It was true. The two women looked forlornly at each other, overwhelmed. How could you go on? The adventure of the stolen vegetables had just about saved them, so far. It had been one in the chain of little miracles that had enabled them to survive at Hunters Head. Andy had paid one butcher's bill. The illness of Mr Hetherington – no, Mrs Arbuthnot's goodness of heart – had given them the rooms available for the passing guests, whose timely arrival had itself arisen from one light-hearted misreading of a map. Miss Spinks had produced the vegetables. And now, quite suddenly it seemed, the Americans were leaving, the supply of free vegetables was at an end, and in fact it looked as if it was all going to be the end. You must face up to selling Hunters Head and giving everyone notice and taking Uncle away somewhere. You couldn't pay the electricity bill with extra sausages. What the Americans were so generously paying you would meet the next quarter, but then... . It looked like the end of the miracles.

'Miss Jane,' said Miss Spinks. 'I know that my usual breakfast is toast and marmalade, but this morning I would like to have eggs and bacon. My dear father always had that before going on a journey.'

Chapter Nine

Departure of the Americans

P hotos, and even final photos, were over at last, and the visitors were about to drive off.

'And now, folks,' was the cry, 'just one more, with Miss Jane on her own in front.' Jane stood in front of the house, feeling that with all this business of saying 'goodbye' and 'for the last time', she would be ready to burst into tears, not that that was going to help. She seemed to herself to have lost control of the situation, and when the departing guests urged her to accompany them to the village, 'for a photo, the very last, of you standing outside The Hunters Arms', she weakly concurred. Goodness knows she would have to hurry if she was to get back in time for lunch. But did it matter? It looked as if more than one lunch would all too soon be disrupted.

Finally, with Jane squashed in on top of the luggage and the great piles of mementoes, the party drove off. There was a heart-rending moment when they stopped to turn back and wave with a chorus of 'Goodbye, Hunters Head, goodbye, Hunters Head.' To Jane this seemed an unhappy omen.

At Hunters Head, Mrs Arbuthnot automatically took charge of the unexpected situation; even if Miss Jane was out, there was no need to let things slide. 'Caroline, you look after your husband. Miss Spinks and I will go in and clear up the breakfast things.' Miss Spinks meekly divested herself of hat and gloves, and set about helping.

'Clearing up breakfast' turned out to include 'getting ready for elevenses' and 'seeing to the papers and the flowers'. There was quite a bustle as Mrs Arbuthnot organised her rather meagre troops. Miss Spinks for once was much too preoccupied with her own thoughts to rejoice at the change of mood in Mrs Arbuthnot. That formidable lady appeared to be much mollified after the previous evening. After all, she reflected, it *had* been kind of Mr Jackson to take them to the theatre, and it was not his fault that that Caroline had made such an exhibition of herself. Come to think of it, Caroline was quite a good-looking young woman. Not perhaps all that much of a *young* woman in years when you came to think about it, but just as Uncle Silas always thought of her as 'Miss Caroline', Mrs Arbuthnot tended to classify her as 'that young woman'. It was nice, thought Mrs Arbuthnot, to be home again at Hunters Head. 'Miss Spinks, would you please bring that other vase down to the kitchen?'

The ringing of the telephone brought 'that young woman', or Caroline, in a rush. Had Mrs Arbuthnot been a sociologist, she might have noted that over a certain age, you use letters as a means of communication, and

69

under that age, it is the telephone. The speed with which Caroline reached the telephone did not, as one might have thought, indicate that she feared some sudden disaster; just that she was answering the telephone.

'Hello, yes, this is Hunters Head, and this is Mrs Hetherington speaking. Miss Jane is out. It's... who did you say? The line isn't very good, is it? I didn't quite catch. Who? Oh, it's The Hunters Arms. Yes. And Miss Jane is not coming home to lunch? Because she's going home with – with who? – she's going to have lunch with the Gregsons at The Barton. Okay. Ta for ringing. Yes, I'll tell everyone. She's out to lunch. Yes, cheerio.'

Caroline happily passed on the news. 'Miss Jane's gone out to lunch.' That meant, thought Caroline, that they would have to have a cold lunch at Hunters Head, but as there would be that rather decent chutney that Miss Jane made, that would be okay by her. Mrs Arbuthnot was made of sterner stuff. She commandeered the somewhat unwilling Miss Spinks ('you can go for your little walk after dinner, dear') and set out to prepare a good meal for everyone. It struck her as decidedly odd that Miss Spinks should seem so unready to help, so unlike Miss Spinks, who was always one to be relied on. And come to think of it, it was very odd indeed that Miss Jane should have gone dashing off to lunch like that, without leaving any instructions. She had the same sense of uneasiness that Andy had at anything unusual. She stood stock still, Mr Silas's special breakfast in her hand. Was something... well, was something up? Before she could explore this thought further, she was distracted by the smell of milk boiling over. As Jane had already found out, running a household is not the best of situations for pondering the future. Mrs Arbuthnot coped with the milk, and concentrated on getting the dinner ready.

Dinner was again rather an odd meal. The actual food was all right, even if the potatoes were not quite of the same excellence as Miss Jane's... crisp and brown outside, but not hard inside. The food was all right, but there was a slightly unsettled atmosphere, as if everyone was waiting for a car or the doctor or a train... or something. Mr Silas had either not heard or not understood the original explanation of where his niece was, so punctuated the meal with continual remarks that it was not like her not to be in, and did Mrs A think they should keep some warm for Jane?

Mr Hetherington, it is true, was in excellent form. Caroline had wheeled him out for a walk. She had, of course, done this in order to avoid the obligation of helping to get the dinner ready, but she and her husband had found a great deal to talk about. He had thoroughly enjoyed the company of his young wife, and now he was looking forward to having an hour or two to himself without the company of his young wife. He had discovered that there were great advantages in Caroline's having what amounted to a separate sitting-room of her own. He no longer had to choose between putting up with Caroline playing noisy records, or putting up with Caroline putting up with *not* playing any records. Yes, he was looking forward to his afternoon. He was less put out than the others by the absence of Miss Jane. He was quite content with Mrs Arbuthnot as the matriarchal figure necessary for any well run household.

The rest were less happy. Mrs Arbuthnot had tired herself

out with being matriarchal and was more than ready to have a good lie down. Miss Spinks, unknown to anyone else, was on the verge of desperation. She had nerved herself to go up to the castle immediately after breakfast, to... well, to 'own up'. A lot of her courage had ebbed away. Would she ever get to the castle? And then, would Lady Pomeroy by any chance be able to see her? And when she did, what on earth would Her Ladyship say? And of course, what was really much more important – only she had stopped looking so far ahead – was the financial position of the Marners... and of all of them.

At last, dinner was over, and washing up done. The party departed to its various projects, and quickly before anyone had time to say 'Miss Spinks, will you set out the things for tea?' Miss Spinks seized her hat and gloves and departed.

Caroline's thoughts were on two new records (Leslie was very generous) and on a skirt that needed altering (Leslie had said that she must not be too extravagant). She had enjoyed talking with her husband that morning, and she was satisfied with herself for having helped. She was a good-natured soul, was Caroline. You could justly say that she was the sort who wouldn't hurt a fly, provided you also realised that she wouldn't save one either if it meant any extra effort on her part. She had not made a particularly marked success of anything in her life, possibly because of the effort that always seemed to be needed. Marriage to a man much older than herself had been a real boon, except that her talents had not included running a house. It was a happy chance, for the Hetheringtons, that had landed her back in that area at the precise moment that Uncle Silas had been ready to let Jane take in guests. It was real nice living at Hunters Head, and Caroline saw herself as one of the helpful members of the household, always ready, for example, to put up with cold meat and chutney rather than do any cooking. Now, should she slip out to the village to get some Silko, or might it be better to leave it till next week?

Mr Silas had greatly enjoyed the whole bustle caused by the visit of their American guests. He had also just enjoyed his dinner, even if it had not been quite up to the standard of his niece's cooking. Usually he had a nap after dinner. Today, though, perhaps unsettled by the absence of Miss Jane, he felt like... like not having a nap. It would have been better if Jane had got back. If he was not going to have a nap, what would he do? A sudden thought came to him. That was it; he had not done any painting for a long time, and it would be good to get down to a picture, a picture of the castle with the autumn tints showing on the few remaining elm trees. Yes, that was what he would do.

He hesitated as he thought of having to go up two flights of stairs to reach his paints. Then, even his diminished hearing indicating to him that Miss Caroline was about, he thought of getting her help. 'Miss Caroline, I mean Mrs Hetherington. Ah, thank you for coming. I wonder if you would be so kind, so very kind, as to go up to my room for me and fetch me down my painting things. To save my old legs.' Caroline had never been up to the top floor, where Mr Silas's and Miss Jane's rooms were, and she was quite prepared to go up to save Mr Silas's legs, especially as she could then have a little look round too.

She again had the pleasant if erroneous impression of herself as a little busy bee helping others along life's way. She pointed out to Mr Silas that in any case he wasn't 'really' old, my goodness no.

Uncle Silas laughed, and gave her detailed explanations of where everything was. 'You open the *left*-hand side of the cupboard, the left-hand side, of the brown cupboard, and then on the bottom shelf et cetera, et cetera' She went up, found the cupboard (the brown one) the door, the shelf et cetera, and came down again with almost everything he wanted.

Chapter Ten

Offer of a horse

Jane, in the meantime, found herself in the village and did not return till long after tea. In unusual despondency that morning, she had allowed herself to be commandeered. First of all it was by the Americans. At last, the photo (the *very* last one) had been taken outside The Hunters Arms and the guests had driven away. Then the vicar appeared. He was a most likeable young man. He hailed Jane. 'Jane, the very person I wanted to see.' Explanations followed. Mr Silas was to have read the lesson next Sunday, but there had been some changes, and would Mr Silas mind if he read the lesson on the Sunday after that instead? Jane said that Uncle, she was quite sure, would be quite agreeable. Uncle always prepared well for reading the lesson, and it was a constant surprise and pleasure to him as he made fresh interpretations. He would not have been reading Ezekiel but for preparing the lesson, and now he would be just as interested and surprised when he came to study the next week's lesson. Jane did not understand the vicar's farewell reference to 'drawings of the Temple', but then it was Uncle and the vicar who had been reading Ezekiel, not Jane.

Aunt Min then sallied out of The Hunters Arms; Jane having been so busy, had not been down outside her front door for ages, and there were things that needed discussing, particularly the church's autumn fair. The youth club, of all people, wanted a stall; what did Miss Jane think? Could they be trusted? Perhaps Miss Jane would be able to keep an eye on them. Jane obediently went into The Hunters Arms, and momentarily forgot her own troubles in the planning of the autumn fair. Some of the youth club, particularly two of the older girls, were very responsible, and she was sure they would manage very well. More people came into the bar, greeting Jane as if she had come back from Australia. 'Haven't seen you down here for ages.'

Her thoughts turned to her own troubles. If only the youth club stall had been her chief worry. Perhaps the time had come to seek advice... but from whom?

Her friends, the Gregsons, arrived. They were not really taller and broader than anyone else, but just seemed it as they exuded such friendliness and good cheer. They were accompanied by a selection of the Gregson dogs, all of whom shared the family characteristics, friendly, bouncing, self-confident, cheerful. Aunt Min felt surprised when they left the horses outside, though on this occasion they had come in vehicles. They were delighted to see Jane, as well as all their other acquaintances. Jane stayed home too much, they said. She had started missing things in the village. And now she was out, what about coming home with them for a spot of lunch? And she must meet Mamie. A sudden ray of hope appeared to Jane. She needed advice, about money and property, so who better to ask than the Gregsons? Yes, she would come with them, if Aunt Min would get someone to ring Hunters Head and tell them. It would also, thought Jane, be interesting to see if Mamie was Mrs Gregson's sister or a new horse. So, seeking for someone who might be able to give her advice, Jane accepted their invitation.

Lunch with the Gregsons, as a less troubled Miss Jane would have realised, was not going to be a very auspicious occasion for asking or giving advice on anything other than horses. There would be dogs, cats, children, and unidentified boy cousins, and sundry older women, Aunties this and that. The Gregsons farmed and fed extensively and well. A nice jolly no-nonsense family, whose idea of neighbourliness usually was to lend you a horse or sell you a promising young filly.

The Gregsons finally disentangled themselves from the rest of Aunt Min's customers. Jane found she was the only one going with them – it would not have surprised her if everyone else had come too, as she was sure they had all been invited. What a family. They seemed overjoyed to be taking her back with them. 'Such ages since we have seen you, and you're looking slimmer than ever, isn't she?' As they drove the short (but adventurous) way back to The Barton, Jane thought about them. The Gregsons were the biggest landowners in the village, not counting the castle. They were numerous, hard working, jolly, breeders of beef (on the lower fields) and of sheep (in the area adjoining the moor), and owners of horses and dogs, who seemed as much part of the family as did the younger children. Probably they were treated not dissimilarly; the wits of the village asserting that older horses slept in bedrooms and younger children in stables. It did seem to Jane that this fine no-nonsense family might be the very ones to advise her. *They* were managing a farmhouse, that with its ramifications dwarfed Hunters Head, and obviously they had plenty of money. What they had spent in a few minutes in The Hunters Arms that morning would have made a sizeable contribution to Jane's housekeeping. One of the Gregson children spent part of the brief journey in explaining to Jane that Amanda had just had puppies, and it would be lovely for her to have one of them, so she must come and choose one. It was another good reason for going with the Gregsons, even though Jane was quite certain that she was not going to take on anything that had a mouth and required feeding.

When they arrived at The Barton, there was some altercation (friendly and loud, as were all altercations at the Gregsons') about whether they should have lunch first, or take Jane to see the new puppies, and of course the newest foal. Lunch was decided on, and Jane found herself next to a pleasant woman of her own age. Perhaps this was Mamie? Jane would hardly have been surprised to find a horse along with them. The woman may have known something about Hunters Head, and promptly enquired how many Jane had beyond her kitchen. When Jane replied, in some surprise, that there was only Miss Spinks, she was told that they ought to have at least one more, as they would be company for each other, even in separate boxes, and if she needed another stable door, Greg was sure to have an old one he could spare. Jane found herself much cheered by the thought of Miss Spinks as a horse, peering over a stable door, with another one next, in what would have been a converted pantry. The other woman was disappointed to find that Miss Spinks was not a mare, and turned her attention to someone with more equine interests. Jane looked along the table; she could not help reflecting on what it all must have cost... great lavish helpings of roast meat, and frozen peas, which she was sure the Gregsons had not frozen, and mounds of three different kinds of ice cream. Amanda, or a dog very much like her, was amicably sharing a saucerful with a small female Gregson.

Jane moved round to see if she could have a word with the head of the family, and Mr Gregson, finding there was business to be discussed, took Jane into another room. 'Can't go into the office,' he explained. 'I've got a damn good secretary, and she says I mess things up when I get loose in there.' He led Jane into a sitting-room, ensconced her in an armchair, and then, under the same impression as the female cousin had been, namely that Jane wanted a horse, enumerated the progeny and immediate ancestors of a mare that a neighbour was seeking to sell. 'Just right for you, my dear; steady, but a lovely mover. Always been treated well. In fact just a bit spoilt, but I know you wouldn't begrudge her the odd carrot and a few lumps of sugar.' Once more Jane explained that she did not want a horse, but it was about Hunters Head. Mr Gregson at once jumped to the very reasonable conclusion, which was partly right, that Jane wanted to rearrange things at Hunters Head. Well, that was simple enough. His wife, Mrs Gregson, knew several places where 'rooms' could be recommended, so that would be Jane's four lodgers out of the way, and then she should go to a Yeohampton firm for any repairs, only not to do too much, and then of course the really important thing was to choose the right estate agent; Hunters Head would not be all that easy to sell... you would need the right agent, so he would recommend Messrs so-and-so in Exton. Quite simple. All very nice, very straightforward and full of commonsense. The family began to seep into the sitting-room, and Jane was taken off to see a lot of the farm.

The visit to the Gregsons was not producing much in the way of helpful advice but Jane could not help enjoying the whole unruffled atmosphere. A hospitable family probably gives the impression to outsiders of having no problems itself. After the children had escorted Jane out, Mr Gregson permitted himself another cup of coffee and a glance at the local paper, and he mentioned to his wife that he hoped everything was all right at Hunters Head.

The afternoon was ending when Jane finally left. It was impossible to go on feeling downcast in such a family. She was wind-blown and refreshed when she accepted a lift home – but in a vehicle, not on a horse. She wondered where she would have put a horse. Presumably in one of the old sculleries, next to Miss Spinks. As she thought of Miss Spinks, she wondered how *she* had been getting on at the castle.

Chapter Eleven

Lifeline for one

T here were always plenty of jobs to be done, and Jane occupied herself with tidying up, and then went and got the supper ready. By the time Miss Spinks finally returned, supper was being served up, so that it was not till after supper that the two women found themselves on their own. They sat in the kitchen and Jane passed a cup of coffee to an undeniably triumphant Miss Spinks, who sat there with the unmistakable air of the rabbit that has turned and bitten the stoat. She accepted the coffee, and then made her surprising announcement.

'Miss Jane, dear, I have such good news. I am, as it were, going away.'

'Yes,' replied Jane bleakly. 'I know. So are we all. We are all going to have to go away. I think we can manage without saying anything till after the harvest home.'

Her voice fell. The harvest home. One of the very nice events in the village, when everyone somehow took part.

This would indeed be their last, certainly their last from Hunters Head; she had always supplied the shortbread.

'Miss Jane,' said Miss Spinks. 'You have not quite understood. I mean, it is my fault, but in my excitement I did not make my meaning entirely clear. This is a miracle that has occurred, another miracle. I am leaving but I am not going away.'

Jane visualised her astral body floating over Hunters Head while her corporal body searched unhappily for 'accommodation for gentlewomen'. It seemed hardly less unlikely than what had already happened. Normally Jane would have been amused at the thought, but not any longer... now you just waited for the final catastrophe.

Miss Spinks continued: 'I have had an offer, a singularly convenient offer of employment. Of *paid employment*.' She made it sound like a lease of the Crown Jewels. 'As you already know, Miss Jane, I had to go up to the castle. It was fortunate, for me I mean, that Lady Pomeroy was able to see me straightaway. I explained everything about the vegetables, and about...' for a moment the voice quavered as Miss Spinks sought for the right word... 'about my wrongdoing in taking them. Naturally Lady Pomeroy was surprised, but also – something amusing must have happened – she almost seemed to be laughing, and she wasn't in the least bit put out. She almost seemed to be implying that I might in some way have been justified. But perhaps she was just recognising that I had behaved correctly in coming to inform her.'

Jane, knowing Lady Pomeroy, was not in the least surprised to hear the way in which she had received Miss Spinks's revelation.

There was a pause. This was not the end of the story, but only the prelude. 'While I was there,' went on Miss Spinks, 'visitors arrived, and I was able to be of some assistance to Lady Pomeroy. It appeared that her daughter was out and that there was no one in the kitchen. I was therefore able to help in bringing some of the things along from the kitchen. Of course, I had had no intention of staying when tea was served, but Her Ladyship asked me to stay, and then... well, actually I was able to be of some assistance, because I was able to answer the telephone and take several messages, while Lady Pomeroy was occupied I mean.'

Jane felt that she could imagine this scene rather more easily than the previous incident in the garden. Yes, certainly Miss Spinks could have been 'of some assistance' to Lady Pomeroy, and, moreover, the ladylike Miss Spinks would then have effaced herself, being far more aware than Lady Pomeroy of the need to maintain social distinctions.

'And after the visitors had left,' continued Miss Spinks, 'it was of course up to me to offer further assistance. I had had my tea with them. So I asked if I could help, and we did the washing up together, and, and Miss Jane, you will find this hard to believe... I can hardly believe it myself... but Lady Pomeroy has asked me to go and work for her, to go and be what I can only describe as a part-time confidential help. This is not to be voluntary. I am to be paid. There!'

Miss Jane thought rapidly. Yes, she could see that Miss Spinks, so careful and reliable, would indeed make a useful help at the castle.

'You will have perceived, Miss Jane, I am sure, that I

am much better in a self-effacing role.' (For a moment Jane was tempted to laugh, as she thought of the way in which the self-effacing Miss Spinks had that morning rounded on His Lordship's unfortunate gardener.) 'I have inherited from my dear father a very clear mind, and in fact while we have been living at Hunters Head, I have been the one who has remembered Mrs Arbuthnot's engagements. Not that she has so many now. But there are all the things like the appointments with the doctor and the dentist, and the oculist, and keeping the addresses of the people we write to at Christmas, and those we write to at Christmas *and* Easter. And then the birthdays, even though there are a little fewer of those. I think I should be a help to Lady Pomeroy. I could take messages accurately for her, and remind her of appointments. I am quite good at flowers, and I could help. And naturally I could mend or wash when the maids were away.' Miss Spinks's careful watch on the castle's inhabitants in the last weeks had given her a good impression of what went on in the daily routine. She would have liked to add that she knew how to behave, but felt that the incident with Mr Stanley prevented her ever saying that again.

The more Jane thought about it, the more she could see what were the advantages from Lady Pomeroy's point of view. Miss Spinks, the utterly ladylike, would always look the part assigned to her. If required to dine with the family, she would do so without embarrassment. Jane envisaged Miss Spinks as knowing when to refuse a second helping if anything was short (if one could envisage such an unlikely event at the castle). And when *not* wanted, she would suddenly *not* be there. Further, there would be no need for the Pomeroys to worry about gossip. No juicy morsel about what Lady Pomeroy had said on the phone to her daughter or her bank manager would ever be regaled by Miss Spinks to acquaintances outside.

'I know,' went on Miss Spinks, 'that I am not good at getting on with absolutely everyone like you are. You are so good too with all the young people. But I think that this will be a safe position for me. It is really quite providential. As my father used to say, the Lord works in mysterious ways sometimes.'

A doubt was creeping into Jane's mind. The ways of the Lord were mysterious, and it all sounded very nice, and very suitable for the castle, but what was to happen when the Pomeroys went away? And what if they got tired of Miss Spinks? And in any case what about Mrs Arbuthnot?

'Also,' said Miss Spinks, answering Jane's unspoken questions, 'and this is where I have to consult with you, Mrs Arbuthnot has something to occupy her now, even though Mr Hetherington is so much better. She does not need me like she did. In fact, it is better for Mrs Arbuthnot to have something to occupy her. But it would not be right for me to leave her completely, and indeed, I think it is always better to have one's own place. It would be the intention, dear Miss Jane, for me to keep on my own little room here, for which I would now be in a position to pay rent. Dear Hunters Head would still be my home.'

Jane considered the matter. Of course Miss Spinks could keep her room, the skilfully adapted ex-scullery or pantry, no question about that. One less to feed, and extra rent for one small room would hardly save Hunters Head. A lot more than that was going to be required. All the same, the Lord's mysterious ways might stave off the evil hour for a little, and it might lead to a safe haven for at least one of them.

Miss Spinks was thinking about Mrs Arbuthnot. 'Mrs Arbuthnot is really well occupied here. If this enables her to stay on here, it will be well worth any small sacrifice on my part.' Tears stood in Miss Spinks's eyes. 'Oh, Miss Jane, you can't imagine what difficult times Mrs Arbuthnot and I had before we came here. After Mr Arbuthnot was taken, there was some trouble over the money... I did not understand exactly what and we could not keep on the house. The estate agent said that we sold it at the wrong time (I am not sure what he meant, as we were having to sell it then). And we went and stayed in so many places. Mrs Arbuthnot could not accustom herself. It wasn't really the conditions – quite nice places some of them were – but she was not *used* to being beholden to other people. She did become a little bit domineering.'

Jane had sometimes wondered what the bond was between these two people. 'A little bit domineering', as a description of Mrs Arbuthnot, would have seemed, only a month or two earlier, the under-statement of the year. But since 'that morning' when Mr Hetherington had so suddenly been taken ill, and which, according to the calendar, was less than two months ago, Mrs Arbuthnot had started showing sterling qualities. And now it transpired that Miss Spinks was truly devoted to that lady who in most people's opinion was more than a little bit domineering. Miss Spinks could have managed in other people's houses, but Mrs Arbuthnot had always been the difficulty. Miss Spinks would not have complained; she would have raised no objection to being told the times when she might use the bathroom; she would have accepted strong tea and fried bacon as a staple breakfast diet. But she had a real affection for, at first sight, the unprepossessing Mrs Arbuthnot. So every time that that lady had decided that 'things' were too difficult, they had moved.

'If only we can stay on here,' concluded Miss Spinks. 'I can manage, quite well, and with my own little room here I shall be all right. If only we can stay. It was dreadful before. It's home, the way we live here.'

It was hardly necessary for Miss Spinks to explain further. Her whole voice had conjured up the previous visions of discomfort and discomfiture... the unfortunate little incidents when you were queuing for the bathroom; the difficulty in drying the little bits of washing; the unpalatable meals; tea when you wanted coffee; other residents peering at your letters; the central heading too hot, or your bedroom too cold; letters that were important to you somehow gone astray. Miss Spinks was right when she summed it up by saying that Hunters Head, 'the way we live here', had become their home. And Mrs Arbuthnot too had also become a great deal happier now that she had found so much to occupy her.

Miss Jane was only too happy to agree to the new arrangements proposed. Anything that promised salvation for even one of them was welcome; the extra money she had begun to translate into extra days... or even weeks?

There was one final message from the castle. 'Lady Pomeroy also said,' (and Miss Spinks blushed a deep red) 'that you were to have any vegetables that you wanted. Mr Stanley will come in to see what you want.'

That was the end of the conversation. Miss Spinks retired, in her usual noiseless fashion, presumably to inform Mrs Arbuthnot of this turn of events. Jane felt a little bit guilty about the prospect of accepting vegetables as a continuing gift. But it was a well meant offer and was it not a welcome one?

She sat longer than she usually allowed herself over her coffee. She was beginning to feel that she had been doing everything possible, for a long, long time. It was true that in the last couple of months help had come from unexpected quarters. Mrs Arbuthnot had become helpful, reliable and irreplaceable instead of domineering. Andy (she smiled reminiscently) had certainly helped her round one corner. Maisie had been a great help. Uncle had brought along the welcome American guests. And now Miss Spinks (Miss Spinks of all people) was about to start paying a little more money. Profoundly thankful as Jane was for these miracles, her commonsense told her that they were not going to be enough. She must be glad that this little group of people had been so happy together at Hunters Head. Now... now she must face with resolution what might well be their last few weeks together. Their last weeks should be... another oasis for them all, something to remember afterwards, something to give them strength to face the discomforts that were awaiting them. It was not all that long to Bonfire Night, and she would see that everyone had a lovely evening. And not long after that would be Christmas.

She winced at the thought of 'a last Christmas' at

Hunters Head. She tried to envisage the future. That Caroline would survive was fairly certain, but what about Mr Hetherington? The quiet Miss Spinks would find herself a welcome in some unlikely niche, but Mrs Arbuthnot would go back to being the unpopular dragon. And Uncle? Uncle, for whom Hunters Head had always been home. Poor defenceless Uncle. Jane drank her coffee, unhappy, unsure, and with the words of the departing American guests re-echoing in her mind, 'Goodbye, Hunters Head, goodbye, Hunters Head.'

Chapter Twelve

Message for Jane

What happened next was what in a more rational world might have happened earlier. If you wanted help with moving the furniture, you asked someone who could do just that, and for meat you talked with the butcher's boy! So whom did you consult about money? You consulted someone who knew about money, not only their own, but money in the abstract. Mr Gregson might have given Jane useful advice, but it took *time* to consult Mr Gregson about anything less abstract than horses. What Jane did not realise was that people who know about money usually like to have time to reflect on a situation.

This simple thought had not occurred to Jane. The idea of even consulting the Gregsons had been but a passing whim. What was the basis of Jane's financial calculations was the maxim inculcated in her childhood: 'If you look after the pennies, the pounds will look after themselves.' Money now was something of which you had barely enough, and if you were very careful, somehow you had managed. Or had she got to the stage when somehow she did not manage? There were, she knew by hearsay, such things as overdrafts, and she had heard people talk about 'bridging loans', but she couldn't see where any bridging loan would lead to, and in any case she could not have embarrassed that nice man who lived in the village and was your bank manager in Exton, by asking him for money that she could not hope to pay back. Loans to Miss Jane's family had carried overtones of Newgate and imprisonment for debt. As you could not repay, you did not borrow, you managed – at least she had managed up to now.

It was Uncle Silas who ushered in the next chapter, some few days later. He had been for his morning stroll. Jane, as so often, was in the kitchen preparing for the next meal, alone apart from the castle cat installed on the windowsill. (The cat knew it would not be fed, so this was a gesture of pure friendliness on its part.) The strains of a tune, number something in the charts, came from Caroline's room, and had put an idea into Jane's head. Mrs Arbuthnot was helping a lot, and Miss Spinks was paying more, and even that Caroline usually did the washing up. What about Mr Hetherington? Nobody seemed to know much about him. Might it be possible for him to pay a bit more? Jane wondered.

Uncle came into the hall and down to the kitchen. He always had news to tell after his excursions to the village. It was surprising what happened from one day to the next. Jane waited, cooking knife in hand, to see what the morning's revelations would be. Uncle, to her surprise, seemed just a shade uneasy.

'Janey, dear, do you know who I have just seen?'

As it was half-term, *and* the Women's Institute monthly market, Uncle might well have encountered almost any one of the able bodied members of the community, as well as several of the less mobile.

'Who, Uncle?'

'Lady Pomeroy and Miss Spinks. And they were together. Going up to the castle. Carrying things. And together. Just like old friends.'

'But, Uncle, I did tell you. Miss Spinks lives here still, but she does work for Lady Pomeroy, so it is quite natural that they should be going up to the castle together.'

Uncle agreed that she had told him. He also smiled to himself as he had a mental picture of Miss Spinks as a castle employee driving one of those big lawn-mowing machines. He had never been a comic artist, or he would have put it on paper; perhaps she could have had a sunshade up as well. It was a pleasant notion, and he moved across the kitchen. He absentmindedly stroked the cat, and picked up some beans from the draining board.

'Beans for dinner again. They do look nice.'

'Uncle,' replied Jane. 'They certainly are nice ones. They are some of the late ones that you can only get from the castle.'

Uncle picked up three of them and made a triangle. 'Jane, we are not sufficiently aware of things, very often. Look how lovely these beans are.' He broke one in half. 'Look at that colour.'

Presumably he had not come down to the kitchen for the sole purpose of admiring the colour of the inside of one runner bean, which was not particularly different from any others. There seemed to be something on his mind.

'Did someone give you a message for me?' asked Jane suspiciously.

It would not be true to say that Mr Silas had become very much aware of the financial position, but at least he had begun to feel that his niece might be having some slight difficulty. He ignored her question. 'Jane dear, you know I don't always understand things. I don't know how I could have managed without you. Janey, I hope I am not putting too much on your young shoulders.'

By now, Jane had become convinced that someone *had* sent her a message, and that it was a message that Uncle had either not understood or not liked. She moved over to the beans, and started preparing them, while keeping a suspicious eye on him.

He moved back to the window. 'Oh, by the way, I didn't exactly understand it, but Lord Pomeroy was in the village too, and he said that he wanted to come and see you. He asked if you would be in, and I said that I didn't know.'

This was a distinct evasion of the truth. Uncle Silas's usual reaction was to invite anyone along – errand boy, bank manager, bank manager's wife, doctor's daughter, grocer's son, anyone. He must have been put out in some way to have hesitated. Jane put down what she was doing. Uncle must not be upset. 'Uncle Silas, it's quite all right.' She dredged up a degree of apparent serenity. 'If Lord Pomeroy, or anyone else for that matter, wants to come and see us, of course they are welcome. You know everyone always has been.' She was giving quite a convincing performance, to herself as well as Uncle, of a gracious hostess with unlimited means at her disposal. This was just as well, for neither of them had heard Lord Pomeroy making his entry into the kitchen, number ten on the charts being even noisier than number twelve.

'I did ring,' His Lordship was explaining. 'Good morning, Mr Silas, good morning, Jane. I think your bell is out of order, so I came in.' (Jane knew it was out of order, but was postponing paying for a man to come and put it right.) He laid a bunch of very fine carrots down on the table. 'I was coming to see you, and Mr Stanley asked me to bring you these.'

Mr Silas, now quite recovered in spirits, beamed on the unexpected visitor. Visitors who feel free to walk into your kitchen, and carrying carrots, can hardly be harbingers of disaster. All the same, it had been funny, sending that message to Jane, almost, he thought, as if something had been wrong. There was some old Latin phrase he had learnt at school, about the Greeks bearing presents (or was it the Assyrians?) that he was sure was applicable. It was not about carrots though. Jane produced coffee, and the visitor was made welcome. Mr Silas enquired if His Lordship thought that the Romans or the Greeks had eaten carrots. The castle cat, after a suitable pause, deigned to walk over and indicate acquaintance with Lord Pomeroy. It was a pleasant moment... the sun shining, a kettle boiling, the cat purring, and a nice easy conversation between the men about nothing that was really important. The church clock could be heard striking, and even the strains of whatever Caroline was listening to sounded quite pleasant at that distance. Jane had a horrid glimpse of a future when these unexpected interludes did not take place.

Presently Lord Pomeroy mentioned that it was Miss Jane he particularly wanted to see. No, it was not about the flowers for the church next week – that was all arranged; but actually it needed more time than that, and he wondered if she would mind coming up to the castle, early next week, to talk about something. Jane's thoughts flew to Miss Spinks. Had Miss Spinks...? Or had Lady Pomeroy...? Had this promising arrangement not worked out? Was this a prelude to the dismissal of Lady Pomeroy's new confidential help? If a replacement were needed, Jane could hardly see Mrs Arbuthnot or Caroline as candidates. Lord Pomeroy was suggesting Tuesday evening for their meeting – 'Miss Spinks and my wife will be out, as they are both involved in getting ready for the group meeting on Wednesday, so if you could come up to the castle after your evening meal?'

Jane agreed, and His Lordship departed, followed shortly by His Lordship's cat. The memory of his kind but very straightforward manner remained with Jane and helped her through the usual round, getting meals, looking after Uncle, checking things with Mrs Arbuthnot, clearing away meals, talking to Mr Hetherington, but not about money. It was a pleasant enough round, usually, but less so when you were facing a growing anxiety about what the future will bring. Like Uncle, she could remember something about Latin quotations. Hadn't she learnt one at school about black care sitting behind a horseman? She might not be a horseman, in spite of the Gregsons' attempts, but she knew about black care perching on her shoulder. If only.

All the same, Lord Pomeroy's manner had in some unexpected way given her a feeling of confidence. She began to anticipate Tuesday with interest.

Chapter Thirteen

Sacrifice by Caroline

It was Saturday, the next day. Maisie made her way up, as she often did on a Saturday, to Hunters Head. She was in a somewhat more pensive mood than usual. She had, she realised, started to become very fond of that Hawkins boy. And that brought its own problems. What was the reason that he had, well, changed somehow? At one stage she had wondered if there was 'anything going on' (marvellous the shades of the English language) between Andy and Miss Jane. One visit had confirmed her feeling that 'that' – again, how expressive is the English language – 'that' was out of the question. All the same Andy was changing.

Given then that Andy was becoming more serious, that meant that there was another thing worrying her. Why had a more serious Andy lied to her about having gone out, or not gone out, with that French girl who had been au pairing at the River Café during August? Maisie would have liked to talk it over with someone. The question was, who?

The first person she encountered at Hunters Head was Caroline, from whose room floated out the strains of number one in the charts. Maisie stopped short to listen. She had not got this particular one, and it was real nice to be able to hear it properly to make sure whether you wanted to get it. Caroline, who always enjoyed a bit of company, invited Maisie in, and they had an animated conversation.

'Do you know this one?'

'Oh yes, isn't it a smasher?'

'And have you heard...?' This one was put on, and another, and then another. Caroline, with a generous husband behind her, had a much larger stock of records then anyone else in the village, the castle and the Gregsons excepted, and the two young women thoroughly enjoyed themselves.

Caroline suddenly realised her role as hostess, and went to put on the kettle.

'We have a kettle and instant coffee handy in the dining room now,' she explained, quite unnecessarily, as Maisie had done several Saturday mornings' work at Hunters Head. 'It saves having to keep on going down to the kitchen, and it helps Jane a bit.' She giggled. 'Actually I'm the one who really likes instant. The others go on so about having "proper" coffee, but I'd just as soon have instant. It costs more now, so it must be better.'

Maisie concurred. She too preferred instant to 'real', though she was not sure whether to agree that costing more made it better. Anyhow, it was a nice cup of coffee.

She was beginning to wonder if Caroline might be a good person to confide in. After all, Caroline wasn't all that much older than she was (though when you got near, you could see that she wasn't all that young), and as Caroline couldn't really be said to belong to the village, not what you mean *belong*, she wouldn't be so likely to repeat things.

Actually, it was Caroline who brought it up. 'You're going out with Andy Hawkins, aren't you? I say, isn't he a good-looker? Are you going to get engaged soon? I bet he'd like that.'

This indeed was the question that had begun to occupy so much of Maisie's thoughts. But there was this other problem. She decided it would be best to have it out, there and then. Caroline might be able to resolve it for her. No use beating about the bush. It would be better to have it out than to go on thinking about it. Maisie thereupon opened her handbag, produced a little plastic bag, undid that, and took out a carefully folded lady's handkerchief.

'There,' she exclaimed dramatically, like a detective who has found the blunt instrument. 'There, see those initials in the corner. JM – that's that Janine Martineau or something, that... that dolled-up French girl they had au pairing at the River Café in August. It was in Andy's pocket,' she wailed, 'and he said he hadn't been out with anyone but me since the July fair.' Maisie worked up to a rousing crescendo. 'There were other girls before, and I knew, but he said he hadn't been out with anyone else since July, and Janine – JM – didn't come till August. He lied to me. And I hate him.' She glared unconvincingly.

Caroline took one look at the offending handkerchief and laughed. She recognised the mark JM. The initials were the same – it was Miss Jane's. 'It's all right,' she explained. 'You don't have to worry. It's nothing to do with Janine. That's the mark Miss Jane has on her hankies. JM, Jane Marner. Look, I've got one of hers that I was just going to return. Nothing to do with that wretched Janine.'

Caroline seemed to share Maisie's opinion of the beautiful Janine.

Maisie gave a great gasp of relief. Never mind how Andy had come by one of Miss Jane's hankies. That didn't matter. 'You're sure?'

Yes, Caroline was sure, and indeed spread out the one that she had borrowed, clearly marked, in exactly the same way, JM, Jane Marner, not Janine something-or-other.

What had been bothering Maisie was indeed not the handkerchief, nor the fact that Sandy had 'been around', but that he had, as she thought, lied to her. No one was perfect, and you must have a bit of give and take, but deliberate lying wasn't going to be *her* idea of give or take. But now it looked as if no one had lied to anyone, and in any case the legendary Janine had long ago returned to her native France.

'Oooh,' said Maisie, 'I'm glad I asked you. I've been so worried.'

Caroline considered the matter. Andy, she was sure, was very keen on Maisie. It looked as if Maisie was equally keen. Now wasn't that nice? Being of a practical turn of mind, she went on to consider where Andy and Maisie would live. 'Would you live with your people, Maisie, or would you go and live at the Hawkins's? It's a bit small, isn't it?'

Maisie opined that living at her home would hardly suit Andy, and she didn't see herself as fitting in with Mrs Hawkins, not, she added hastily, that Andy didn't get on really well with her people, or that she didn't like Mrs Hawkins, but... well, but.

Caroline, for once in her rather self-centred, if not selfish life, decided to do something to help someone else at the cost of some inconvenience to herself. If she offered to stay on the ground floor, then Andy and Maisie could have the vacant rooms on the first floor. She proceeded to expound her idea. 'Maisie, I've got an idea. My husband and I have been here in the ground floor rooms since he was taken ill.' (This fact was of course known by the whole village.) 'But we should soon be moving back to our rooms on the first floor.' (This was news.) 'They are really the best rooms, you see, and the bathroom is on that floor. Now, what I've just thought' (Caroline became quite enthusiastic) 'is that we can stay here, and actually it is quite convenient, and I can ask Miss Jane if she would let the first floor to you and Andy. You would have to be married of course.'

Their minds had worked so fast that both young women were already visualising the delightful ceremony at the church, and all the presents. Caroline, unable to be the chief bridesmaid, was seeing herself next year as godmother to the first baby, a boy, whom the grateful couple had named Leslie after her husband. Caroline would be a nice name for the first little girl.

It was Maisie who suddenly came back to the fact that

at the minute there was not even an engagement, and that even if Janine had gone away, there were plenty of others 'like her' in the village, ready to pounce on a good-looking young man like Andy. She, Maisie, had better be off back to the village and see him as soon as possible.

'I must go now, and see Andy. Thank you ever so. You do have some good ideas. Thanks for the coffee. Bye for now.' Maisie made quite a hurried exit. She was glad to have everything clear in her own mind. Fancy thinking that Andy had lied to her. What a relief to find that he hadn't. And what an idea about finding somewhere to live when you did get married.

The more Caroline thought about it, the more she saw it as a good idea. She quite liked living on the ground floor. Nice rooms, even if the view was not so good; Leslie with that big desk in their bedroom and room to spread out all his papers and things, not that Leslie was one to spread things out much. And she with her own sweet little room and her records and things for daytime. Even Caroline, it must be noted, was becoming daily aware that money might be a difficulty for Miss Jane. The idea that extra people permanently in the household had to fit in with those already there was not one to occur to Caroline. The first-floor rooms were free, and you needed the money, so hey presto, you let them.

She ran down to the kitchen to explain what she was thinking to Miss Jane. Miss Jane (funny how things turn out) did not seem as receptive as she had expected. It was very kind of the Hetheringtons, of course, and one did appreciate their kind offer, and one would go and look again at the Hetheringtons' nice rooms on the first floor. How kind of Caroline to have thought of it.

Caroline returned to her own room to put on again that record that Maisie had liked so much. Oh well, she had made the offer. It was up to Miss Jane now.

Jane had thanked Caroline, and sincerely too, for having had the idea. But having said that, Jane could think of a large number of reasons for not seeing this offer as one more in the line of miracles that had so far saved them. For example, the only bathroom was on the first floor. And what she was really and truly thinking was that Andy and Maisie might not fit in. To everyone else, Hunters Head had become 'home'. They all fitted in.

Chapter Fourteen

At the castle

T he next two days went pleasantly enough. The village was fortunate in its vicar, and he probably thought he was fortunate in his parish. Certainly, you had a very good attendance at evening service that Sunday. Jane thought the sermon an unusual one, and had a most interesting discussion afterwards with Mr Hetherington about it. She had missed their little talks and discussions while he had been ill.

On Monday, Mr Hetherington wanted Jane's help in posting various letters at the post office. Mrs Arbuthnot took on the cooking. It was one of the days when Jane's 'lovely homemade chutney' would make a lot of difference. Jane returned from the post office, feeling more acutely than ever the warm welcome from Hunters Head. She wished she could have envisaged Lord Pomeroy suddenly handing her a cheque, but this, like having Andy and Maisie on the first floor, she knew was no possibility.

All the same, now it was Tuesday and it was nice to be going up to the castle to see Lord Pomeroy. Lord Pomeroy had retired prematurely, gladly and successfully, from a business career in the City, and things you discussed with him always seemed easier. Jane wondered what it was he wanted to see her about.

Arriving at the castle, she was greeted by Lady Pomeroy and firmly shown into 'the master's study'. 'He wants to see you on his own,' she said. 'Miss Spinks and I are banished.' Lord Pomeroy installed her in an armchair, made certain that she was comfortable and then tabled the subject of the interview. He had, he said, been startled by what Penelope had told him about Miss Spinks and the vegetables, not, of course, that he minded about the vegetables. He had not realised, regrettably, that the finances of his old friend Mr Silas were in a precarious state. He was not insulting Miss Jane by offering her advice or charity, but if she would like to tell him what was the exact position as regards money, he would be glad to listen.

If Lord Pomeroy had offered sympathy, or money, the interview would have been short, friendly, and totally inconclusive. But he had hit on the right note, the respect that we accord to someone whom we regard as a colleague, an eminently reasonable colleague, who happens to have a passing problem; one might indeed find it helpful to explain what the problem is.

Jane began, first of all rather tentatively, to explain the situation. As she went on, she gathered confidence. There were further questions, all given in the same calm manner, the same suggestion that Jane was reasonable but might have had a little less experience on this problem than her listener.

Who, might he ask, was their accountant? Ah yes, that used to be one of the better people in the county, but certainly not as well up to things as they used to be. Who held Mr Silas's portfolio? Jane said that Uncle didn't really have a portfolio now, as he hadn't done any painting for a long time. This complete *non sequitur* had the effect of reminding Lord Pomeroy that the use of technical terms can easily make someone else feel an outsider. Apparently a 'portfolio' had some meaning, quite unknown to him, in connection with painting. He must be careful to avoid his own financial 'jargon'. Who exactly at the firm handled – I mean who does Mr Silas see? Jane wasn't sure, but produced a name, recognised by Lord Pomeroy as a leftover from a bygone age. If this was the man who was looking after Mr Silas's investments, they could indeed be in trouble. This was a man of integrity, but dated. Lord Pomeroy smiled to himself. That man in his extreme youth had been likened to a more famous 'Mr Five Per Cent', and the habit had stuck.

It transpired that Mr Silas had not discussed his investments for a long, long time. Jane said that Uncle did not like talking about money nowadays, and as he had so little, it did not seem worth bothering about. She added that if you looked after the pennies, the pounds looked after themselves.

Lord Pomeroy had arrived at his present very happy condition of life by bothering a great deal about pounds, and by frequent discussion with other people who were also bothering a great deal about pounds, and dollars, and

Deutschmarks. The world was not always a very kind place for people who were afraid to seek advice. There were plenty of true stories about elderly people whose savings were locked up, and whose investments, properly managed, could have given them a reasonable degree of comfort. Lord Pomeroy thought appraisingly about Mr Silas and Miss Jane. His old friend was exactly the sort who, having made arrangements many years previously, had now put thoughts of money on one side. And Miss Jane? Lord Pomeroy reflected a little testily that women in the past had either been very extravagant or very parsimonious. Look after the pennies, indeed, when it was pounds you wanted. He had never thought of Jane as poor, but it was becoming obvious to him that circumstances had indeed made her extremely careful.

He made a few enquiries about her household. Jane, by now revelling in the luxury of having an intelligent and sympathetic listener, explained how they had managed. At some vague stage in the past, Uncle's income seemed to have dwindled. At one time there were servants. Then there had been a daily 'help' and a jobbing gardener. The gardener had come every day. Then, the daily help went. After all, you didn't really need a maid with only two of you in the family. And then you started to manage with sharing a gardener. And as it was really cheaper to manage for four people, Uncle had invited the Hetheringtons. Well, you see, Uncle *had* been under the impression that Mr Leslie was a distant relative, and of course that might be true. And Mrs Arbuthnot? Jane smiled. Well, as a matter of fact, Uncle had not intended to have Mrs Arbuthnot, but Mrs Arbuthnot had said they were coming. It was Lord

Pomeroy's turn to smile. The Mrs Arbuthnots of this world tended to do this, and it was not hard to understand how she had steam-rollered her way into Hunters Head. What was surprising was that she was still there.

And, finally, as of course Lord Pomeroy now knew, Ed, the part-time gardener, had had to go too.

The eliciting of the whole story took some time. Lord Pomeroy, early in a business career, had learnt when to hurry a client and when to take time. The financial details that he wanted could have been obtained in under five minutes from someone else in a business world. But there were times when you had to establish an atmosphere of trust and confidence, and this was one. Financial considerations put him in a different world from Miss Jane. 'Gilts' to Jane were pigs, and 'growth' was what your roses showed too much of in a wet summer. And a portfolio was either some kind of a case or else Uncle's great folder of the pictures he had – long ago – been painting.

The position gradually became clear and Lord Pomeroy blamed himself for not noticing earlier the plight of anyone in the village. He would like to come and talk to... he was about to say 'your uncle', and realised in time that Jane would resist anyone nagging Uncle. He changed it to 'come and have a real talk'.

This was as far as he could go, he felt, that evening. He was turning over in his mind whether Jane would prefer a lift home or to be left to walk. If Penelope were here, she would know; she always knew things like this. The ever timely entry of Miss Spinks supplied the answer. 'I am just going home. If Miss Jane is ready, we can accompany each other.'

The two women walked the short distance home in friendly silence, enjoying the sight of the stars over the hill – that one must be a planet – and the sounds that float from distant farms and from the village, making progress in one's own village so pleasant and so secure. The light in the farm meant that Bluebell was calving, and the light at Hunters Head meant that the kettle was on.

Chapter Fifteen

At The Hunters Arms

Lord Pomeroy, as the younger son, had not been brought up to inherit the castle, and had 'gone into' banking, with a considerable measure of success. An unexpected death had brought him back, to be the lord and master of the castle, of its grounds, half the village, and a large slice of that beautiful stretch of the county. He and his wife had been delighted and they now paid for their good fortune by giving help in the village, including sage financial service to a large proportion of the inhabitants.

They now conferred as to where the proposed meeting with Mr Silas and Jane should take place. If it was at Hunters Head, Jane might have half her thoughts on preparing the next meal. If they met at the castle, Mr Silas might have the feeling that he was not a free agent. Somewhere neutral would be better. What about The Hunters Arms? Very suitable, provided they could find an occasion there when they could be undisturbed. The proprietress of The Hunters Arms was Mrs Stone, Henrietta Stone. She was the older sister of Mrs Hawkins, so aunt by blood to Andy, as well as titular 'Aunt Min' to half the village. When approached, Aunt Min entered into the plot with great enthusiasm. What she could do, she suggested, was to open up the rarely used coffee room for them. She herself would then see that no one else strayed in there after them.

So, after a number of telephone calls, and a final message transmitted along with some Bramleys by Mr Stanley, the parties concerned converged on The Hunters Arms shortly after opening time on the Friday morning. It was a damp day, not exactly raining and not exactly fine, in fact an ordinary autumn day for that country just to the north of the moor.

Jane was feeling a little bit guilty at not having told Uncle Silas that they were intended to meet someone. Uncle was pleased to be getting Jane out of Hunters Head to come down to the village with him. Arrived at The Hunters Arms, he was equally pleased to find His Lordship there. Aunt Min said that she was half expecting a coach (funny, thought Mr Silas, this time of year, though he supposed you could never tell with townspeople), so perhaps Jane and His Lordship and Mr Silas would like their drinks in the coffee room. It did just happen that she had lit a fire there this morning.

Uncle Silas liked the idea. Now wasn't that kind of Aunt Min? Indeed, just what you would expect from her. Oh, and how nice the fire looked in there, what a contrast to the mist outside. Those surely were apple-tree logs? You couldn't always tell, he said.

The three went in and settled down with their drinks, Aunt Min carefully closing the door behind them. Lord Pomeroy had calculated on a casual approach, and allowed time for the conversation to turn to this and that. The football club was not doing as well as one had hoped. The yellow chrysanths were lasting especially well this year. A young raven had been reared successfully up above Stony Valley. The café down at the river was still doing well, as late on as this; local people went there more, now that the summer visitors had ebbed away.

His Lordship then led the talk towards more personal items. Did Silas do any painting nowadays? Lord Pomeroy reflected to himself that although he could address his old friend as Silas, his own title seemed to debar him from being anything but 'Lord Pomeroy'. Still, in this conversation, this might be a good thing, as he was getting ready to play the role of elder statesman and offer some unwelcome advice. Had Silas been in Exeter lately? His Lordship wondered if Silas had seen the exhibition at the Senate House, perhaps while doing business in Exeter.

At this stage, Aunt Min looked in to see if they wanted anything further and went out again. Jane, espied by someone in the bar, was called out. Thus left, Lord Pomeroy continued his labyrinthine tactics, until it did transpire that Silas had indeed not done anything at all about his investments for a long time... no, not for a very long time.

There was a pause. Lord Pomeroy waited thoughtfully for the significance of this to strike Mr Silas, who indeed found himself faced with a new idea, rather like a mediaeval explorer who hears that the world is round. Mr Silas spoke with the gravity that the situation demanded: 'Does Your Lordship think that I should go and see my accountant?'

This was precisely what Lord Pomeroy had been leading up to. True, he would have preferred that the matter should be discussed with some younger member of the firm, if not some other firm altogether. All the same, it was sufficient to have reached the point that Mr Silas was entertaining the novel idea of going to see the accountant.

Mr Silas was getting ready to ask another important question. He did not regard discussing his investments with his accountant as anything but a waste of a perfectly good morning, when he could have been up on the moor or planning his next painting, or… well almost anything. The journey by bus to Exeter would also be unpleasant in this weather. But what he was suddenly thinking about was Jane. Several times lately she had seemed tired; more tired than she ought to have been. Was it… good gracious… was she worrying about *money*?

Rather hesitantly, he put this to Lord Pomeroy. 'Lord Pomeroy, we have known each other a long time. I wonder if I might trespass on old acquaintance and ask you what is, what is, I fear, a purely personal question?'

Lord Pomeroy was surprised at this, said yes, and was even more surprised at the innocence of the question that followed.

'Might I put it to you that there is a possibility, just a slight possibility I mean, that my niece is finding some little difficulty in meeting certain of our household bills?' (There, it was out.)

Lord Pomeroy reflected on the extraordinary way in which the members of a family could be unaware of each other's financial circumstances. He envisaged Penelope's reaction to such a situation – and the exact terms in which *she* would have made *him* aware of any great change in their finances. He was tempted to reflect on the good points of his own generation's upbringing, but moved to concentrate on the matter in hand.

Yes, he thought that Silas was right and that Jane just might be having some difficulty. Jane at the minute was having an animated conversation with Aunt Min, and their voices could be heard through the door. It looked as if Jane was well occupied. Lord Pomeroy pressed on. If Silas would allow him, he would arrange for the visit to the accountant's; in fact, if Silas wished it, His Lordship would be glad to accompany him.

Uncle Silas accepted at once. He felt like a non-swimmer being offered a life belt. If Lord Pomeroy would see to this… well, the matter was as good as done, and he would be most grateful to accept this kind offer of help. Yes, most grateful. The matter was as good as done. Many thanks.

They finished their drinks.

Uncle Silas, finding that all this necessary and unpleasant business about money was over, turned to the infinitely more interesting topic of the effect of the light on the view. It was extraordinary the way the mistiness of the air that morning was showing up the castle, or, alternatively, the darkness of the castle had made the drizzly air seem almost transparent. Had Lord Pomeroy noticed this? No? Well he should come out now and have a look. The French painters were the ones who had captured these impressions of light.

Aunt Min in the meantime had been glad to see Jane called into the bar. She particularly wanted to have a word with her, alone, though she would not have interfered with His Lordship's arrangements. However, Jane being in the bar, the opportunity had occurred. Aunt Min didn't waste words.

'Miss Jane, it sounds all right, and it's good of you, but you mustn't do it.'

Jane was a bit taken aback. She had intended to have another drink and then get back to get the lunch ready. She couldn't see anything wrong with either. She smiled at Aunt Min.

'Aunt Min, I don't know what it is you say I am not to do. But if you say I'm not to, then I won't. Only you had better tell me what it is I'm not to do.'

'Why, having Andy and Maisie as tenants or something when they get married.'

Jane burst out laughing. 'Aunt Min, I don't know what you are talking about – I mean, I do know, but we really weren't sure that we were going to have them. I mean, I hadn't spoken to anyone about it. How on earth did you know?'

Explanations followed. To anyone who knew the village, it was simple. Andy was indeed ready and anxious to get married to Maisie, only where would they live? Maisie had told him what Caroline had said, and he had told his mother, and his mother had hot-footed it up to consult her older sister. Mrs Hawkins did not like the idea. Nor did Aunt Min. Young people should start on their own. And if not on their own, well not... she didn't know how to put it, but both women knew what they meant. Not with people of a completely different background, et cetera.

'So there you are, Miss Jane. I didn't think it would do. And I wanted to tell you so.'

Jane explained that she too had been doubtful. 'I mean, they're two nice young people. But it would be awkward having them. There isn't a kitchen there, and our only bathroom *is* there. Though goodness knows, I was glad of the money when you sent us the Americans. And, really, I'm not sure that Andy and Maisie would fit in with everyone else.'

Aunt Min was quite well aware that Jane might be having financial difficulties. The procession of vegetables from the castle to Hunters Head had not gone unmarked. And Andy had dropped a word to his mother. And Mrs Hawkins had just mentioned something to Aunt Min. And in any case, what was mentioned in passing, or discussed, or questioned, at the bar of The Hunters Arms did include most of the business of the village. Now Jane came to think of it, she might have done better to think of consulting Aunt Min than the Gregsons.

She was relieved to find that her own instinct not to offer a 'flat' to Andy and Maisie was supported by Aunt Min. So that was settled.

At that minute, Lord Pomeroy was led out by Uncle Silas, intent on pointing out to him the exact effect of the shadow cast by the castle. Jane said goodbye, and accompanied them.

Aunt Min's final remark had been very odd, but there was no time to go into it. 'If you did want visitors again, why not one of your uncle's friends, like that Mr Mannie he is always on about, the one who's a painter.'

One of Uncle's friends? Funny, she had never heard of a Mr Mannie.

Chapter Sixteen

At the accountant's

Uncle Silas had not, for a very long time, been to see his accountant. As Lord Pomeroy had agreed to make all the arrangements, there was no need for Mr Silas to bother any more about it. This was fortunate, for Mr Silas did not like dealing with money. If it had been the old days of course, with golden sovereigns being pushed to and fro, that would have been different; there was a certain *something* about sovereigns. Come to think of it, what had he done with the sovereign that a mythical great-uncle had presented him with before the mythical great-uncle departed for... was it India?

'Janey,' he called out, 'was it India that your great-great-uncle was going to?'

Jane wondered what had put this thought into Uncle's head. 'Yes, Uncle,' she replied. 'Bombay, you used to say. But now we're going to Exeter, not India. Lord Pomeroy is coming to pick us up, at half past.'

'Yes, of course, I hadn't forgotten,' asserted Uncle with conscious virtue. 'You're coming too, aren't you?'

Jane said yes, she was coming to Exeter, and so was Mrs Arbuthnot, but she and Mrs Arbuthnot were then going shopping and Lord Pomeroy would be taking Uncle to the accountant's. (It sounded, to Uncle's ears, ominously like taking a dog to the vet.) 'And Caroline', she added, 'was getting her husband's lunch.' Not that the last detail was of any special interest to Mr Silas, who enjoyed his food without much knowledge of how the womenfolk contrived its regular appearance. What a kind man His Lordship was. It was a pity it was such a misty day... they wouldn't have much in the way of a view. That nice stretch too, where the land dropped steeply to the north of the road, to show the fields laid out below.

Lord Pomeroy arrived, driving something that his household referred to as the old bus, and that seemed to his present passengers a magnificent equipage. He mentioned to Jane, as she got in and sat down, that he thought she needn't worry about accommodation for Andy and Maisie. Jane was surprised to find that His Lordship had heard of that stillborn proposal. Through his wife, perhaps? Then they were all in and away. Once in Exeter, she and Mrs Arbuthnot went off for their morning's shopping spree, with instructions about when they would all meet up.

Lord Pomeroy and Uncle approached the accountant's. It stood, naturally, near the centre of the city, in what, for fifty years and more, had been a fashionable address. Must have kept some clients, was Lord Pomeroy's thought.

An elegantly dressed young woman welcomed them in. This girl clerk, thought Mr Silas, seemed a little young. Ought she, he wondered, to be dealing with clients' private accounts? The girl clerk, who had just celebrated her forty-second birthday, passed them on to an even younger-looking person, even more elegantly dressed, with a, 'Mr Robinson is going to look after you.' Mr Robinson ushered them in to the sanctum of Mr Five Per Cent.

'The very room,' exclaimed Mr Silas, 'the very room. It hasn't changed, not one little bit.' Mr Silas was as pleased as Lord Pomeroy was dismayed. Lord Pomeroy did not care for dealing with accountants whose offices remained exactly the same for over twenty years. He turned to the young man questioningly. They had expected to meet Mr Five Per Cent. Had he not arrived? Had anything happened?

The young man seemed embarrassed. Mr Five Per Cent had it in his diary, but sometimes he was... er... not able to come, and it was beginning to look as if this was one of those occasions. Lord Pomeroy suggested that they should telephone. The young man sprang to the door, almost as if forestalling any attempt to reach a telephone. There was no telephone, of course, in the sacred sanctum. When Mr Five Per Cent was not able to come, explained this young man, someone else in the office would take it for him. He himself had got all the papers ready. He indicated an aged metal box, on which could be seen on a clearly printed label the name Mr A Marner. So if Lord Pomeroy and Mr Marner would like to sit down, they could proceed to the business in hand. He motioned them to the ancient leather armchairs.

Lord Pomeroy had a very good idea that 'being not able to come' was a euphemism for 'having forgotten'. So far, so good. He regarded the young man with interest. A fashionable haircut – Exeter. The shape of the jacket – hardly London; Paris perhaps, or New York. This could be a considerable improvement. The ancient box and the unchanged room were what he had anticipated. Neither Mr A Marner nor Mr Five Per Cent was of today when it came to talking about investments. But perhaps this young man might be a bit more astute. Robinson, wasn't it, that the young woman had called him?

Coffee, biscuits and sherry were produced, swiftly and efficiently. Uncle Silas's eyes rested on an old minute book on the shelves –'Bless my soul, I remember that,' and he became engrossed in it. Various questions and answers were fast convincing Lord Pomeroy that the young man was of a very different calibre from what he had feared. Years of dealing with all sorts of amounts of money had taught His Lordship that the first step, if you *are* going to go on doing business (which he had not in this instance expected), was to get to know the other man. The young man also appeared to have learnt this lesson.

So they spent some time in an unhurried exchange of views. The young man explained that he was new to the firm; until recently he had been employed by a well known London-based firm, friends of his father's, to do some business in the changing Arab sheikhdoms. He had formed the opinion that the time the Arabs spent in drinking coffee with you was just to allow themselves time to sum you up; he felt that at the end of the day, they would be found to be more shrewd than the quick-acting Americans. And now his father had sent him down here.

'To see how the other half lives?' queried Lord Pomeroy, and accepted more coffee.

The young man smiled. Yes, to see how the other half lived. He decided that he could speak openly to His Lordship. 'Lord Pomeroy, you will understand what can happen in a firm like this. The big people, like the county council, take their advice from London investment brokers now, not from us.' Lord Pomeroy nodded. He had in fact known when the chairman of the County Council Finance Committee had thought of changing their advisers, and had indeed given them a likely name.

'The older generation,' went on the young man, 'leaves its money here. And the old man doesn't let anyone else handle their accounts. It's only in the last... perhaps eighteen months, that he has stopped coming in every day.'

Mr Robinson paused. Lord Pomeroy had the gift of inspiring confidence. Just as Miss Jane had found it possible to talk to him, so did the young accountant, a difference being that the young accountant was taking a shrewd gamble on what he thought would benefit his firm.

'To be truthful,' he said, 'we ought not to have left things to him, but one doesn't like taking them away. He is old, and this firm has been his life, you may say. But now, when he doesn't turn up for an interview, like today, we take all the papers and do the follow-up, and he doesn't seem to mind. I think that really he is glad when he's relieved of the responsibility, only he doesn't want to look as if he is giving up.'

Lord Pomeroy noted, with approval, the firm's concern for its failing chief.

Mr Robinson explained that as Mr Five Per Cent had not yet put in an appearance, they should feel free to get on with the business. He held up the key. 'Will Mr Marner do the unlocking, or would he like me to?'

Mr Silas, recalled from the long-ago world of the minute book, was ready to play his part in the proceedings. He took the key, pointed out who the maker had been, and happily turned it in the lock. Wonderful, he commented, opening as easily as that after all these years. Lord Pomeroy could not help thinking that either Mr Robinson or the young woman in the outer office had been practising with it.

There, inside the lid, was the little piece of paper on which were recorded the dates of opening, the last one being... good gracious, no wonder Miss Jane was finding money difficult.

The first papers were lifted out. Mr Silas was most interested. Yes, he did remember that one. No, he had only a vague memory of that other one. Was this one something to do with a house we own in Torquay? What an interesting set of papers. And how kind of the accountant to have looked after them so well for all these years. Had the young man – Mr Robinson, wasn't it? – noticed the writing on this one? A beautiful hand, beautiful. Mr Silas motioned for a piece of paper and showed that he could produce much the same handwriting. But not for every day, young man, not for every day. And had Lord Pomeroy noticed the colour of the ink?

Lord Pomeroy and the young man smiled at each other. It was evident that Mr Silas had completely forgotten the purpose of the interview, namely, to investigate his financial position. Mr Silas was now willing to stay and potter round this fascinating old office for as long as the others were there. Mr Robinson finally turned to Lord Pomeroy. Might he make a suggestion? If Mr Marner would allow him to take temporary charge of his papers, he would prepare a statement for Mr Marner. It would take a few days, and although it would not be by any means complete, it would give them all a clearer idea of what the position really was.

Mr Marner's attention being gained, he was quite willing to agree to anything Lord Pomeroy thought was right. And if Lord Pomeroy thought it right that this astute and personable young man should at any rate prepare a statement, then this would be the thing to do. How nice. And now, duty done, they could get home again. How splendid. It would be nice to get home again. Though, he must admit, it had been a much more interesting morning than he had expected.

Lord Pomeroy and Mr Silas took their leave, and went to meet Miss Jane and Mrs Arbuthnot.

Mr Robinson was to depart early from his office, bearing with him what looked like several evenings' work on the box marked Mr A Marner. From the glimpses he had had, he would guess that an infinitely more favourable income could be arranged. Not that you could always tell. Sometimes it turned out to be the reverse. Some poor old souls had found that they didn't even own their own homes. But this lot looked promising, very promising.

Mr Robinson could not have been more concerned if it had been his own income he was to decipher. And in a way it was – for if he could not convince Lord Pomeroy of his firm's ability to handle Mr Marner's accounts, he could see that his firm would shortly be one customer down.

Chapter Seventeen

Autumn gold

The party that drove back from Exeter was a great deal quieter than the one that had gone in. Mrs Arbuthnot was tired after the shopping. She leant back, closed her eyes, and peacefully, apart from a few snores, dropped off to sleep. Jane was feeling disappointed. She supposed she was being unreasonable, but all the same, she had expected that Uncle would be leaving the accountant's with a bundle of notes in his hand, or at least a substantial cheque. All that Lord Pomeroy had had to tell her was that he was glad they had been in, and in a few days' time they might be hearing something.

Uncle Silas was wide awake. He was in a state of some excitement; seeing that old writing had reminded him of the pen-and-ink work he used to do in the past. This might be the very thing. He had been thinking that it would be nice if they could give Lady Pomeroy a present, now that she was so friendly with Miss Spinks and seemed to be in and out quite a bit. But what? Even to Uncle's other-worldly eyes, it was obvious that Lady Penelope Pomeroy was very rich and had everything. But a pen-and-ink drawing of, say, the gate to the castle gardens – or better still the silver birch on their boundary? Uncle decided that he would start on this as soon as they got in, only it was a pity that he would have to go up two flights of stairs for his drawing things, and that his room, where he could spread out the paper, would be chilly.

Lord Pomeroy drove fast and smoothly. He was satisfied that a reasonable step had been taken and turned his thoughts to wondering about Mr Robinson. Some potential there. It could make a difference to the firm. You needed young people of calibre to keep up the professional level in an area that was so attractive to the retired and the older people. You needed youngsters like Mr Robinson in the county, and other young men like Andy Hawkins in the village. He thought over the two interesting conversations he had had recently, one with Andy's mother, and the other with the butcher. Lord Pomeroy's business experience made him an invaluable adviser on sums over... well, on money in general. His role of lord of the manor had come to him so unexpectedly on the death in an accident of his older brother, and he was continuing to interpret his role as keeping an eye on the business affairs of the village. Anyone, like the butcher on this occasion, who was contemplating a change in their affairs, was finding it worthwhile to come and have a talk with His Lordship. Lord Pomeroy felt he could almost have put up a sign, 'Nothing too large and nothing too small'. He smiled to himself as he thought again of young Mr Robinson. Fancy negotiating with oil sheikhs one week, and with old Mr Five Per Cent's genteel clientele the next. Mr Robinson would be very useful if he stayed on in the country, very useful. Might get him on the County Council.

They drew up at Hunters Head. Mrs Arbuthnot woke up and took charge. 'Lord Pomeroy,' commanded the loud voice, 'you will help Miss Jane take the things down to the kitchen, by the outside steps.' Lord Pomeroy obeyed. He was regarded by most people in the village with a certain degree of awe, either because of his position as lord of the manor, or, among the less feudally minded, because of his fabulous wealth. It made quite a change to be in the company of Mrs Arbuthnot.

Jane too obeyed, having first made certain that Uncle and Mrs Arbuthnot were on their way in by the front door. She need not have worried, for Mrs Arbuthnot was waiting only to get to her room to take her shoes off, while Uncle was equally anxious to get in to work out his ideas on paper.

The strains of number one in the American charts reminded him that Miss Caroline (he must remember, Mrs Hetherington, not Miss Caroline) would be willing to go up and bring him his sketching block and inks. The hall, with its log fire, would be a pleasant place, and he could spread out the paper on the table there. Miss Caroline was delighted to go up and fetch his things for him. He turned round and became aware that the hall table was occupied. Eggs – vistas of golden brown eggs, and orangey gold chrysanthemums that had not been there when they went out. And a chicken, ready for cooking, more of a white than a yellow, but still an opulent sight. In his mind some of all this was replacing the silver birch on Lady Penelope's greetings card. Yes, he would make it something rich and autumnal, say *Harvest Gold*. No... *Autumn Gold*, or... *Yellow Harvest*. Or should it just be *Eggs*, or something jocular like *Tomorrow's Breakfast*? In view of this number of guests they were always having at the castle, this might be accurate. On the whole, he thought he favoured *Harvest Gold*.

This pleasant reverie was interrupted by the return of Caroline from upstairs with his sketching things, and by the emergence from the kitchen stairs of Jane, accompanied somewhat unexpectedly by Mrs Hawkins. Mrs Hawkins was flushed, either with exertion or excitement. What she was wearing was definitely her best outfit, including a most elegant hat, with rakish feathers, in tones of red and brown. The women in the village could have identified the hat as emanating, via the autumn sale, from the bank manager's wife. They would also have noted that the air it bestowed on its wearer really suited Mrs Hawkins better than its erstwhile owner. Andy's mother had been a beauty of the village 'in the old days'.

It immediately occurred to Uncle that Mrs Hawkins should be the focal point of his picture. She did look the part. A good job he had settled on *Harvest* as the title rather than *Autumn*. He knew that older ladies did not like being reminded of their age.

'Uncle,' Jane firmly attracted his attention, 'Mrs Hawkins has come to tell us the news.'

'Oh, Miss Jane,' expostulated Mrs Hawkins, 'I came to bring you the eggs, as a sort of, as a sort of way of saying thank you to you, but it's all right and you don't need to think of giving up your first floor to my son and Maisie. Though they are getting engaged now.'

Uncle expressed his congratulations. Andy was a very good-looking young man, 'as your son would be' he added, bowing in courtly manner to Mrs Hawkins and getting ready to make his request.

Again he was forestalled. Mrs Hawkins had certainly come to say how grateful she was to Miss Jane. It was partly for the possibility of rooms, but more for the way in which Andy had been influenced. 'He seems altogether more serious like, and I do think that you and Mr Marner have helped him.' This expression of gratitude was followed up with the item of news that was shortly to resound through the village. 'And Miss Jane, you and your uncle can't think how pleased I am. Andy is going to be the chief assistant in the shop. Bill is going off to Plymouth' (Bill being the then chief assistant), 'to a chain of butchers, and Andy has been offered *his* place in the business, *and*, now that he is getting married, he and Maisie are being offered the place over the shop.'

This was news indeed, and what a metamorphosis. Andy as a married man (to be). Andy as the butcher's chief assistant, left in charge of the shop on many occasions. The more Jane thought about it, the more she could see how Andy was changing. The debonair and graceless Randy Andy of the past might indeed be ready to become the go-ahead chief assistant to the village butcher. Maisie would be a help to him too. Not above running down to the shop and lending a hand when things were busy.

A thought struck her. The news was sudden. She looked at Mrs Hawkins. Mrs Hawkins answered the unspoken query. 'No, Miss Jane, thanks be. I did wonder that myself. The Lord has been good to us. I'm so grateful that I had to bring you up a few things.' She indicated the largesse spread out on the hall table.

The general jubilation was interrupted by the appearance at the front door of Lord Pomeroy, who had come up the outside steps from the kitchen. He had delayed for a while in order to have a look at the somewhat dilapidated garden. He was leaving now; would Mrs Hawkins like a lift? Yes, certainly Mrs Hawkins would. So Mrs Hawkins, her empty shopping basket and her exuberant hat, departed with His Lordship.

To tell the truth, their departure left both Jane and Uncle Silas feeling rather flat. Uncle had not negotiated a sitting for his picture, and after the radiance of Mrs Hawkins, the eggs and that pallid-looking chicken seemed a bit dull. Jane too was deflated. She mentally translated the eggs and the chicken into meals – roast chicken, mushroom omelette, chicken soufflé and then soup. Very nice. At least three days. But small miracles, like eggs, even in that quantity, were not enough.

She had hoped, when Lord Pomeroy reappeared, that he was going to say something like, 'I am clear in my mind that the accounts will...' Will what? Give us enough to pay for electricity and the coal and the telephone? The overall prospect was really unchanged. She had expected a lot from the visit today. Discussing it ahead of time with Lord Pomeroy, it had all sounded so reasonable.

She tried to feel cheered by the news about Andy. That really was nice. And the young man deserved it.

All the same, the little miracles weren't going to be enough. And you could no longer take your mind off things by going and sitting in the garden, for that was getting so run down. Oh dear.

Chapter Eighteen

The first floor

Uncle was in good spirits the next morning. The view from the window refreshed him, and there was Jane with his early morning cup of tea. Oh good. Had Jane noticed how white the distant moors looked?

Jane had awoken from a persistent dream of going to Exeter in a taxi, and of a policeman on point duty who kept stopping them and advising her not to let the first floor to Mr Hawkins and his fiancée. Well, at least that had been settled and she need not feel that perhaps she ought to have offered to have them at Hunters Head. The coming marriage, and Andy's promotion, were good news indeed.

Breakfast was a cheerful meal. Breakfasts since 'that morning' continued to take place in the kitchen. Miss Spinks was full of the preparations for Christmas that were going on at the castle, and how many people were coming to stay, and how many other people came every week to see His Lordship. 'Everyone with business seems to come and see him.' Jane's spirits flagged – she had been one of the ones 'with business' and it didn't seem to have done her any good. Mr Hetherington mentioned that in his opinion, as a comparative outsider, the village was fortunate in having such a businesslike and amiable family at the castle. Mr Hetherington was in good health again, happy at sharing the connubial bed with Caroline, and not over anxious to have a joint living-room again. The sound of music from a distance suited him much better.

Mrs Arbuthnot and Caroline were talking over the delightful prospect of the wedding. 'What will you wear, dear? I think I shall have my blue altered…' and so on and so on. Caroline had had a genuinely unselfish desire to help Maisie and Andy when she had suggested the first floor as a home for them, and now felt that she was reaping her just reward in the prospect of a valid reason for getting new clothes. Caroline's much-prized contributions to the village's jumble sales and second-hand stalls were second only to those of the bank manager's wife. Mrs Arbuthnot, who was normally Jane's great ally, seemed to have forgotten that there were financial considerations as she entered into a discussion on whether to alter the blue ('the colour does suit me so well, and I have hardly worn it') or whether to go in for an entirely new outfit. And what would Jane be wearing? And what would they be getting to give as a wedding present? Did Miss Spinks know what Lady Pen and Lord Pomeroy were going to give?

It was Caroline who suddenly exclaimed, 'Oooh, I've got such a good idea. Now that there is no one coming to live in the first floor, can't you let it to some more rich Americans and make some money? Or use it as a picture gallery and charge people admission to see Mr Silas's pictures? He's got ever such a lot upstairs.'

Jane feigned a welcome to these suggestions. Although they were out of the question, they did show a spirit of... she hunted for the right word... a spirit of concern, unusual from Caroline. Also it was good that everyone was assuming that there was to be a communal wedding present 'from us'. If only, somehow, this gathered family could keep its haven. Aloud, she thanked Caroline for the idea and said that they would have to see (the stock answer through the ages to small children).

After breakfast, everyone except Mr Hetherington went off chattering excitedly about the wedding and 'my blue' and the unusual clouds in the west, and whether it meant a storm. Jane was about to embark on the usual tasks. She then realised that Mr Hetherington was still in the kitchen. He gave a little cough, as people so often do when they are going to discuss something embarrassing, like money or sex.

'Miss Marner,' he said, 'might I have a... er... a private word with you?'

Jane wondered if this was a prelude to giving notice or a request that she should try to stop Caroline buying too many new clothes for the wedding. It didn't seem to her that she was in a position to do much about either. However, remembering the unhurried way in which she had been allowed to talk by Lord Pomeroy, she sat down again and offered Mr Hetherington another cup of tea. That he was addressing her as Miss Marner instead of

Miss Jane indicated something of the importance to him of the conversation.

'Thank you, Miss Marner. Well yes, yes please, I would like another cup. Miss Marner...' (pause) 'my wife and I are very happy to be here, very settled' (So he wasn't giving notice.) 'What I want to say is this... I mean, I don't know, I really don't know...' (anyone who read Mr Hetherington's lucid and learned articles would have been nonplussed at his inability to express himself verbally). 'I can't think how we should have managed this autumn without you, and without Mrs Arbuthnot. She is a very kind and thoughtful lady. Now, what I want to say, and I don't want you to misunderstand' (perhaps he *was* going to give notice?). 'I, well my wife and I, I should say we, we like being in the two rooms on the ground floor. I have my papers in the bedroom, which is large and gives me plenty of room for reading and writing. I mean, there is room for my desk and the shelves as well as the bed. And Caroline has the little annexe where she can be and play her records in the daytime. We would like to keep it like that.'

So that was it. Unsuited though these two seemed at first sight, they had the tie of nights together, and were now being mercifully spared long days as well. Well, well, well.

'I would have liked to offer you more money,' he continued, 'but the fact is that my income is limited. I do get paid for my articles, but I'm afraid Caroline has always spent rather a lot. I very much hope that you will feel able to manage with just a little extra.' And he mentioned a sum.

He paused unhappily. Jane, who had not expected any

more money from that quarter (what that Caroline spent… a good job he did get paid for this articles), thanked him and said that the extra he mentioned would be adequate. Either they were all going to have to go, she was thinking, or they could all stay; in any case, even a little would help. At least she could now be clear in her own mind that they were not going to have to get the big double bed up the stairs again, with all the Hetheringtons' things… 'gear' was the in-word, wasn't it? She idly wondered if Michael, who had been so helpful in moving the furniture downstairs, was on his way to Teheran.

Mr Hetherington then followed the rest out of the kitchen, leaving Jane to concentrate on the next meal. No… she would tidy upstairs first. She might even have another look at the first-floor rooms. Perhaps going into them might suggest something to her. She sallied up from the kitchen, and paused in the hall to notice with pleasure that the flowers did not need doing.

She went on up to the first floor, to the rooms once occupied – so long ago it seemed now – by Mr and Mrs Hetherington, Mrs Arbuthnot and Miss Spinks. The rooms, bereft of small furniture, seemed empty, but were enlivened by the photos that had arrived from the Americans and had been propped up on the mantelpieces. She smiled as she looked at them. In fact, it would have been hard not to smile at those cheerful faces, with the greetings inscribed below – from Robert E and Susannah Jackson, and David and Eleanor Cartwright, to our dear second home, and Mr Silas and Miss Jane and all of you. Robert E Jackson – she had almost forgotten their names, what with one thing and another, and all the hopeful fuss over

Uncle's investments, from which nothing so far had emerged. A pity you couldn't hope for more Robert E Jacksons to miss the turning on the way from Tintagel to Glastonbury.

The chief thing that the rooms suggested to Jane was that they were in need of decorating. She must get those spiders' webs down. Mind you, they were still nice rooms, with what the estate agents would have called a southern aspect and extensive rural views, not to mention all modern conveniences on the same floor. All modern conveniences were one bathroom and lavatory. This in fact was the bathroom for the whole house. All modern conveniences seemed to need redecorating. It was a pity, thought Jane, that the best rooms in the house should be empty. But you could hardly have anyone else living there and sharing the one bathroom, certainly not with Caroline as one of the people doing the sharing. In any case... and Jane's thoughts reverted to how well this odd family had settled down together. Anyone else, except passing admirers like the Americans had been, seemed unlikely participants.

Uncle had become aware of Jane pottering about in the first-floor rooms. That was what he enjoyed, a gentle potter. Very interesting the things you came upon, like that minute book in the accountant's office had been. He regretted that Jane had so little time these days for a nice potter. My goodness, how the old angle cupboard showed up now that the room was so empty. A nice piece of furniture.

Uncle went over to the nice piece of furniture and discovered in it some old newspapers that had somehow been deposited there. 'Look, Jane, look at these. This one is surely… yes, it's a picture of Grandmère's dress she wore when she went to Buckingham Palace.' Jane was no longer sure of why Grandmère had been at Buckingham Palace, or under which monarch, or whether she had been accompanied by Grandpère (and if so, why wasn't he in the picture), but there certainly was the picture of Grandmère. Jane was not quite sure whose grandmère it was. Not hers. Perhaps Uncle's?

Uncle reminisced happily. He settled himself by the fairly sunny window, in the armchair, the one that had been 'Caroline's' but had not followed her downstairs to the little annexe. The old newspapers reminded him of so many things. Had he ever acknowledged to Jane that he had always been a bit afraid of the horses? Yes, Uncle had. 'Lovely to look at, of course.' He was also remembering that money had been more plentiful, or rather that you hadn't needed so much of it. He didn't know why, but you seemed to need more now, and you didn't really eat or drink more, or wear more. It was odd. He looked at Jane with sudden admiration. It was wonderful how she had managed, wonderful. He again inspected the pictures of Grandmère.

'You know, Janey,' he said. 'I've no idea why she was going to the palace. Just being presented, perhaps. Here's another picture, on a big horse. Do you think she rode it to get to the palace?'

He chuckled happily. Another thought struck him. 'I think that you deserve to go up to the palace. I'm sure you have done much more than she ever did. You have been wonderful, wonderful, keeping us all going.'

Jane felt a bit embarrassed. She was not used to

expressions of gratitude. She almost had tears in her eyes, till she wondered how one got to Buckingham Palace and had a mental picture of being driven up to the palace gates by Andy in a newly painted butcher's van, with 'and Hawkins' on the side. But, to return to the present.

Chapter Nineteen

Good news

Sunday passed, without message or sign from the castle, or of Michael, or a substitute.

A few days later, the fateful word was relayed, by Miss Spinks, together with two very fine heads of broccoli. Lord Pomeroy had been called to London, but was back and he had a telephone conversation with Mr Robinson, and would like to have a talk with Mr Marner and Miss Jane, and Lady Penelope recommended cheese sauce over them but only a touch of mustard in it. And would Mr Marner and Miss Jane be able to come up that evening as the guild was off? Yes, of course, yes.

By the evening, the weather had changed from a cold bright snap to a murky mist. Away from the moor, it would have been referred to as rain. To Jane and Uncle, and Lord Pomeroy and Lady Pen, and all the other 728 inhabitants, it wasn't any particular weather. In town, His Lordship might even have sent a car to fetch his friends.

On the edge of the moor, one did not feel that weather of this kind merited any special attention. Jane and Uncle cheerfully put on their raincoats, once Jane had recovered Uncle's from where he had abandoned it earlier in the day, and set off. To Jane's surprise, Uncle seemed quite glad to finish the short walk and get to the warmth of the castle.

The warmth was both physical and spiritual. Lord and Lady Pomeroy welcomed them in. There was a fire alight in the study, and drinks were brought in. And... of course... there was that nice young Mr Robinson from the accounts in Exeter.

To Jane's wary eyes, it seemed that there was an appearance of good news to come... but she told herself not to hope too much.

They took their places. Then Lord Pomeroy, rather like a conjuror producing a rabbit from a hat, invited Mr Robinson to explain to Mr Marner what his financial position was. Mr Robinson produced some sheets of paper, and embarked on a careful and accurate explanation. There were phrases like 'when interest rates world wide fell sharply', 'bank minimum lending rate followed the trend cautiously', and 'the long awaited downturn as FIFO accounting turns stock profits into stock losses having yet to manifest itself' – which meant nothing to Jane. When Mr Robinson finally referred to 'gilts moving unsurprisingly', she had a clear memory of the morning that the Gregsons' pigs got out, and was forced to own that she did not understand what Mr Robinson was saying. He immediately apologised; he had been so concerned at making the position clear to Lord Pomeroy that he had forgotten that he was using what to his clients was a language as foreign as Swahili. He then altered his words, and explained, perfectly clearly, what the position was. One third of Mr Marner's money could not be reinvested; it had to stay, just like this, as it was... he grasped an imaginary ball firmly in his hands. But the other two thirds, and here he made a fine gesture of flinging open his arms, the other two thirds could be used, if they would take his advice, to produce a sum each year of... and he mentioned the sum. It was true that against that Mr Marner would incur rather higher tax, and that there would be accountant's fees. But even allowing for that, this gave a satisfactory amount of disposable income.

There was a momentary silence as Jane and Uncle Silas tried to digest this information. Then a smile broke out on Uncle Silas's face, and he turned to Jane with a look of love and thankfulness. 'Janey, I think Mr Robinson is saying that it's going to be all right.'

Jane just sat there, dumb with wonder and gratitude, not knowing if she was going to laugh or to burst into tears. It was going to be all right. They would be able to manage. It was going to be all right. Thank God, thank God. Uncle would not have to move.

Jane found the tears pouring down her face as she tried to express satisfaction. She got as far as 'Oh, Nunky', and put her head on her knees and unashamedly wept. Uncle patted the shoulder nearest to him and blew his nose. Lady Pen, dabbing a hanky at her own eyes, moved next to Jane and put an arm round her. For a moment no one spoke – a moment of quiet and profound thankfulness, shared by them all. In a more religious age, one of them would have called, a little histrionically, on God to bless them.

Lord Pomeroy stood up and raised his glass. 'Mr Chairman' (he conjured up an imaginary chairman in an empty armchair), 'Mr Chairman, ladies and gentlemen, I propose a toast. Will you be upstanding and join me in drinking a health to... to the future of Hunters Head and its family. May they remain prosperous, blessed and a treasured part of our village. To Hunters Head.'

They stood and drank. The solemn moment ended and there was a babble of conversation. Neither Jane nor Mr Marner really understood what it was that Mr Robinson was reporting. That this could be done, and that that could not, but that something else – I think so, Lord Pomeroy, but what would be your opinion? None of this meant anything at all to the Marners. All Jane knew was that even allowing for tax and the fees of the accountant, there would be enough to pay the fuel bills and the telephone, and even some new clothes for Uncle as well as herself for the wedding. As for the rest, she could manage somehow. Never mind about the decorating and any repairs and the garden. She would manage.

She turned to Lord Pomeroy. 'We have so much to thank you for.'

He smiled. If he had known her thoughts about 'just managing somehow', he would have been less pleased. He did not believe in 'just managing somehow'. He believed in adequate planning. He would have liked to see rather more income and rather fewer liabilities. That poor garden!

Penelope's voice recalled him, to 'Look at this card that Uncle Silas has done so beautifully for me.'

143

It was indeed a pleasing card, a picture of eggs and some lively little yellow and brown chicks that had become a spring greeting rather than an autumn one. Uncle shook his head. He had meant to put more into it. He mumbled something about 'not being as young as he had been', and he refrained from saying that the room where he painted was too cold; he did not want anyone to think he was complaining about his niece's arrangements for the household.

The evening lingered pleasantly on, with lots of conversation alternating with pleasant little pauses. Jane was usually the one who remembered what time it was and when to leave. On this particular evening, she was still contemplating the prospect of having money (*money*) when Uncle stood up and started saying goodnight to their hosts. 'Oh yes, yes, goodnight, and thank you, goodnight.' It was going to be all right.

Chapter Twenty

The final miracle

There was a general convergence towards church on the Sunday morning.

Lord Pomeroy was walking along discussing with his wife the business affairs of Hunters Head. He was not quite so optimistic as Jane had been. He was satisfied with Mr Robinson's competence; the papers were by no means completed, but the overall picture was not going to be markedly different. It might vary, it might vary perceptibly, but on the whole one could see that, counting the contributions from Mrs Arbuthnot and the Hetheringtons and the Sphinx, there was going to be enough income to meet the ordinary household bills. What worried the Pomeroys was the lack of a foreseeable margin with which to meet the unforeseeable. There must come repairs, and there would be decorating. You could of course do wonders yourself with decorating, but even if the labour was an affair of love, you still had to buy the paint and the paper.

And repairs. Lord Pomeroy shook his head. He had had a good look round the day they came back from Exeter, and he did not care for what he had noticed of the gutters at Hunters Head. You did not, as Jane had opined, 'just manage somehow'. You planned, and you foresaw.

Jane and Uncle made their way to church. Mr Hetherington had intended to but wanted to finish an article. If Miss Jane would excuse him, he would not accompany them this morning. Mrs Arbuthnot had volunteered to get lunch ready, and had commandeered a not unwilling Caroline to help carry things from the kitchen.

There was a good congregation, even though most mums and several dads were busy getting ready for Christmas. Jane was so overcome with thankfulness that she would not have been surprised to see the church bedecked with a banner announcing something like 'salvation has come'. The rest of the village though had presumably been unaware of the financial troubles hanging over Hunters Head, the rest of the village, that is, with the exception of Lord Pomeroy and Lady Pomeroy, of Andy, Maisie, Mrs Hawkins, the bank manager, the bank manager's wife, the butcher, Aunt Min, Aunt Min's husband, and of course the one or two other people who had somehow heard or suspected.

It was a good service. The vicar happened to be preaching on miracles, not the brilliant series of miracles that Jane felt she could have told him about, but ordinary day-to-day ones like sight, and hearing, and other people being raised from the dead, and why we enjoy working with others in some communal task. Jane agreed with most of what he was saying, though *her* miracles had been Mrs

Arbuthnot's transfiguration from dragon to saint, and Miss Spinks's dramatic visit to the castle, like David defying someone. Jane wanted to stand up and say, 'Listen to the miracles we have had at Hunters Head.' She was beginning to feel that she was a bit light-headed. When the service was concluding with a prayer and a benediction, she wanted to add, 'And may God send us one more quite small miracle and enough money to finish the job.'

The service over, they walked down the square. The Hunters Arms was open, and Aunt Min, who must have been watching from the window, beckoned them in. Andy was there, and Jane had the very distinct impression that Andy and Aunt Min had been talking about her. Rejoicing probably. Aunt Min served Mr Silas, who was glad to stop and have a chat, especially as he was joined by His Lordship.

Andy escorted Jane over to a chair, apparently in response to vehement nods from Aunt Min. Jane would have liked a quiet word with Lord Pomeroy, but there seemed to be a conspiracy to allow Andy to say something to her. Odd, Andy did not usually need urging to speak or act.

'Ma was saying,' he began. Clearly, he was about to make a request, but couched like this, the way would be left open for Miss Jane to refuse. It was only some sort of outsider, like Caroline, say, who asked you something direct and gave you no polite way out.

'Ma was saying to Aunt Min,' continued Andy, thus strengthening Jane's suspicions that this was going to be a request for her to do or give something quite considerable. Well, in a way she felt she owed Andy something; she had not forgotten that long-ago evening in the summer when she had avowed her troubles to him and started to face up to things. Perhaps she would be able to do something now to repay this personable young man.

'Yes, Andy,' she prompted.

He smiled, and plunged into his story. 'Look, Miss Jane, you see, it's like this. You know I'm going to be number two in the business. And the old man is getting on. And Maisie and I want to develop the business more. The old man doesn't want to change things, not really. His idea of something new is to cross out "sausage meat" and put "beef burgers" instead. They are very good beef burgers, of course,' he added conscientiously. 'What Maisie and I have been thinking is that the old man wouldn't mind if we had a go at the greengrocery side. With fruit and peppers and special vegetables and things, especially in the summer when all the village has got visitors staying. Could we use the bottom half of your garden? The walled bit, out of sight of the windows I mean. And I could get those two greenhouses mended,' he concluded.

Jane could see nothing against this. In fact, far from being something that she was to do to help Andy, it looked as if this would turn out to be something to help Hunters Head. She wished she could have found exactly the right word. 'Yes, yes, certainly,' she said, feeling it was a bit inadequate. She wanted to stand up and make everyone in the bar drink a toast. But not only would it have been out of character for her (though Uncle could have done it), but her knees did not feel too good.

Aunt Min bore down on her. 'What do you think of the idea, Miss Jane?' Jane said how wonderful it all sounded and looked on a trifle vacantly while Andy explained how this or that could be done, with a new path *here* (indicating with his finger a line on the table), and Aunt Min added the suggestion of a path over *there* (a further line). Uncle joined them, and had the position explained to him. He thought it an excellent idea, but would suggest a new path rather like *this* (a further line, with two bends). He called in Lord Pomeroy, and there was an enthusiastic conversation, in which Jane took little part, while the chief participants outlined where each would put a new greenhouse. Lord Pomeroy, who had in fact already had the matter broached to him, gave a qualified measure of approval. He did not see it as a scheme that would make a lot of money, but he approved of projects that kept young married men from spending so much time in the pubs. He ordered more drinks.

Jane's head was aching and her throat hurt. If Andy had the use of part of the garden... the brain was trying to impart the news that this might be a help, but the news was not getting through. Perhaps she would feel better in the fresh air.

She got as far as the doorway, where she leant, hearing as from afar the cries of, 'I'd put it more to the left' and 'polythene would be better' and 'personally we roast them' – then she recollected why she had particularly wanted to see Aunt Min, so she tottered back in. One did feel better after just a little fresh air.

Did Aunt Min know if Michael was abroad or coming home? Aunt Min knew that Michael was abroad, even if not in Teheran. Why did Miss Jane want him? Not moving furniture again?

Jane explained that yes, she and Uncle *were* having a shift round; she and Uncle were going to move down from the top floor to an infinitely warmer and now empty first floor.

Ah well, Aunt Min knew that Michael's friend Tony was staying, and no doubt he would be willing to come and do a few hours. Students always were. But wasn't it a pity to have those top rooms empty? Wouldn't some of Mr Silas's artist friends, like that Mr Mannie he was always on about, like to rent a studio in the country? Or that chap who had been down before, who had kept such odd hours and come to The Hunters Arms for bread and cheese at two o'clock in the morning?

Jane became aware that she was not well, and once more retreated to the open air. She therefore missed hearing the conversation that, quite by chance, sparked off the final miracle. Thinking it over afterwards, she felt it should have been ushered in by a body of celestial trumpeters. As far as she was concerned, as she sat on the seat outside the pub, leaning back with her eyes half closed, there could have been whole squadrons of angels, and the Salvation Army band as well, for all the notice she was capable of taking.

The final miracle emanated from Uncle, engaged in passing a casual reply to Aunt Min. Yes, apart from Manet, who was French and had been dead for some years, he did still have that artist friend in London, the one who had always wanted to have a studio in the village for the summer. And, yes, of course he would pay. Funny that Aunt Min should have connected him with Manet... there was something reminiscent in the style. He must tell his friend. What was that Aunt Min was saying about paying? Oh, no, his friend wasn't a poor man any longer; he was making good money. You see, his pictures had 'caught on'. Uncle then embarked on an explanation of what was implied by 'catching on' and whether it was, or was not, a good thing for his friend's artistic development.

Aunt Min looked at Uncle severely. Bother his friend's artistic development. Surely Mr Silas realised the anxiety Miss Jane had had trying to manage. Surely... no, it was obvious that such domestic details did not enter Mr Silas's head. But the important thing now was that apparently this artist fellow wanted to come and could pay. She questioned Mr Silas further. Would his friend, who was not Mr Mannie and not French and not dead, but whose pictures were selling, would he really like to pay to have the top floor of Hunters Head for a studio, which he would use in the summer but pay for with an annual rent? That would be splendid for them. Aunt Min felt that she could welcome the artist every night at midnight for bread and cheese if that would mean that Hunters Head was saved. Aunt Min, like Lord Pomeroy, knew the difference between planning ahead and 'just managing somehow'. What Mr Silas was telling her sounded most promising.

The thing he must do, at once, insisted Aunt Min, was to go and *tell Miss Jane*; then they could communicate with his friend and make it all definite.

She guided him out to the front door. Jane, they saw, looked proper poorly, but was determined to walk home. Aunt Min set them on their way, neither Jane nor Uncle aware that the final last piece of the puzzle had just turned up.

Chapter Twenty-one

Not the end

Hunters Head was saved. Mr Robinson's handling of Mr Marner's accounts was adjudged satisfactory, even by His Lordship. Altogether, the income would be adequate. Miss Spinks, nicknamed the Sphinx, in tribute to her capacity not to gossip, was happily working at the castle. Mrs Arbuthnot, a much *slenderer* woman than she had been the previous summer, alternately domineered over and protected Mr Hetherington and Jane. Caroline played her new series of records, and kept everyone up-to-date with the details of the coming wedding. Andy and friends were bringing part of the garden back into some sort of order. Uncle was looking forward to the visit of the artist friend, whose works had 'caught on' to such an extent that he could pay handsomely for a summer studio.

Jane herself had 'gone down with a virus'. As recounted by Ma Hawkins, it sounded like a rather nasty animal, probably shaggy. Fortunately the move from the cold north-facing rooms on the top floor had taken place in time for Jane and her virus to occupy one of the nice south-facing rooms on the first floor. She lay in bed, watching the clouds racing across from the west. What a year it had been. The gathering anxiety of the spring and the summer. And then the series of miracles, so that here they were, at the end of the autumn, safe at Hunters Head.

Jane reflected that, in the Victorian novel, she would now be lying on her deathbed. Angels would be appearing from the clouds in the sky, and she would be hearing the distant strains of the harps. The door opened. The sound of 'Good King Wenceslas', played by a famous choir in a cathedral city, floated up from Caroline's room. Mrs Arbuthnot came in with a nice cup of coffee.

The two women looked at each other, and just for a moment it seemed that time stood still.

Time stood still. If an angel of the Lord had appeared at that moment, and offered the two women immediate and painless extinction, they might each have had a fleeting impulse to accept.

Then Mrs Arbuthnot would have asked him (this was the correct way to address it?) if she might first go downstairs to put the stew in the bottom oven and leave a note for the others. Jane, on reflection, would have felt that there were things she *must* stay and find out. Would Michael get his job next summer? Would Andy finish up by becoming 'the butcher'? Would by any chance Uncle's artist friend get a picture of their sky, with its contrasting dark over the moors and light over the sunlit lower slopes, into the academy? Would Mr Robinson stay in Devon? Would one of the Gregson girls become a vet? And... yes...

.

very important... had Maisie decided who was going to make the wedding cake, the Exeter firm or the River Café?

In fact, grateful though they would be to the angel of the Lord, for the moment of perfect happiness, perhaps he would kindly go away again.

Jubilee

in Chapel Street

Chapter One

It was very surprising, very surprising indeed, but Chapel Street decided to celebrate the Queen's Silver Jubilee. It was not that kind of a street, and it did not contain the kind of people who can organise that sort of thing.

Take, for example, the one good house in Chapel Street. This was number 7 and it was inhabited by Mrs Smith. Mrs Smith was old. She was not particularly dirty. She was certainly not a bastard. Fucking was a very inappropriate description. But 'dirty fucking old bastard' was how the rest of the street referred to her.

This was not in any case a reflection on Mrs Smith. This was how the street talked, and the way the street talked was the way it felt about things in general. It was not a very attractive street. It lay near the centre of the town, and it typified what the town planners mean when they talk about 'an inner city area'. There was a derelict shop at the corner. Ex-bicycle, ex-grocer's, ex-everything. Then three little houses, two of them boarded up (by the council? by their absentee owners? Nobody knows, nobody cares). Then the pub, The Rising Sun, an odd misnomer of a name, as the only thing rising there was the smell from 'Here it is'. Then some council houses, of a type now referred to by the housing department as 'archaic' and by certain committee members as 'a bloody disgrace'. And so on. A dirty and unprepossessing street. Here was the one good house, opposite the pub. This was a real Georgian house, a listed building, but untouched for many a year by paint or decorator, and inhabited by the Mrs Smith laconically referred to by the rest of the street as a dirty fucking old bastard, or – in its more urbane moments – a dirty fucking old geezer. This, it must be reiterated, was no reflection on Mrs Smith's character, though it did reflect her retirement from the outside world. Some of the street remembered that her deceased husband, Joseph Smith, builder, had once long years ago been the mayor of this prosperous little town. The Smiths in fact had built and owned the houses in Chapel Street. Now, Mrs Letitia Smith lived alone, with Pussums and memories of dear Joe, and tea and toast, and she seldom went out.

Why Chapel Street should have decided to celebrate the Jubilee was something of a mystery. It was not loyalty to the royal family ('lazy fucking layabouts, wish I had a quarter of wot they get'). It was hardly a spirit of community with the rest of the town ('the bloody town council... them buggers are the worst of the lot'). Perhaps it was a desire to outdo the neighbouring street – Jubilee Street. If Chapel Street did have any communal purpose in life, apart from dodging the police and the rent collector and the hire-purchase man, it was to out-do its rival, Jubilee Street, which, perhaps because of its name, was setting out to celebrate in a big way. It had been built by an earlier generation of Smiths, builders, in 1897. It had come to be inhabited by the industrious and ambitious. Many were self-employed craftsmen. They bought cheap, worked hard on their properties, sold, and moved on to the more select Closes and Crescents away from the centre of the town. Jubilee Street's celebrations would be good.

The children of the two streets were the liaison to pass on the news to each street of what the other was up to, even though the children of Jubilee Street were of a different calibre from the kids of Chapel Street. Jubilee Street children sometimes had their pictures in the local paper, smiling, and clutching certificates, over captions like 'Junior Record Breaker' and 'Family of Four Win St John Ambulance Badges'. News about Chapel Street was more likely to be found under headings such as 'Gang of Four' or 'Stolen Goods Found in Back Yard'. All the same, the children carried the information.

It was Bob Stiggins who relayed the news... that in Jubilee Street they were collecting money, together, and – he added – buying presents for the kids. Chapel Street could understand the kids getting presents – the church or the welfare or someone usually produced the Christmas presents. But collecting money yourselves. That was going a bit far. Everyone in the street, except perhaps Mrs Smith, had plenty of experience in handling money, their own, and what they could get off social security, and indeed, not to put too fine a point on it, what they could nick off other people as well. If a gas meter was broken into within half a mile, the police started their investigations in Chapel Street. Bloody interfering bastards. So no one in Chapel Street wanted to entrust even a modest donation to anyone else. Trust it to that lousy bugger? Wot djer think I am? On my way to the loony bin?

The fact that money had to be collected, if Bob Stiggins's report was right, postponed the start of any arrangements. Most streets were considering what to do with their surplus before Chapel Street had started collecting.

The problem was solved, unexpectedly, in the unlikely person of little Mrs Green. Mrs Green lived opposite the untidy Stiggins household. This did not differentiate the Stiggins household from the rest of the street, but it marked out Mrs Green as different. 'Little' usually implies something rather endearing, like a dear little kitten or a pretty little flower. Applied to Mrs Green, it meant someone thin and anxious, a figure more likely to attract the belligerent boot than a protective arm. She was not, it was thought, physically beaten by her husband, but she had been forced to live in a guilt-ridden silence about the large quantities of cigarettes, et cetera, et cetera, that he habitually brought home. Their family comprised their two idiot children, the idiot girl, aged nine, and the boy, aged eight. Politer streets would have referred to the children as mentally retarded, but not Chapel Street – Chapel Street was the archetype that called a spade a bloody shovel, and the children were known as the idiot girl and the idiot boy, or, collectively, as the little bleeders. The bloody welfare came and took 'em off somewhere every day.

As it happened, Mr Green had also been taken off, by the police. His continuing absence (in Barfield Gaol) was giving Mrs Green some respite from her usual anxiety. On her way back from the police court one evening, she had actually called out goodnight to the mechanics at the garage round the corner from Chapel Street. And when the police car came into the street one afternoon – a signal for all to vanish – little Mrs Green had stayed at her front door and spoken to them. Clearly such a respectable woman was the person to whom one might entrust money with some hope of seeing it again.

Mrs Green collected the money with a surprising amount of success. She had been told, by the ubiquitous Stiggins children, that in Jubilee Street *everyone* was being called on. So she proceeded to call on all the non-boarded-up houses, and the pub. She hesitated about number 7. Unlike the rest of the street, Mrs Letitia Smith was held to be a lady: she was also felt to be a little bit odd. Mrs Green, emboldened by her success at the pub, called. The visit was most successful. Mrs Letitia Smith turned out to be real sweet. She gave a sum according to her means, which might have seemed paltry in some streets, but a princely donation in Chapel Street. She also promised to come to the party, poor old geezer. She embarrassed Mrs Green by asking solicitously about 'your poor little ones', and then, with a vestige of mayoral protocol, asked for and noted the time at which she should arrive.

Mrs Smith had given the final boost to the arrangements... a decision on what time the party should start.

Chapter Two

There were other difficulties too. Mostly, they sprang from the fact that the street had never worked together or *with* anyone. It was up *against* the law, and each other, and the bloody fuzz, and of course above all, up against Jubilee Street.

One question had been how to have the street closed so that they could have tea in the street. If Jubilee Street was having its tea in the street, and it was, then so would Chapel Street. But how to get it done? It goes without saying that nobody was willing to go and see the council. Writing was also out of the question. It was asserted that some of the schoolchildren could have written a real proper letter, but the most likely one, the fifteen-year-old Alan Stiggins, was off in the remand home or somewhere. Very unfair, as he'd only borrowed the car for half an hour, and then there had been an accident, and the bloody cops had got him for being two years under age in any case. Bloody unfair. The question of how to close the street was solved by Big Bill Hoggins. As he put it, getting anyone's leave didn't fucking well matter, as he'd pick up a couple of those bloody 'No Waiting' notices from the depot, and *he* would close the street himself. It was their bloody street, wasn't it?

No one liked arguing with Mr Hoggins. If Big Bill said he was going to do anything and anyone argued, he clouted them one. Although this did not make him a popular character, it was an argument that was understood in Chapel Street. So if folk hero Hoggins was going to close the street, the rest of Chapel Street would bloody let him.

It was the landlord of The Rising Sun who had finally done most of the organising. As a man who prided himself on knowing what was what, he had been mindful of what was happening in preparation for the Jubilee. He decided that anything that gave Chapel Street a good name (filthy stinking place though it was) might, just might, be good for his trade. He didn't hold with this tea-and-lemonade business, but he reckoned, rightly, that if there was no celebration being held in Chapel Street, then its denizens might go off somewhere else, the rotten lot of cadgers, and not be back for opening time. Or if they did come back early after a do somewhere else, it might lead to fights, and he didn't want any lousy constable along. Careful and mercenary calculations had led him to the conclusion that he must help organise Chapel Street's Jubilee tea party.

So there they all were, at three o'clock on a distinctly damp June afternoon, and there, to everyone's admitted surprise, were the trestle tables, right across the street, and cardboard cups and saucers, and red, purple and blue bunting. There wasn't any white, as the source of supply had been unwanted streamers from the political parties, and the fucking Liberals had only had purple, not white. But it looked all right, real pretty.

In view of the amount of distrust and dislike that constituted Chapel Street's normal way of life, the celebration didn't promise too badly. There were crisps and cakes and sausage rolls, and a big cake, with 'jubillee' misspelt in red icing across the top, and someone had provided two large jellies for the fucking kids. Mrs Green had got some red, white and blue pencil cases, and Mrs Smith was going to present them, also to the fucking kids. It was three o'clock and it did all look smart.

Mrs Smith regrettably did not appear. This was the start of the disaster. Mrs Green must have failed to tell her the right time – nearly as much of an idiot she must be as her two blasted kids. Mrs Green burst into tears, which was a bit out of character, but she had had the children home all day as welfare were on holiday. The idiot girl then followed suit, but instead of just standing there bawling, grabbed a handful of crisps, and belted off towards the end of the street. The police van – trust them buggers to turn up when not wanted – arrived at that very moment to pick up the illegally erected 'No Entry' signs, and the idiot girl hurled herself against what might have been the bonnet of the car. The driver managed to swerve, hit her a kind of sliding blow, and collided with the front of one of the empty shops, which disintegrated.

It is not hard to imagine the rest of the scene. The kid was carted off to hospital. There were tears and arguments and recriminations. Big Bill squared up to the police under the hazy idea, induced by too much beer drunk in The Rising Sun at midday, that the 'No Entry' signs were his private property.

A second police car arrived. Big Bill got taken away as well, though not to the hospital. A dog from Jubilee Street was found to have jumped up and knocked the sausage rolls into the gutter. And to crown it all, Alan Stiggins's blasted young brother Bob, who had been scouting in Jubilee Street, came back to tell them that Jubilee Street was having a *smashing* party. His dad clouted him one of course, which was a bit unfair as the boy was only reporting the truth – Jubilee Street *was* having a very fine party. Bob didn't mind the blow much, as it was only one for show, but his mother took umbrage, gathered her brood about her and departed indoors, shutting the door with as much of a bang as she could considering that the hinge was off.

That was the end of that day's party. The woman who had made the jellies (that slut Mavis Tompkins) took them dispiritedly home and stood them on the scullery window sill. The kids pinched the crisps. The publican and a few of the more responsible members of the street collected what was left of the food and dismantled the tables. Mrs Hoggins, relieved of the presence of her husband, took the big cake over to that poor Mrs Green and the little idiot boy. Bob sneaked out and went back to join the party in Jubilee Street.

That, however, was not the end of the story. Punctually at three o'clock on the next afternoon, Mrs Smith came out from the Georgian house, resplendent in the red, white and blue costume she had worn for some bygone civic occasion. The sun was shining and she carried her parasol carefully, so that her face was shaded. This may have been why the street saw her before she could notice that the street was remarkably empty for a street about to celebrate the Jubilee.

Perhaps the street was just a bit ashamed of itself for its behaviour the day before. It hadn't intended any harm, and yet somehow the whole thing had been a disaster – the shop in ruins, Big Bill in the cells, the little girl in hospital, goods all spoilt, no presents for the kids, et cetera, et cetera. Perhaps it was shame, or the fact that the sun was shining, or the knowledge that the cake was untouched, or even a feeling of compunction for the disappointment it was going to cause 'the poor old geezer'. Whatever it was, the street came to a tacit communal decision that it would have its party, if only for Mrs Smith. Poor fucking old geezer, dressed up so smart and all, a real credit to any street.

Quickly and surprisingly efficiently, the party took shape. Everybody was helping. There were taps on communicating walls here, and the kids sent with messages there, and someone distracting Mrs Smith's attention by taking her to inspect the ruins of the shop. The police of course had now put 'No Entry' signs up. The trestle tables came up again. Kids were sent to the nearest shops for more crisps. *The* Jubilee cake was brought back by a beaming Mrs Hoggins. Mrs Green allowed her son, mysteriously dearer to her than on the day before, to carry out the coloured pencil cases. The jellies were all right, the stray cats that had sniffed them over in the night not liking the flavour of strawberry much. There was suddenly an abundance of food and drink, with bottles of fizzy lemonade *given free* by The Rising Sun. And it was not only the food and drink that looked so good; somehow everyone was willing to enjoy themselves. Oh, hooray!

The crowning moments were still to come. Bob Stiggins, carrying out his unofficial task of liaison with Jubilee Street, came to report that Jubilee Street was wild with envy at Chapel Street having their celebration still in hand, and on this nice sunny day. The Chapel Street revellers looked at each other and smiled. What a moment of triumph. Then two little kids, who were in their turn scouting from Jubilee Street, appeared at the end of Chapel Street. Young Terry Stiggins (seven-year-old half brother to Bob and Alan) waved a belligerent fist at them and urged them to 'sod off'.

Chapel Street was delighted. This exactly expressed their feelings. Oh joy, oh jubilation. Sod off, indeed, Jubilee Street and everyone else. Three cheers for the queen. Hip, hip, hooray! Three cheers for the whole bloody royal family. Hip, hip, hooray! Hip, hip, *hip*, hooray! Hooray! Hooray!

And the cheers re-echoed over the roofs, to Jubilee Street and the rates department and as far as the police cells, as Chapel Street celebrated the Jubilee.

Chapter Three

The next day dawned fine, and the sun rose over Chapel Street as well as over the rest of the town. The only difference was that the rest of the town had had a day in which to settle down after the Jubilee celebrations, while for Chapel Street it was the morning after. Chapel Street however was flushed with the unexpected success of its celebrations, and woke in a more victorious mood than usual to face the day's problems.

Mind you, one day's celebrations does not entirely do away with problems, particularly if you have the kind of problems that are endemic when you are the sort of person who lives in the sort of street that Chapel Street is.

Take, for instance, Mavis Tompkins. Mavis Tompkins was the lady who had provided the jellies for the poor little buggers. Mavis awoke and was immediately sick. This served to remind her of her particular problem, which has not been solved by ignoring it.

Mrs Green's idiot boy woke to the desolation of being alone, that is, without his idiot sister. Mrs Green woke as usual to anxiety. She did not know of a Latin poet's famous lines about 'black care', nor indeed had heard of the poet, but the lines could have been voiced by her. The only thing that made this morning different from any other was the cause of the anxiety. Today, this sprang from the need to reconcile two different and apparently mutually exclusive needs. She had to be at home when welfare brought her son home in the afternoon. Then she had to get to the hospital, which was in the next town, to see her daughter. When you have no car, and no friendly car-owning neighbour, and no money for a taxi and, needless to say, no telephone, this leaves you in a quandary.

The landlord of The Rising Sun made his usual start to the day – a count of glasses broken the night before. The number turned out to be very small, considering the amount of money taken, and although he was not a man given to making extravagant gestures, he rubbed his hands together in satisfaction. Yes, from his point of view, the Jubilee had been worthwhile, definitely worthwhile.

Mrs Smith of the Georgian house had a very different problem. Her problem was simply one of time, or rather of date. The day before had been Jubilee Day, when they had had that nice party. And Jubilee Day, she was almost certain, had been on a Tuesday. So today must be Wednesday. But the milkman had left her a pint of milk that he left her on a Thursday. So it couldn't be Wednesday. Or could it? As she considered this problem, her attention was attracted by the very unexpected sound of a child singing, in Chapel Street.

Children singing in Chapel Street was itself unusual and particularly at this time in the morning. The raised voice of Patsy Stiggins represented the answer that another family had found to the morning's problems. This was the Stiggins family, whose boy Alan could have written a proper smart letter if he had not been off in that bloody remand home, and whose slightly younger son Bob was the liaison with Jubilee Street. It was the family in fact whose next younger son, Terry, had so aptly summed up the street's attitude to Jubilee Street.... 'Sod off'... which could have been taken as the street's motto.

It was Bob, thirteen-year-old Bob, who had the problem. To be more exact, it was Bob who was doing something about it. It was Bob's parents who had quarrelled on the Tuesday night, after the party that hadn't taken place. On the Wednesday, mellowed by the success of the party that did take place, followed up by a number of drinks at The Rising Sun, the parents had patched up their differences, and gone home to an amorous and drunken sleep. So Thursday morning, which was school again, saw Bob surveying a pretty empty kitchen, two sleeping younger sisters, and a somnolent Terry. Bob felt that he must get them up and off to school. Perhaps it was fear of the school welfare officer. But, mingled with that, was a certain newly acquired pride in his street. Chapel Street had shown 'em, hadn't it? You couldn't let your street down now, could you?

He cuffed Terry awake. He shouted at the 'little 'un', the five-year-old Patsy, until she came down. He considered how to wake Charlotta. Charlotta was ten, nearly eleven, next down to him. Charlotta was small. He could have hit her of course. It was not gentlemanliness on his part, or fear of her nails, that stopped him. It was rather the respect she had won by her attitude to authority. For some reason, you had a certain respect for the inconspicuous Charlotta. If Lotta would wake up and give him a hand... Patsy and Terry were demanding something to drink. He gave each of them a small sip of the sherry, there being nothing else available. He then went upstairs and tried yelling to Lotta that Ma wanted her. Charlotta made vague sounds. He went downstairs again, to discover that Patsy had had a great deal more than a sip of the sherry. The altercation that ensued, in which he prevented Terry also having more than a sip, brought Charlotta downstairs. She seemed to be on Bob's side, and the two older children managed the gathering of things together that constituted getting ready for school. Finally, at the proper time, Bob triumphantly led out his little party, unwashed, unfed, and the five-year-old Patsy inebriated... but, in time for school. Whether school was going to see this as a particularly victorious action remained to be seen. Bob had already surmounted more obstacles than some people were going to meet in the whole of their pleasant and well organised days in the nicer areas of the town.

It was the unmelodious singing of Patsy that had attracted the attention of Mrs Smith. She would probably have been thinking 'dear little child' if her mind had not been focused on the problem caused by the delivery of Thursday's milk on what she had so for assumed to be Wednesday. Had she made a mistake? Experience led her to think that this was indeed possible... it was so difficult now to be certain which day it was... and that the milkman was probably right. The children, or at least one of them, told her that it *was* Thursday. Well, well. Thursday. She would slip in again and tell dear Joseph. Thursday, then. Come to think of it, if it was Thursday (and the children had seemed quite certain), that brought another problem. So she would certainly go back indoors and tell Joseph of her mistake. She smiled. Joseph would be amused. And she would give Pussy a nice saucer of milk.

Mavis Tompkins, meanwhile, was making an uneasy way to the sink. She vomited. God, what a life. What a mess. She was thinking figuratively, God what a mess. She must be pregnant. It was true that this was hardly a surprise. She had suspected it for some time, and then what with one thing and another, she hadn't done any of the things she might have done. God, what a bloody stupid mess. Funny though, come to think of it, how your pregnancies varied. She hadn't been sick at all the last twice, and now... ugh. She trailed back to bed. What really was funny was that in spite of everything, she didn't feel too depressed. You missed Big Bill of course, but... well, it had been a better party really without that bloody great bully about ('thinks 'e's fucking wonderful'), and it had been nice to be on speaking terms, so to say, with his wife, the second Mrs Hoggins. The kids had been civil too. In fact, it had been a good day. You began to wonder if you might after all keep the kid. It might be nice to have a kid of your own. Mavis recalled taking out the jellies and how pleased the kids had seemed, especially that Bob and his sister Charlotta (bloody stupid name for a girl in Chapel Street). Mavis dropped off to sleep again, with quite a pleasant expression on her face.

Transport arrived to take the idiot boy, Mrs Green's kid, off to wherever it was that he blasted well went. Strange to relate, the driver knew all about the little girl being in hospital, and he was ready with the solution to Mrs Green's problem… or at least the immediate problem. Chapel Street never ceased to wonder at the way in which 'the welfare' knew things. What of course was foreign to Chapel Street was the ability to take trouble and to find things out. One of the reasons for not finding things out, Chapel Street felt, was that they did not have a telephone. This was one of the street's perennial grievances – not that they did anything about it. The few private phones had long been disconnected, over questions of payment. Even Mrs Smith's had gone, as the actual timing of the payments eluded her. Someone had bust up the kiosk. Someone had always bust up the kiosk. Jubilee Street had a kiosk, which reputedly was in order, but you hadn't got any change. In any case who would go to the fucking trouble to go round to the phone in Jubilee Street when the welfare or the police or someone would have done something for you? And if they hadn't, then it would be too bloody late. This was the philosophy of Chapel Street, whose inhabitants continued to be amazed at the network of information that enmeshed them whenever they encountered 'the welfare'. There were times, it was admitted, when they benefited from all this. This was one of the occasions. The driver of the vehicle that collected Mrs Green's little boy was able to tell her that she must get to the hospital on her own, but a driver from some group or other in the town would be there to fetch her home before welfare brought her son back. And she was to meet this driver at the enquiry desk in the front hall.

After the children had gone to school, the street relapsed into quiet. The kids and the people who had jobs to go to had gone. The rest of the street, the Mavis Tompkinses, the unemployed, were indoors. It looked as if a kind of Sabbath slumber was on the street. And it still had problems, many problems. All the same, yesterday had been a good day.

Chapter Four

One of the people who had greatly enjoyed the Jubilee celebrations was the genteel Mrs Smith. Having learnt from the children that the day was, unaccountably, Thursday, she retired within her portals. She did not, of course, retire to spend the morning in bed, as various other inhabitants of the street were doing. She had first to acquaint Joseph with the news that it was Thursday, and then to do something about it.

Her problem, like Mrs Green's, would to some people have been a simple one. It was that Joseph's brother, Alfred, together with Alfred's wife, Emma, were coming to see her for lunch, it being the Thursday that they came, and she had for lunch just one tin of meat. What she was wondering was whether she should go over to The Rising Sun (and she imagined Joseph's start of surprise), later on of course, at whatever was the proper time for going over to the pub, and get a bottle of beer. This revolutionary idea shows what an effect the Jubilee had had on at least one inhabitant. It was quite a long time since Mrs Smith had left her house, except for the party. It was not that she feared to venture out in Chapel Street. She had just got out of the habit. After the death of dear Joseph, she had stayed indoors, more and more. Perhaps it was becoming something of a fantasy life, where she still lived with her admired husband, and consulted his wishes, and found him less impatient about her mistakes than at times in the past. She did not notice the deterioration of the street, and the lives of the inhabitants were mercifully concealed from her. She could not think that Joseph would be interested in the Greens and the Hogginses, who now occupied the houses once rented by artisans working for the firm of J Smith, Builders.

Now – as to lunch. The landlord of The Rising Sun had seemed quite a pleasant person at the party, and she remembered that gentlemen liked a glass of something at lunch (she winked knowingly at Joseph – not lemonade) and a bottle of beer would make up for having forgotten the cucumber. She had never before felt that she knew the landlord, but now, after that nice party, you felt you could go over there, in an emergency only of course, as this was. Yes, decided Mrs Smith, she would go over, at the proper time, and buy a bottle of beer. There still remained the question as to what would constitute the proper time, but in the meantime that was settled. She would allow herself to have a second cup of tea. All work and no play makes Jack a dull boy, as Joe said.

The Stiggins children were having a less disastrous morning at school than might have been expected. Bob had to turn in at the gate of his schools and could think of no reason for accompanying the inebriated Patsy on to her school, the entrance to which happened to be beyond his. Even if he had gone, he could see that it wouldn't help, as what they wanted to do was to conceal the fact that Patsy was drunk, not to advertise that something was wrong. He stood disconsolately at his own school entrance, watching impotently while Charlotta piloted the two younger ones to the combined junior and infants' entrance. He felt anxious about leaving Lotta to cope by herself but there was absolutely nothing he could do. Oh dear, and now it looked as if some sort of a fight was breaking out at the junior entrance. He could do nothing. He turned away and went into his own school. Pressing problems awaited him there too, but some change in the timetable had meant a games period, and Bob forgot about the rest of his family.

Charlotta would not have admitted that she too was worried about Patsy's condition. One thing to be thankful for was Mrs Smith's question of 'is it Wednesday or Thursday today?' This had had the effect of changing Patsy's song from a very rude lyric, clearly and articulately rendered, about a midland ram, to a nice song you had learnt in school starting ''Twas on a Monday morning'. True, the one you had learnt at school had enumerated the days, while Patsy's song was a reiteration of ''Twas onner *Thursday* morning'. But that was better than the first song. 'Better' to Charlotta simply meant 'less likely to get us into trouble'. Whether the first song was one that was suitable for a five-year-old little girl to be singing did not enter into it. It was just that that particular song was likely to attract attention when you didn't want it.

As they reached the school entrance, deliverance came. It would be truer to say that Charlotta made brilliant use of a situation provoked by someone else. As Bob had seen from afar, a fight had started. A quick and unnoticed shove from Charlotta, and Patsy was on the ground with a blood-stained knee, her song changed to a wail. Charlotta grabbed her by the hands, yanked her up, and was towing her away to the sickroom before you could say 'Jack Robinson' or 'Wolves okay'. A harassed member of staff was alerted and produced a rug and disinfectant. Charlotta thanked teacher and firmly took charge. No, she could manage all right, thank you, on her own. She made certain that sufficient of the disinfectant was spilt round to cover up the lingering fumes of the alcohol. She made Patsy lie down and covered her up with the rug. Unknown to herself, she was earning a reputation of 'helpful little girl, the older Stiggins'. Teacher came back to leave a cup of coffee. Charlotta thanked him demurely and assured him that she could manage. ('That child is getting quite polite.') She then drank the coffee herself. It was true that she needed sustaining more than Patsy did, as Patsy had had the sherry and she had had nothing. The late hour of going to bed the previous night, combined with what for a five-year-old amounted to a booze up, meant that Patsy was quite ready to fall asleep. So that was all right. Charlotta tucked the rug round her, and thankfully slipped away to her own classroom. She succeeded in getting unnoticed into her inconspicuous place. She had long known that the great thing in life was not to attract the attention of authority. She looked attentively at her exercise book. Phew... it had been a narrow thing this morning. Good job sir had left her to see to Patsy. With any luck, the child would sleep till dinnertime and no one would have noticed anything. Charlotta discreetly observed what her neighbour was doing, and did the same. Exercise 4a, explain why you think Robin Hood was surprised.

Back in Chapel Street, Mrs Smith was spending the morning in carefully setting out the exiguous lunch for the expected Mr and Mrs Alfred Smith and herself. It was a meagre lunch as regards the content, but everything else was right – white tablecloth, the table napkins, the silver and, especially for today, three glasses. Everything looked right. She wondered a little about the number of glasses, but put three. The cat was duly shut out of the dining room.

Mrs Smith then decided that it was time to go over to The Rising Sun. One of the things she had learnt from her Joseph was that you could be slow to make a decision, but once made – *voilà* – so over she went to The Rising Sun. She had a little difficulty in finding the right doors but finally entered by one marked 's oon bar'. She wondered if you pronounced it 'soon' or 'so on'. A 'soon' bar, or a 'so on' bar?

Her own mild surprise about the title was as nothing to the shock her entry caused in the 's oon' bar. The usual couple of dirty old geezers (the description fitting them better than it did Mrs Smith) were sitting at a small table, with as much beer as they could afford on their pittances from social security. The landlord had found four more broken glasses and was again casting up their value against money that he had taken for extra drinks. He was now wondering what had induced him to come to such a bloody lousy street. And in stepped Mrs Smith, the heroine of the previous day's celebrations. The Rising Sun pulled itself, slightly, together. The landlord's first reaction was that there had been an accident, and he moved quickly to conceal the brandy, in case someone expected him to make a fucking present of some to some lousy bastard.

Mrs Smith took the few steps necessary to reach the counter. She wondered if she might ask the advice of the landlord as to what she should take. She wanted a bottle of beer for lunch. It was not for herself, she added. It was for her brother-in-law, whom she was expecting to lunch. This fact of course was known to the whole street – not that anyone fucking cared who it was for. To the landlord's surprise (and the astonishment of his two regular customers), he heard himself recommending a pleasant beer that was not the dearest he stocked. Mrs Smith thanked him, said that she would have one bottle, paid, smiled at the others and departed, the bottle of beer held carefully upright in her hand.

One of the two old guys actually stood up as she passed, mellowed into muttering something that sounded more like a greeting than his customary profanity.

'Fancy the old girl coming in here,' summed up the view of the 's oon' bar and Mrs Smith was promoted to the position of 'funny old geezer'. 'Came in here, the old girl did. Coo. And bought a bottle of beer. Funny old geezer.'

Chapter Five

Mr and Mrs Alfred Smith lived in quite a different part of the town, in a new and commodious house, with a spruce and commodious garden, in what could only have been described as a nice road. Alfred had been the youngest of the family, and now was the only survivor of his generation, apart from the two unmarried sisters, known to their own contemporaries as 'maiden aunts'. The whole family was greatly respected, and had indeed done much for the town. Some of the more recent members of the local council, with socialist backgrounds, were not slow to point out that the Smiths and their like had also done well out of the town. When brother Joseph had died, many years ago, Alfred had asked his relic, Letitia, if she would like to move out of Chapel Street. But no... Mrs Joseph Smith had spent all the pleasant part of her life there and saw no reason for moving. What she did not mention to her unimaginative brother-in-law, what in fact she could not possibly have said, was that in a way she still felt near to dear Joseph at 7 Chapel Street.

As the years passed, she had allowed herself to foster

this feeling, until it came to exclude the more real aspects of life in Chapel Street. At 7 Chapel Street she could still talk to dear Joseph – to a dear Joseph who became a more compliant listener than the Alderman Joseph Smith, Mayor, remembered by the town. The street came to know less about Mrs Letitia Smith than it did about the rest of the inhabitants, not that it cared one whit more or less. What the fucking old geezer did all day long was no concern of the street. An earlier age might have thought of burning her as a witch, except that no one, but no one in Chapel Street, would have offered a communal match to start the thing off. It had been an event unprecedented when Mrs Green in Jubilee fervour had called on the old girl.

Mr and Mrs Alfred Smith, their invitation not accepted, conscientiously went to visit her once a fortnight, on a Thursday, which accounted for the extra milk. On this particular day, two days after their own road had had its pleasant, decorous and indeed extremely well organised Jubilee party, they approached Chapel Street. Mr Smith liked to leave the car round the corner. It was kept too clean for anyone to write on it the name of their favourite football team, and nobody had ever – yet – let the tyres down. But Mr Smith felt – and rightly – that you couldn't be too careful about what you left unattended in Chapel Street. So they always left the car on the forecourt of the garage round the corner in Bond Street. It happened to be a good garage, very competent, and always willing to do any special job for Mr Alfred Smith while he visited his sister-in-law.

Mr and Mrs Smith left the car, as usual, and proceeded to walk the rest of the way. They were halfway down

Chapel Street when they caught sight of... good gracious, what appeared to be their Letitia coming out of the dirty old pub with a bottle in her hand. Alfred and his wife instantaneously looked to each other for reassurance. Had they each seen the same thing? They looked again. Yes, there was Letitia, bottle in hand. Like the landlord, they had a first thought that there had been an accident. But if there had been, they would have seen it and in any case dear Letitia now saw them and gaily waved with the bottle.

They finished their walk down the street in some trepidation, but found that the rest of their visit followed its customary lines. Letitia led them up to the room on the first floor that had been Mr Joseph Smith's dining room, which had then looked out on to a well tended garden. Now it was a sort of riot or burgeoning of green growth. Mrs Alfred Smith commented on an old-fashioned climbing rose that reared some unexpected blooms above the greenery. 'Quite like Sissinghurst,' she said politely.

Mrs Letitia Smith equally politely agreed. She had not the slightest idea what Mrs Alfred meant, but then so often she had not known what dear Joseph meant. 'Yes,' she said, 'quite, isn't it?'

And now, would Mr Alfred and his wife like to take their usual places at the table? Alfred and his wife would, and the lunch proceeded on its usual uneventful lines. Alfred commented with approbation on the unexpected glass of beer. Surprising, he thought, the old girl producing a decent glass of beer like that. In fact the old girl did seem in rather good fettle, apart from some confusion over the exact day of the Jubilee celebrations, which, according to her, had been on the previous day, when everyone knew that they had been two days previously.

Mrs Alfred ignored the lack of cucumber. After all, she and Alfred would be having their own 'proper meal' in the evening. And although dear Letitia's meal was always on the sparse side, the table looked so nice, so impeccably right, that you quite enjoyed the occasion. After all, you were there to do a duty, not to enjoy yourselves.

The Smiths were extremely grateful that their sister-in-law kept so well. At times she sometimes seemed a little odd (like today, over the date of the Jubilee celebrations), and they had always kept in mind that they would help 'if anything happened'. They were not entirely clear as to what they would do or even what 'anything' was. They often wished that there were some reliable neighbours who could have kept in touch with them. From what they saw of the street, it was obvious that whatever the street did have, it *did not* have respectable neighbours. But one had offered to help dear Letitia, and if she chose to remain in this dubious street, perhaps it was for the best. After all, she was in her own home and her occasional oddness was not likely to cause comment in Chapel Street.

At the usual time, they prepared to leave. Letitia, somewhat surprisingly, elected to walk up the street with them. It was therefore a party of three that was almost outside Mrs Green's door when the little incident or accident occurred. 'The welfare' drove up to leave the idiot boy. The welfare nodded pleasantly to Mr Smith, who happened to be the vice president of something. Mr Smith halted, to gaze with approbation on the wonderful work being done by welfare, and everyone waited for the door to be opened. Welfare knocked repeatedly, and it soon became obvious that the door was not going to be opened. A passing child (Terry? Tommy?) informed them that 'she' wasn't back yet from the 'ospital.

The arrival of the welfare car had of course been noticed, and, by some sort of street communication, everyone knew. But no one, no one at all, was going to come out and help. This was the kind of situation that happened so often in Chapel Street, and that left the welfare (or the police or the probation or whoever it was) furiously doing overtime to overcome what could have been solved by a little neighbourliness. The welfare had brought back the idiot boy, and the boy's mother was out. So what? So bloody what? You don't expect any of us to do the job the fucking welfare's paid to do?

This was the normal reaction of Chapel Street. Then it seemed that Mrs Letitia Smith, who did seem to be unusually lively, was willing to stay with the poor little boy for a while, while Alfred, finding himself a part of Chapel Street, went round the corner to the garage and phoned the hospital. He phoned. It was all so easy. 'Good afternoon, Sister, this is Mr Alfred Smith speaking. Would you mind finding out for me, et cetera, et cetera?' Sister found out, and back he came with the information. Yes, it was all right. There had been a delay, something to do with an ear specialist, and Mrs Green was already on her way home. So the Smiths waited, and in quite a short time were able to hand over the little boy to his mother, all safe and sound.

Mrs Letitia Smith did not accompany her relatives further. This had been quite an expedition for her already. She returned to her own end of the road, and was about to go indoors when she noticed some of the schoolchildren returning. She looked at the group, and it seemed to her that one of them might be the dear little girl she had heard singing in the morning. She would thank the children for letting her know which day it was. Then she would go in, let the cat out of the kitchen, have a nice cup of tea and tell Joseph all about the day's events. What a lot there was to tell. My, what a lot.

She did not hear what one dear little girl called her in response to her thanks. Normally, Charlotta would not have allowed her little sister to use such words, but Charlotta was immersed in conversation with Bob.

Bob's presence with them was unusual. He would mostly come home well behind the younger ones, but he had kept wondering about them during the day, and so just happened to be at the entrance to his school when they came by. Charlotta, without ever admitting it openly, was devoted to Bob. She did not usually waste words in telling other people what had happened at school, but her instinct told her how anxious Bob was to know how things had gone. After all, she and Bob had together turned this morning's affair into a bit of a family triumph, even if no one else knew it, and now Bob was walking home with them, even if he pretended not to be. So Charlotta explained everything, how she had wondered what on earth to do, and how one of those Hoggins buggers had started a fight, and how she had pushed Patsy over, and then – triumph, triumph – had got her unnoticed into the sickroom and poured disinfectant over everything. Bob looked at Charlotta with admiration. Coo, she really was a good 'un. It was jolly decent of her too, to tell him about it. Living with Charlotta meant that you didn't get many explanations. He appreciated this one. With some care he pulled a bar of chocolate out of his pocket and offered her half. She selected the larger half and they proceeded home, ignoring the younger ones, and chatting amicably. It was a bit like Indians smoking a ceremonial pipe of friendship; it meant more than an onlooker could have guessed.

They arrived home to find, to their great surprise, a smell of cooking. This was Ma's way of making up for this morning. She had not intended to oversleep. And she had been shocked to find that there had been nothing in the house for the kids' breakfast. She remembered running out of tea, and she must have forgotten the bread, and a cat must have got in and had the remaining margarine, and the milkman wouldn't leave anything more without money down. Oh well. By the time the kids came home though, Mum had got some mince cooking, and some potatoes and some baked beans, so there was general jubilation. Five-year-old Patsy was especially lively, but of course you didn't explain to Ma about the sherry and about Patsy sleeping all the morning. Ma would have assumed that Pa had drunk the sherry before doing off to his shift.

At 10.30 Mr Stiggins returned, having done a fair eight-hour shift. Chapel Street was quiet. You couldn't expect every day to be a day of triumph, like the day-late Jubilee celebrations. But several people had spoken to each other politely. A momentary gleam of something like feeling for others had come into the street. For Bob and Charlotta it had been a day of achievement. Mavis Tompkins had given Mrs Stiggins some milk. The street as a whole took the credit for looking after Mrs Green's kid while she was on her way from the hospital, overlooking the fact that some of that credit should have gone to Mr Alfred Smith.

It had indeed been quite a good day for Chapel Street, even if several households were facing unsolved problems.

Chapter Six

A new social worker sat in the area office. She had not expected to land this particular appointment, and was feeling both elated and apprehensive about her first day. She had spent the morning getting to know one and another, and now, with the senior away at County Hall, she was on her own for the afternoon.

She looked again at the files that were now 'hers'. What a lot of the people seemed to live in Chapel Street! Stiggins, S; Stiggins, A; Green; Green; Hoggins; Hoggins; Hoggins. Her first appointment outside was to go and see Mrs Eliza Hoggins, second wife of William Hoggins, first wife deceased, address 16 Chapel Street, to discuss with her the charge of grievous bodily harm being brought against William Hoggins, or, to be more exact, to discuss with Mrs Hoggins the household conditions likely to ensue from William Hoggins's absence. She noted the number and age of the children, and tried to visualise what sort of a person the second Mrs Hoggins was. She tried to see herself as somehow helping the street, and pondered on the age-old problem of why some streets are like Jubilee

Street and some like Chapel Street. Had some malicious fairy once…?

Her departure for the interview was interrupted by the arrival of an affable Mavis Tompkins, of 18 Chapel Street. If the address was anything to go by, this must be the next-door neighbour of the Hoggins family. The new social worker had not been prepared for the arrival of a Mavis Tompkins, affable or abrasive. Perhaps Mavis was concerned about the Hoggins family and had come to offer help? This extraordinary explanation did just occur to the new social worker. It must be remembered that she was new to Chapel Street. In looking at her list, it appeared that Mavis Tompkins, next-door neighbour to the Hoggins family, was one of the few inhabitants of Chapel Street whose detailed history was not there for the reading. What the social worker did not at this stage know was that Mavis Tompkins was the same as Mavis Ferrers and that the outstanding peaks, or troughs, of Mavis's thirty years were there recorded. There were more troughs than peaks.

Mavis was relieved to find that there was a new social worker in the office, as there had been difficulties with the previous one (interfering old bitch, what could she understand?).

Mavis, on being invited to sit down, made that simple operation last as long as possible, as she tried to decide what role to play. The good girl unexpectedly let down? She doubted if she could do that very convincingly. The naïve simple young thing? Actually, that was a very nice role, and the only thing that held her back was the conviction that few naïve simple girls lived in Chapel Street.

She ran her mind over the inhabitants: Mrs Smith and the idiot girl were about the only candidates. That little Patsy even, to judge by the language she used, was hardly naïve and simple. You couldn't tell with Charlotta; a quiet child; probably a dark horse.

'Would you care for a cup of coffee?' Mavis's thoughts were interrupted by the social worker. 'And do you take sugar?'

'Oh, yes, thank you,' beamed Mavis. 'But no sugar. Because of my figure.'

Mavis realised too late that in the circumstances this was a silly thing to say. As she seemed to be slipping into the third role – the 'you-and-I-are-women-of-the-world' – as the only viable one, she proceeded to play it as well as she could.

'I wanted to talk to someone reliable,' she said. 'The fact is, living in Chapel Street, I do feel so isolated.'

The new social worker, who had visited Chapel Street during her training, had not thought of it as an area where isolation was a problem. However, she smiled expectantly, proffered biscuits (accepted in spite of the figure) and waited for Mavis to unfold the reason for her visit.

'I expect you've noticed,' continued Mavis, 'that I am going to have a baby.' The new social worker nodded. 'This is not my first child, but two of the little ones were adopted. I was on my own then and I couldn't afford to do what would have been right for them.' Mavis said this with as much conviction as possible. It was a statement that was not likely to be challenged, at least by this social worker. 'They went into very good families. But I'm not sure what to do now. I've got my own place. Well, I mean, it's a council house, and they'll have to re-house us if they redevelop, won't they?'

It was unlikely that Mavis had dropped in in order to discuss the future development of derelict council property. If one had been in contact with the welfare before, she presumably knew of the help possible for unmarried mothers. The new social worker wondered what the particular difficulty was, and then decided to go ahead and find out certain necessary details. Did Mavis know when the baby was due? The answer was less clear than one might have expected, even though more exact than the 'not yet' and 'quite soon' category of answer.

The next question should have been something meaning 'Who is the father?' – a polite euphemism for 'Do you know who the father is?' Instead, the new social worker, on the first case that was really hers, asked what she really wanted to know. 'Are you on your own?' Unwittingly, she was helping her client over a hurdle. Mavis knew, or at least was pretty sure, that it was either the foreman at work, or her neighbour, 'that bloody Bill 'Oggins' with whom she had had a brief and explosive relationship during the absence on holiday of her more regular associate, the foreman at work. This had been her difficulty. If you said no, you didn't know, then it made it look as if you were on the game or just too bloody stupid. But on the other hand, if you said yes, you did know, then welfare just possibly might start prowling round and asking questions, and neither of the two gentlemen or their wives would be likely to think it particularly funny. But... are you on your own? That was an easy one to answer.

'Oh yes,' answered Mavis, 'I am quite on my own apart from Tommy.'

It took a little time for the social worker to establish who or what Tommy was. Even in her limited experience, this description could have applied to a husband, present or 'away', a friend, a dog, a cat, or even a budgie. No, Tommy was none of these. Tommy was a twelve-year-old boy, going to the local school. Mavis described him – not entirely truthfully – as 'my sister's boy'.

So then one went into the question of where Mavis lived, which was in a house that the council had bought and where she was quite happy. And where would she have the baby? That again was easy. In the maternity ward of the district hospital. And what would happen to the infant? Here there was a good deal of doubt. Mavis thought that she would like to keep it, especially if it was a boy. She did not explain to the new social worker that much would depend on who it looked like, and whether the Hoggins family were still living next door. Plenty of time for that. And what about Tommy? asked the social worker. 'What about Tommy?' repeated Mavis. Well, what about Tommy? It took a little while for her to understand that anyone reckoned anyone ought to do anything about Tommy. After all, he'll have the place, won't he? and he gets school meals. He'll be all right.

The interview finally came to an end. Mavis was ready to depart, pleasantly aware of a duty fulfilled. The social worker was ready to return to the perusal of the file marked Hoggins, W. She was wondering why there appeared to be no file marked Tompkins, M. It appeared that the client had had considerable dealings with the social services.

Perhaps though… yes, that must be it. Mavis Tompkins was a newcomer, whose file reposed in some other authority's office.

The telephone went. It was the social worker from the accident centre, where the idiot girl had been taken. Was that social services? Ah good: now they wanted to discuss the eventualities for the little girl, Green of Chapel Street, the one who had been knocked down by a police car on Jubilee Day. She was doing quite well, quite well. There was no cause for anxiety. But did the mother know how deaf the child was? This was not the result of the accident, at least not this accident. No, no. Injuries to the left leg and the left arm. But fortunately nothing to the head. Only did the mother know about the child's deafness? It was difficult to talk much with the mother, as she was always anxious about getting back for the boy, and of course the father… . They would be so glad if social services would investigate, and let them know. Thank you, thank you very much.

Mavis Tompkins was sitting with her legs akimbo, by now relaxed and at ease. The new social worker seemed quite nice. She had not asked the embarrassing question one had feared, and now one could sit back and leave it all to welfare. It even occurred to Mavis to offer the information that her own previous contacts with the department had been under another name. She imagined herself as saying, 'Excuse me, but when I was here before, I was Ferrars, Mavis Ferrars.' She also envisaged the resulting explanations. Why you had been, at one time, Ferrars, and were now Tompkins. Then again, if you had been really sure of yourself, it would have made explanations easier. So Mavis Tompkins-Ferrars smiled gently, unloosed the top of her skirt, and relapsed passively into waiting. The new social worker seemed all right, but you didn't bloody well want to do their work for them, did you? They were bloody paid to do the job, weren't they?

It was the typical attitude of Chapel Street. What the street felt was reasonable. That Big Bill hitting people about all the time was going a bit too far, but having said that, you didn't want to start doing all the things welfare was supposed to do. With any luck, the new social welfare might end the interview by offering to give you the money for a taxi home instead of your having to go on the bloody bus.

The new social worker was trying to work out how much she could fit into the rest of the afternoon. She had to see Mrs Hoggins, and the sooner the better, and it wouldn't hurt to check on what Mavis Tompkins meant when she had described her home conditions as ''s all right'. And now too there was Mrs Green to go and see.

'I'm coming along to Chapel Street,' said the new social worker. 'I can give you a lift.'

Mavis was delighted. Actually, delighted puts it rather too strongly. She was glad not to have to bother about the bus, and it saved the fare, and it would enable her to have a nice gossip with madam. Pity she wouldn't be able to stop and buy cigarettes, but she could send Tommy out to get some.

The car and the two women set out, and arrived in Chapel Street just as Tommy and the other schoolchildren were drifting in. Mavis had already imparted a great deal more information than she realised, in the nice chat she had had in the car. The new social worker prepared herself for a new meeting with Chapel Street, in the flesh as well as in the files.

Chapter Seven

Are those the Stiggins children?' asked the new social worker, and on being told yes, ticked them off in her mind. That boy – rather alert-looking – must be Robert. It was his older brother, the fifteen-year-old Alan, who was 'away' after taking a car. And there was a seventeen-year-old older sister, also away... but that was another story. The girl with him would be the next down, Charlotta. What a name for an undernourished little shrimp of a girl. She was not pretty. All the same, noted the social worker with some surprise, there was some quite unexpected poise, something indicating that she knew what she was about. At that moment, the young Charlotta turned to see what a smaller child was doing, and to adjure 'Patsy' to 'come along'. Charlotta and Bob then resumed their conversation together. The new social worker received an unexpectedly vivid impression of two people bound closely together. It happened sometimes in families. It was particularly nice, she reflected, that a family in Chapel Street should have brought forth some relationship of love and trust. Or was the girl not Charlotta at all but Bob's girlfriend? An alert-looking boy like Bob would have had no lack of applicants.

The ever ready Mavis was explaining that these were the Stiggins kids. 'That Bob's quite a good kid. He's ever so good at football. They think a lot of him at school. And that's his sister with him. Lottie, the next down. I don't know much about her. She's sort of quiet. I mean she doesn't get into trouble as much as some of the other fucking kids... oooh, what have I said?' Mavis gave what she hoped was a refined titter. 'But they can be little horrors, can't they?'

The car passed 'the Stiggins lot' and pulled up outside Mavis's. Mavis got out, and wondered whether to offer a cup of coffee or not. She decided it would be worthwhile cultivating the new social worker. 'Tommy,' she screamed as she got out, 'get in and put the kettle on. We've got a visitor.'

The new social worker was quickly becoming the centre of attraction. Chapel Street had a kind of hidden communication shared by all except Mrs Smith, which told them when authority was approaching. Sometimes this told you to slip unnoticed into your back garden. Sometimes, on the other hand, it might be worth being noticed. On this occasion, it waited to make up its crafty communal mind until it had seen the newcomer in action.

The first to make a move towards the new social worker were Bob and Charlotta. First they held a whispered consultation together. Actually it was less of a conversation than a mutual sharing of views, which hardly needed words. There had always been a bond of affection between these two, and in the last little while, since the Jubilee party, and with Alan away, Bob had come to find in Charlotta an ally rather than a little kid. Charlotta for her part had always been ready to champion Bob against the flashier, showier, and less kind older brother Alan. So Bob and Charlotta were now, as the new social worker had divined, a close alliance.

Charlotta had very mixed feelings about Alan. Bob, on the other hand, thought the world of him. So the alliance demanded that they must now find out, if they could, what was going to happen to Alan. Probation had not been forthcoming. The police had been quite unfriendly. The newcomer in the car could be a new social worker. And social workers will sometimes tell you things.

So they approached the car.

'Miss,' said the boy, 'do you know what they are going to do with Alan?'

Charlotta's figure appeared. 'We thought that you might be someone from the social services department,' explained her careful little voice. Charlotta was one of the only inhabitants of Chapel Street who did not use 'the welfare' as a generic term covering everything except the police, prefixed of course by either of the local adjectives. 'We thought you might be able to help us if you're from social services. We're trying to find out when we shall see Alan again.'

It was a sad commentary on Chapel Street that the girl did not find it necessary to explain who Alan was. Alan, at fifteen, was becoming as well known a trouble maker as Big Bill Hoggins. The social worker felt a sudden dismay.

What a street. She already knew about Mrs Green and the mentally retarded children, about the pregnant and unsupported Mavis Tompkins, about the Stiggins family's two oldest children and about Mr Hoggins. She paused briefly, wondering how often she would come here to face the same questions. 'Miss, when's Alan... ?' 'Will welfare... ?' 'I didn't know the child was... .' Can I get a grant for...?'

Before she had time to explain anything about Alan, there was a noise behind her of some sort of ill-boding altercation. Her eyes still rested appreciatively on the good-looking Bob and his polite younger sister. Here at least were two nice kids. Then she turned her attention to whatever it was that was causing the disturbance.

It turned out to be the arrival of the two aged drunks who normally sat in the 's oon' bar of The Rising Sun. They had been down the market. On market day, there were certain pubs that stayed open well into the afternoons for the convenience of farmers, auctioneers and the drunks from the Chapel Streets of the town. Mr Alfred Smith had always regretted this casual drinking, though naturally you could not interfere with the legitimate trading activities of the town, and with the deals, which were brought to a conclusion only in the sheltering arms of The Blue Boars and The White Lions and The Red Cows.

On this particular day, the drunks were in a belligerent mood, though it was not clear, even to them who or what had triggered off their belligerence. Normally, even on a market day, they were only quietly drunk. Someone at the market, some stranger perhaps, or a farmer who had made a successful bargain, had been inveigled into giving free drinks, so that the two drunks had arrived in Chapel Street in that state of inebriation which was marked by hostility. They would have liked to go into The Rising Sun. But The Rising Sun was shut. They would have liked to lie down, but nowhere convenient appeared. Failing that, they wanted to – well, to land out at the whole bloody fucking unfriendly buggering universe – like that, wham. Drunk number one nearly fell over. Drunk number two wavered uncertainly off the pavement, and made off up the street. Drunk number one recovered his balance, lurched after number two, and with a sudden uncoordinated burst of speed, passed him. Drunk number two was labouring under the delusion that *he*, number two, should be in the lead. He therefore aimed a rather inconclusive blow at number one, and by sheer chance hit him. Number one then halted, turned, and squared up to number two. The new social worker assessed the situation. That the two drunks were about to start a fight seemed obvious. It was equally obvious that they were in no condition to do each other much harm. So it might be better if she ignored the whole uproar, distanced herself from Mavis Tompkins's offer of coffee, and concentrated on her original task of interviewing Mrs Hoggins, not to mention also finding out if Mrs Green was aware of her daughter's deafness.

The drunks were not actually coming to blows. They were still lurching up the street, their shouted threats sounding quite sinister, as number one asserted what he would do to number two, and number two retorted with his own version of what he would do to that... son of a... . The words were not unknown to the social worker. Social workers probably hear them more often than do their friends, due to the people they mix with. All the same, the new social worker was sorry to hear these expressions being used in front of the young boy and the polite little girl. It was true that neither the young boy nor the polite little girl was showing any surprise.

The altercation continued. Mrs Green appeared at her front door, either to see what was happening, or, more probably, because welfare was due about now with her son. A door of The Rising Sun was seen to open, and a man cautiously put his head out, surveying the scene. Tommy reappeared, and Mavis's far from dulcet tones could be heard admonishing the little bugger to go and fetch the lady in. Drunk number one hit Tommy, certainly by chance rather than by intent. Tommy wailed. Mavis appeared, and clouted Tommy for a start, clearly under the impression that whatever had happened must be his fault. Tommy hit Mavis back. Mavis upbraided Tommy, and lunged at him with a saucepan she happened to be holding (for the coffee?).

A woman further down the street appeared, wearing an apron and carrying a frying-pan. This new arrival was later identified as Mrs or Ma Stiggins, the mother of the young boy and the polite little girl. The frying pan was not, as one might have thought, a hastily clutched weapon for use against the drunks. It was just a frying pan that Ma Stiggins had succeeded in borrowing from a newcomer in the street. Mrs Stiggins always hoped that her boys would not get into trouble, and on this occasion became a somewhat ineffective ally as Charlotta quickly pulled her brother away from the path of the drunks.

Drawn by the noise, other people, housewives and the unemployed, came to their street doors. Returning schoolchildren hurried to join in – or rather to do what the French mean by *assister*, to be present at without actively partaking.

The new social worker, seeing that no one was in real danger of being hurt, except perhaps Tommy if his mother's threats were to be taken seriously, remained sitting in her car. She therefore had a clear view of the arrival at the far end of the street of police patrol car number 135 XZ. The effect was instantaneous and very revealing. As one inhabitant after another realised the police were approaching, one after another vanished. Mrs Tompkins grasped Tommy, and hand clutching hand, they dashed indoors. The little girl did call out 'Goodbye' as she followed Ma and her brother into their house. The door of The Rising Sun closed, as did all the others. The only people left on the street, apart from the new social worker, were the two drunks, and they could now be seen gravely supporting each other as they perambulated up the street, decorously increasing their distance from the patrol car.

The new social worker had known that Chapel Street housed a number of cases. The sudden emptying of the street on the arrival of a police car was to remain with her as embodying the way of life of the street. It was a pity though for that young boy and his polite little sister.

The street relapsed. There might or might not have been an affray. Mavis and Tommy might have had a fight. That was not the street's business. The street's business was to keep out of the way of the bloody fuzz and let the fucking welfare get on with the work they were fucking well paid to do.

The street's Jubilee-induced good will seemed to be over. Or almost over? True, the landlord could be seen peeping out of the window and making sure that the police had not intercepted anyone. Perhaps he was just counting his customers. Mavis and Tommy were amicably sharing the coffee destined originally for the social worker. Mrs Green had reappeared, ready to welcome her son. And Bob, the lively-looking youngster, and his polite little sister, Charlotta, would soon be studying an abstruse mathematical problem that Bob had not only been set but intended to jolly well do.

Chapter Eight

The summer passed. The summer holidays passed. Small boys, and older girls, got into trouble. The continued absence of Big Bill Hoggins, Alan Stiggins, and cunning Mr Green made the street a less dangerous place. Mavis increased in girth and affability; sometimes she gave Tommy a cooked tea. The little Green girl was still away and her mother was delighted over the progress her erstwhile idiot daughter seemed to be making now that she was having instruction to teach her to recognise sounds. The holidays ended with no one else in custody.

On a Friday afternoon, the second of the term, the members of Stenson School and Hilton Junior were having their termly conference. These were the schools where the children of Chapel Street spent their lives. The termly conference between the two schools was by way of becoming a regular event in the procession of the year.

The schoolteachers were another force that wrestled with the problems of Chapel Street. They were different of course from the welfare. One difference was that individually they were all dedicated to their own pursuits, like photography, or fabric printing, or cookery, or rural science, or football, and therefore saw their little charges as potential artists and cooks and athletes. Many of the schoolteachers were also young and enthusiastic. Most of them had little to do with the parents, and really hardly knew the truculent Mr Hoggins and the ineffectual Mrs Stiggins. The one occasion that Big Bill had come to the school, he had been routed by an elderly and resolute PE mistress, an exploit still remembered in the staff room.

This termly conference had been the idea of one of the heads. Staff grumbled at the extra time that it took, but all the same, you had to admit that it did help you over some of the kids. For the PE and sports staff the occasion was of real value. You could tell the senior school of any promising footballers coming along. Not to mention netball and gym, now that some of the girls' activities were becoming so important. And it was nice to know that young so-and-so, who had started poorly, was now one of the best forwards the first team had ever had.

Talk turned to the Stiggins family. That older boy, Alan, what a good player he had been. Brilliant even, at times. Pity he had kept getting into trouble. He started pinching cars at the finish and then he was heading for real trouble. His younger brother Bob now – he seemed steadier; also a jolly good footballer. He was in the under-fifteens, even though he wasn't thirteen yet. Or was he thirteen, headmaster? Alan and Bob were both outstanding, but Bob had always been – in the shadow, somehow, when he was with Alan. He seemed to be coming out now. Had quite a following in his own form. And who was the girl you saw him with out of school?

One of the PE teachers explained that that might be his young sister, or it might be Eileen Radford. The more junior football teams, sir explained, had decided to emulate the school first team and to take *girls* with them to school concerts. A girl each, he meant. So everyone had to have a girl. And Bob had very sensibly joined up with this new girl, Eileen Radford. She was one of the best netball players, wasn't she? A games mistress agreed enthusiastically. Eileen Radford had a good home behind her; she would be properly fed at home as well as having school dinners: the stamina would show. The headmaster contributed the fact that the Radfords lived in Jubilee Street in one of those houses that had been looked after. Probably make quite a bit when they sell it, as that sort do, to move on to something better. Had a good report too, did Eileen, from her previous school. But the girl you saw Bob with out of school, that was more likely to be his kid sister. Charlotta, her name was, or Caroline… something like that.

The senior school went on to enquire about the kid sister. Was she like her brothers? Was she going to be any good at games? The staff of Hilton Junior knew all about Bob's progress and were very proud of it. But the girl? Her name did begin with C – Charlotta. No one knew much more than that. Not very good at anything, or very bad. Someone volunteered the information that she had been very helpful one day last term when the younger sister had hurt herself. But there was a young brother too – Terry, a curly-haired, dark-eyed kid, half brother probably – now he could really run, a lively little kid – might be worth keeping an eye on.

The prospects of the school teams were thoroughly discussed, and congratulations given on some unlikely scholastic successes. Stenson School and Hilton Junior did their best, but some of their raw material needed more attention than any education committee was able to pay for.

The meeting drew to its close. Coffee was brought in by some of the home economics second year, including Eileen Radford. Yes, there was a nice-looking girl for you. Looked like a games player. Clean too. Looked in fact a thoroughly nice girl, which was more than you could say about some of the others.

The senior sports master noted the figure of Bob Stiggins sprinting by outside. Funny, how much more dependable he was getting. If you'd seen his older brother Alan sprinting by like that, every car owner on the staff would have been in full flight to make certain they had not left their vehicle unlocked. But Bob, you felt, would be on some worthwhile errand, almost certainly connected with football.

Bob hurtled into the road, in time to intercept the family party on its way home from the junior and infants' schools. He grinned at Terry, and gave him a friendly cuff. 'Wait till you can run like that, young 'un,' he boasted.

It was obvious to Charlotta that he had not taken the trouble to meet them just in order to admonish Terry. It was equally obvious to her, from Bob's voice, that it was not bad news. So she urged Terry to see how quickly he could cover the distance to Chapel Street, and happily loitered on beside Bob, while keeping a tight hold on Patsy. Some quirk of town planning had left a marshy field between the schools and Chapel Street. Reeds grew alongside the path, and an occasional duck could be heard. The paths were over narrow for the school population at the beginning and end of the school day, and the authorities constantly battled with cyclists bent on taking shortcuts. Over-populated by day, it would be a nasty place at night, Charlotta always thought. Not many people went that way at night: somehow, even the grown-ups avoided it. Charlotta was in general not an imaginative child, but she suddenly thought what it would be like to be coming across here at night, in the dark. How glad you would be to see the lights of Chapel Street getting nearer.

She giggled at the thought. Fancy being glad to see Chapel Street.

Bob looked at her in surprise. Charlotta wasn't a giggly sort of girl. He would have liked an explanation, but knew better than to ask for one. Also, he had his own good news to impart.

'Lotta,' he said. Everyone else called her Lottie or Lot, except the headmistress, who called her Charlotte, but Lotta was Bob's name for her. 'Coo... Lotta,' he was almost speechless with the excitement, 'Lotta, they're saying that I'm pretty certain to be chosen as *captain* of our team. And I might get a place in the under-sixteens.' This was triumph indeed. Lotta stopped dead, and even let go of Patsy's hand. She wanted to say that the whole wide world was now radiant with joy, that the afternoon had become of a rich golden hue. What she actually said was, 'Oh, good.'

Bob was quite content with this. In the last month or two, he had come to find that he enjoyed confiding in Lotta, whether it was bad news or the occasional bit of good news. This afternoon it was the good news. And he enjoyed her praise without needing any more expression in words.

Patsy sped on, and Bob and Charlotta ambled their way home. Charlotta, not being pressed for an explanation, decided that she would explain her sudden burst of hilarity.

'Bob, I was just thinking. If you were coming home across here, and it was quite late... well, if it was dark, you might be real glad to see the light at the end of Chapel Street, mightn't you?'

Bob considered this gravely. It had not ever occurred to him that you might rejoice at the prospect of arriving in Chapel Street. Yes, it was possible. 'Yes, if it was dark. And,' he added truthfully, 'if someone was after you.'

So even captains of football were apparently a little bit afraid of crossing the old cut after dark. But now it was light, and no one was after them, and Charlotta had Bob with her, and Ma might have got the telly back.

They sauntered on, in great contentment, contemplating the news of Bob's success and the idea that you might be glad to see Chapel Street.

Chapter Nine

A beautiful September was followed by a mellow October. People in Chapel Street and in more prosperous Jubilee Street, and in the exclusive Squares and Crescents and Closes, said it was nice weather. Humorists remarked that it wasn't much for the ducks. Mrs Alfred Smith sniffed appreciatively at her autumn roses and decided she would take some to dear Letitia.

The affairs of the rest of the street were not progressing with such dramatic splendour as Bob's. Nor did most of the individuals have such a loyal companion as he had in Charlotte. If there had been a bit more communal support, the street might have been better. Mrs Green might have wept a bit less about her idiot son if someone could have referred to him as anything but 'the little bleeder'. The new social worker didn't call him that, but then she wasn't a real friend, just someone who was paid to be nice to you.

Or to take another family, the Stigginses. Mrs Stiggins continued on her amiable but woefully improvident way. She was still surprised when food left on the kitchen table was pilfered – cats? kids? your own or other people's? She still hoped that neighbours would not have mysteriously 'just run out' of anything she tried to borrow. On the credit side, Mr Stiggins continued to hold his job, there were often baked beans for tea, and she was sure that they would soon have the telly back.

She and Bob, if the truth were known, were the only ones who bewailed the continued absence of Alan.

The faint gleams of communal help initiated by their success in the Jubilee celebrations still lingered on. Or did they? It would have taken a very dedicated sociologist to have logged the evidence.

There was a bit more help from one to another. Or was there? How much was due to the prodding of 'the welfare'? How much to the absence of the street's bad characters – the flamboyant Alan with his penchant for pinching cars, the bullying Bill Hoggins, and the more rascally Mr Green?

To Mavis Tompkins-Ferrars-née-something-else, the months were passing lethargically and not unpleasantly. The new social worker was really awfully nice, and didn't seem over excited about Mavis's own lack of conviction over the paternity of the coming child. Mavis worked out, yet once more, the financial implications. The welfare would get you so much, and rent rebate was so much, and if you kept the kid, you'd get... she worked out how much more. It'd be awkward if it looked like that bastard Hoggins. But if it didn't, you might keep it. Twelve-year-old Tommy was going through a phase of saying, ''E'd like to keep it,' and ''E'd help.' Not that Mavis paid too much attention to that. A little girl she now thought – so that you weren't always on your own with men. Tears of self-pity slid easily down Mavis's cheeks. She decided that she would be magnanimous and get Tommy's tea ready. She opened a tin of baked beans.

An unpredicted result of the *joie de vivre* of the Jubilee celebrations was the growth of a relationship between the ever ladylike Mrs Letitia Smith ('funny old geezer') and the two disreputable drunks of The Rising Sun. Regularly every second Thursday the milkman left her a pint of milk. Regularly every second Thursday lunchtime Mrs Smith donned what she thought of as her 'walking out' costume, and decorously made the journey across the street to the door that was now marked saloon bar. Here she would pause, and knock, and then enter. Although this foray had not made any great difference (she hardly mentioned it to Joseph now), it had imperceptibly changed the saloon bar, on alternate Thursdays. The two old drunks had acquired new (well, newer) jackets. One had a sports jacket, and one a blazer, both obtained through a Salvation Army girl who had vainly come collecting in The Rising Sun. Every other Thursday they wore them, the days when the funny old geezer came in. Some Thursdays, if the Wednesday had been a day for much drinking, they referred to her as the 'fucking old bastard', but most Thursdays it was the 'funny old geezer', and, without acknowledging the reason, they dressed up in their new clothes and sat up alert and chatting, waiting for her arrival.

The landlord had turned 's oon bar' into saloon bar. He knew, even if Mrs Smith was not always aware, which was the week when her in-laws came. On those Thursdays he dusted and polished the counter. On it was set out the beer that Mrs Smith would buy. The thought crossed his mind, more than once, that it might be nice to have – well, say, some pork pie or pasty or something like that, tasty and filling, that he could offer her. He let the thought cross his mind. He was pretty sure she didn't get enough to eat. He did not get as far as actually providing the pork pie, but he congratulated himself on his unselfish generosity in thinking of it.

Today was the Thursday, and he whistled as he polished the bar. However, when the door opened, it was to reveal not Mrs Smith but the new social worker. Had he a telephone that she might use?

Well, of all the bloody stupid questions. As if he was going to have a phone that every Tom, Dick and Harry, and probably the fucking police as well, would want to use. He thought that. As if he wanted to get mixed up with all these people, who probably wouldn't have the change to pay. He knew what people were like.

What he said aloud was, 'No, miss, I'm afraid I haven't.'

Miss departed, leaving the habitués to exchange glances. They even wondered what she had wanted to phone about. It was quite a relief when 'their' Mrs Smith came in for her bottle of beer and they could slip back into their usual routine.

The new social worker retreated to the street. The phoning would have to wait. Probation had certainly said that there was a chance that Alan Stiggins might be coming out, for a period under supervision. She pondered on the possible results of his presence. The Stiggins family belonged to the probation officer, not to her. Earlier on, when the older girl had gone off, social services had been involved, but that had been one of her predecessor's cases. Her own contact with the Stiggins family was an informal one, largely springing from casual meetings and enquiries from that bright young boy and his polite sister.

The boy seemed to miss his elder brother, and was always agog for news. Did she know if Alan would be back soon? Could she find out? Come to think of it, it was usually the sister who did the asking. She always asked very politely, in quite a grown-up way.

The new social worker wondered if the little girl was really as anxious as Bob to see the older brother out. Probation would of course have to decide about Alan's future; in view of the record of his offences – one car after another, not to mention the truck – one wondered. And if he came out, what difference might that make to the rest of his family?

Chapter Ten

The rumour that Alan was returning that day proved to be wrong. His case was in fact being discussed at a high-level conference, and his immediate future being weighed up. There were those who reckoned that if he came out now, he would soon be involved in something more serious than joyriding. There were others who said that a short sharp period of detention had done its work, and the sooner he came back to his family, the better. The discussion continued, Alan stayed 'away', and the friendship of Bob and his sister deepened.

The pattern of Bob joining Charlotte on their way back from school became a fairly common one. Sometimes he was not there. He had had to stay on at school for mysterious 'selections' and 'squad tactics', as well as 'match practices'. He and his vice captain would sometimes stay on and talk gravely with sir.

Charlotta had fewer duties. Although she was in the top form of her school, she was not of the stuff of which monitors are made. Others might make themselves conspicuous by volunteering to do odd jobs for sir and miss, and then more conspicuous by failing to turn up at the allotted times. Not Charlotta. Life to her was a potentially dangerous experience and you did not challenge fate by thrusting yourself forward. You looked after the little 'uns, you revelled in the companionship of your brother Bob, and you never ceased to be thankful for the freedom from anxiety now that Alan was away. Alan was not a nice brother. He could be *nasty* to anyone smaller and weaker. And the 'larks' he was always up to used to end in trouble, trouble that for some unexplained reason always seemed to involve Bob. You read in stories of people going into churches to say prayers and if there had been a pretty little church in the street, or perhaps a Madonna at a shrine, where everyone stopped, you would have said thank you for keeping Alan away.

In Charlotta's little world, Bob was the centre. Bob was nice. Bob was an ever present centre of companionship, of sharing. Bob helped you look after the little ones. Bob was wonderful. Bob had – she didn't know the word – a zest, and a good-natured acceptance of other people. It was Bob who had made some of Alan's larks enjoyable.

The flowering of her companionship with Bob was making the autumn a time of joy. It showed in her face, and one or two of the more perceptive teachers remarked that the older Stiggins girl occasionally looked beautiful. Not a beauty born of colouring and dash, but something almost spiritual. The teachers who could remember the family seven years earlier remarked on the welcome difference from the oldest Stiggins girl, who had disappeared into the capital, certainly up to no good, but thank goodness she's left this town.

Bob and Charlotta were walking back across the cut. Bob was a little late, and it had taken some ingenuity on Charlotta's part to dawdle sufficiently till he came. Just as well she had, she thought, for Bob seemed to have something on his mind.

Bob was silent for a minute or two. She began to fear that he was no longer captain of his football team, though that seemed unlikely with a team that was surpassing previous records.

'Lotta.' It was the voice of Bob-with-a-problem. 'Eileen Radford has asked me to go out with her and her family next Saturday week.'

'Go out with Eileen's family?' Lotta was evidently as shocked as he was. 'But why?' She nearly added, 'You haven't...?' but refrained, as she hoped that that was so clearly out of the question.

Sex was sex in Chapel Street, the same as everywhere else. The difference was that in Chapel Street it was earlier, more indiscriminate, and more transient. If Bob *had* with Eileen, it would have been no very new thing for the thirteen-year-olds of Chapel Street, but Charlotta and Bob were quite, quite clearly aware of what was sex in the way of fancying someone, and what was demanded of sex as a social relationship. Big Bill Hoggins, who probably didn't fancy his second wife very much, would go back to her when he came out. Mr and Mrs Alfred Smith, who looked to Charlotta a bit grand and restrained for what she knew was a relationship, were a married couple and would go on being one. By the fashions of that particular year, at that particular date, the football captain had to have a female figure at his side at school concerts, so what more suitable than the clean respectable netball player Eileen Radford? Except for not producing children, it was rather like the dynastic alliances between Hapsburgs and Bourbons and their ilk, no more and no less. Bob and Charlotta both understood this perfectly. They now began to wonder if Eileen did too. Fancy her parents asking him to go out with them.

What Bob and Charlotta did not understand was that this particular dynastic alliance, between Bob, captain of his football team, and Eileen, shooter in her netball team, was being played out against very different social backgrounds. The very words used for relationships in Chapel Street were different in meaning from the same words in Jubilee Street. In Chapel Street you referred to someone as 'Daddy' or 'my mum', when that gentleman or lady had been fulfilling these duties over a number of years. 'My mum' was often, but by no means always, the biological mother. 'Daddy', though much more problematic biologically, did represent a definite and stable relationship. 'My mum' was the pivot of the family. If Daddy was away (and there were some quite reputable reasons for this), then Mum might have a friend. This figure was always transient, and he was always referred to as 'Mum's friend'. Kids often did very well, in sweets, tips, et cetera, while the 'friendship' lasted. The one thing that it wasn't of course was a friendship, and the danger was that Mum might finally go off with the friend.

Uncles were different from friends. Apart from uncles who were uncles by being related, there were other gentlemen, sometimes in a metamorphosis from lodger to friend to a more stable relationship with Mum, which might even end up as Daddy. The bickering and fights that might or might not accompany these changes were as much part of the background in Chapel Street as the changes of weather in the more salubrious streets. 'Lodger' incidentally was not an amusing euphemism for a boyfriend. It was a pecuniary and often very necessary relationship.

The explanation for the Radfords' well meant invitation to Bob was something that lay outside the experience of Chapel Street or the imagination of Bob and Charlotta. It was simply that the Radfords were kind people, and although they were not enthusiastic about their daughter's special friendship with a boy from Chapel Street, they were ready to invite him to join them on a visit to the nearby town of larger size. They thought it would make a nice afternoon. The social nuances that such an invitation held in Chapel Street escaped them.

Bob, on Lotta's suggestion, finally worked out what would be a polite refusal. He would say that his own father had arranged to take him out. Bob wanted to add *where* but was restrained by the more cautious and practical Charlotta. As she pointed out, once you started saying where, you had to make up more things. It wasn't that she minded telling lies, but her experience was that it was easier not to tell them unnecessarily. If you didn't volunteer information, you were that much less likely to have to substantiate it. Whether the information was true or false was totally irrelevant – you used truth or a fib according to the situation in which you found yourself in a hostile world. Bob should simply say that Pa was taking him out.

When Bob offered Eileen the unlikely explanation that his father was taking him out, the Radfords accepted this without question and were politely sorry. Eileen was unconcerned. She was a good games player. She had her own friends, and a very nice family whose outings were not solely to the police or the welfare. In the world of school, it was quite pleasant to be invited to appear with Bob Stiggins for a partner on ceremonial occasions. She was quite content with that position in his life. Quite a hero he was becoming in school – you should have seen that last goal – coo. To give Eileen her due, she had some inkling of what football meant to him, and she would certainly have abstained from anything that might have done damage to the progress of Bob and his team. Netball meant rather less to her, but enough to give her a good deal of understanding.

There was no doubt that Bob's team was doing well. Some good footballers, said the sports master concerned, and there's a jolly good team spirit, jolly good. That Bob Stiggins is turning out to be a very good captain. He's really making something of that team. Bringing in other kids too, like that Tony Bloxey, who lives on the council estate. Making him quite a good vice captain. Bob Stiggins has come on well.

Chapter Eleven

The question of Alan's return kept recurring. Would Alan be returning yet? If not this month, would he be home next? The new social worker was convinced by now that the boy was much more anxious than Charlotta to see Alan again. And from what could be gleaned from colleagues, it was the little girl who was right. Alan sounded just the sort to come into trouble... and to bring others with him. And at the minute, Chapel Street was experiencing an unwonted period of tranquillity.

Chapel Street was actually in a period when progress was being made. Take for example the erratic and lazy Mavis Tompkins. She had thrown herself into the role of mother-to-be. She had given up her job, and was ostentatiously making preparations for 'my little one'. Bright orange curtains now gave a colourful background to the dilapidated dustbins and broken bicycles that were still the main ornaments in her small front garden. Or perhaps one should say that these were now subsidiary. The welfare had obligingly produced a pram, prominently displayed there in all its shining beauty. The history of the pram, which had first been seen at a children's and babies' exhibition in the county town's leading outfitters, could well have illustrated the social gradations of the area. Few had been prouder owners than Mavis Tompkins, and blood-curdling were her threats to Tommy if 'e laid a hand on it.

Mr Alfred Smith and his wife had begun to remark on the improvements in Chapel Street. They liked the new social worker. Mr Alfred Smith's position in the town brought him into contact with such people. He had retired a little early from the Bench but flattered himself that he knew what was going on. Those who had appeared before him could have told him even more, but were not asked to. Mr Alfred Smith attributed more of the improvement in Chapel Street to the new social worker than was really justified. She had no such opinion of her influence, but went steadily on. Mr Smith knew that one of the Stiggins boys was coming out on probation. He thought that he would mention this to the social worker, if she happened to be in Chapel Street, as so often, when he was there.

What was more important to him at the moment was that they had changed their car, from the eminently serviceable and reliable 1800, which they had planned to keep for another year. An unexpected legacy had brought this about and Mr Smith was now the proud owner of the newest and most resplendent 2300. He would not have spent the money himself, not this year, but an aged aunt had left him more money than any of the family knew she had. The Smiths were not imaginative or over-perceptive, but they did their duty. Old Auntie, away on the other side of the country, had appreciated nephew

Alfred's regular Easter, birthday and Christmas cards. She had noted especially the Easter cards, as so many of her nephews and nieces no longer kept up their religion – you really didn't know what the country was coming to. But Alfred – now there was a good boy. So – hey ho – a large legacy, and there were Mr and Mrs Alfred Smith, in the opulent new car, the 2300, on the way to visit dear Letitia. It was a proud journey.

Alfred would have liked to drive right down Chapel Street and to have pulled up with a flourish outside Letitia's. But he had to admit that dear Letitia was unlikely to notice what car they came in. She might conceivably have noticed if they came with a horse and cart, but, as Mr Smith laughingly remarked to his wife, you couldn't even have been sure of that. The only people to notice would probably be that surly landlord and the out-of-works. Mr Smith turned the matter over in his mind. Chapel Street had certainly improved. He was greatly tempted by the idea of driving in instead of walking from the corner. He almost felt that Chapel Street deserved it, as a sort of reward for improvement.

More mature reflection brought him to the conclusion that it would be more prudent not to take the new car into Chapel Street. If he left it, as usual, on the forecourt of the garage in Bond Street, they would get their due need of admiration from the garage staff, and the car would be safe. Yes, that is what they would do. It was a pleasant day, and they would leave the car as usual at the garage. And while it was there, he would get the mechanic (a promising young man, in whom he took an interest) to check the adjustment to the headrest behind the passenger seat. It was nice to find such a reliable garage so conveniently near to Chapel Street.

At the garage, the car received the homage due to it. Mr Alfred Smith, the proprietor and two mechanics walked round the vehicle, admiring it from every angle. One might have cracked some little joke, say about not letting some other customer do a swap, but one does not jest in an atmosphere of worship. So Mr Smith gave his instructions, took his wife by the arm, and rather in that state of euphoria that he sometimes felt after going to church, proceeded towards Chapel Street. He could hardly believe in his good fortune. They had done their duty by old Auntie, without expectation of recompense, and now... . Heaven had indeed rewarded them.

Chapter Twelve

Everything was in place that Thursday, like a Greek tragedy, poised ready. Mrs Letitia Smith had been over to The Rising Sun and collected her beer. The two drunks had said, 'Good morning, ma'am.' Mr and Mrs Alfred Smith had arrived, had lunched, and were now passing the requisite time in polite conversation with Letitia. Mrs Green's 'little bleeder' was away at the welfare, and would soon be returning. Mavis Tompkins was sitting in her front room, peeping out from behind the orange curtains. Mrs Stiggins had borrowed some tea from a new neighbour. Mrs Hoggins was out, possibly visiting the old man in gaol. The stage was set, the scenery in position, and the characters in their places. Behind every window curtain were neighbours, ready to play the part of spectators or chorus.

Into this picture came the probation officer's car, bearing the figure of what was hoped was a now repentant Alan. So it *was* true – Alan was due home. The new social worker, happening as so often to be in the street, noted his arrival. Ma Stiggins rushed up and embraced him as he got out of the probation officer's car. One of the drunks from The Rising Sun appeared and waved. Mavis Tompkins's curtains twitched. Mrs Green came to her front door. It was true that she had been under the impression that it was welfare's car bringing her son home, but she too waved across to the jubilant Mrs Stiggins. Mrs Stiggins waved, expansively and indiscriminately, to all whom it might concern, rather like royalty at a fête, and led her prodigal son indoors.

The probation officer and the new social worker conferred. That Bill Hoggins wasn't likely to be out too? Without needing to say it in words, both knew that the Hoggins household was a far happier place without its nominal head. And Alan Stiggins? What were the prospects there? The probation officer said that they had all liked Alan and that they had high hopes that he would make it outside. A lot would depend on the family, and they certainly seem to be the kind who would help. The social worker added her impressions – two very nice younger siblings, and a stable atmosphere, now. Ma and Pa were both the parents of the whole family, except for young Terry, who appeared to be Ma's and not Pa's. Ma was, well, a bit feckless, and tended to put off things, but Ma was all right, and basically it was a pretty sound family – for Chapel Street. Alan stood a not unreasonable chance.

The probation officer looked at the social worker's car, clean, reliable, well kept. 'Mind you keep it locked,' he advised her, 'now that Alan Stiggins is back.' The social worker laughed. You kept your car locked in these streets anyway. The probation officer, having given this piece of advice, went in to see the Stiggins family, to offer more advice, which he devoutly hoped would be taken.

Alan, he told Mrs Stiggins, had behaved well. He was a good lad and he must take advantage of this opportunity. The probation officer declined the offer of a cup of coffee. He would not intrude longer on what was a family occasion. 'Above all,' he concluded, 'no cars, eh, young 'un?' Alan had already determined, like Charles II in an earlier century, 'not to go on his travels again'. It had hardly been necessary to offer him this gratuitous piece of advice. He politely answered, 'Yes, sir. I mean no, of course not,' at the same time using to himself a few of the choice epithets he had picked up while on remand.

The probation officer departed. Alan and his mother sat in peace apart from the telly, drinking coffee and eating the twentieth-century equivalent of fatted calf.

'Ma, what time do the kids get back?' he presently demanded. 'Oh, quite soon,' said Ma happily. She was in her seventh heaven. Her Alan was back, away from those wicked policemen and that dreadful place. And the rest of the kids would soon be home. Pa was on afternoons, and he'd be back soon after six.

'Would you like another cup of coffee, dear? Or some tea? And some more crisps? Or biscuits?' Yes, Alan would like all those things. It was nice being out. It'd be nice too to see his young brother Bob. Particularly now that Bob was the captain of his football team. Jolly good.

Alan was a trifle disappointed when the first to arrive was Charlotta, and not Bob or even Terry. Charlotta was an odd girl. You never knew quite where you were with her. Mrs Stiggins too was surprised to see her daughter so early, but, like the rest of the family, she knew that it was no good asking questions like, 'Why are you so early?'

If it concerned you, Charlotta would tell you. If it didn't, then no word would be vouchsafed. On this particular afternoon, Charlotta was keeping to herself the knowledge that she had come out of school early, in case Alan had arrived, and to forestall if she possibly could whatever he might get Bob into. Ten- and eleven-year-olds do not leave school as and when they like, but she had obtained special permission to leave early, on the grounds that Mum had a migraine. Charlotta had an entirely neutral attitude to telling the truth. It was often simpler to tell the truth. When the truth was unlikely to help you, as in this case, you had to fall back on invention. Sir was unlikely to be meeting Mum to ask about her health, and a migraine sounded vague and important enough to go unchallenged. Provided Charlotta was back on time in the morning, no one would notice, so she had said that Mum was a sufferer from migraine, which would have surprised Mum very much, and had come out early with the full blessing of school.

Alan regarded his sister with disappointment. When would Bob be back?

Oh, quite soon, asserted Charlotta, and used all her wits to regale Alan with what she had gleaned about football. She felt herself without an ally. She divined that Alan would soon be bored. *If* he went out, he would get into trouble. *If* he stayed in, it might be better. Or – dreadful thought – would he at once take Bob out, and the pair of them get into trouble? She battled manfully on. The two teams had won last week. Bloxey (did he remember Bloxey?) was playing well.

Bob had got him as vice captain. Bob had shot in *every* match. Sir made them practise – oh, ever so often. Terry was going to be good too, you could tell that he was pretty fast, and he was proud of his older brothers. She refrained from saying that Bob had encouraged him a lot. Oh, and Bob's form teacher said his schoolwork was improving.

The minutes ticked by. Alan was surprised to find his young sister so interesting. Had they played The Castle yet? Jolly good teams The Castle had always had.

Ma was like a hen clucking over a chick. 'Would you like a cigarette, dear?' she clucked, and when Alan said yes, remembered that she had just run out. She clucked on. 'Oh dear, I've run out. Here's some money and you can go and get some.'

Alan got to his feet. Yes, that was an idea. The pub wouldn't be open, so he'd go the other way to the shop next to the garage in Bond Street.

Alan got up to go. Charlotta got up. Alan went off up the street. Charlotta followed. She was not sure what to do. She must not intrude on him, but she was unhappily certain that if she was with him, he was just that little bit less likely to... less likely to do what? That was the difficulty. She didn't know. Less likely to get into trouble. Less likely to cheek a copper. Above all, less likely to take someone's car and drive off.

Charlotta went up the street after him. At precisely that moment, Bob arrived from school, breathless from running, at the other end of the street. He hadn't enough breath to call her, but cantered along in time to see her vanish round the corner.

Alan bought the cigarettes. He came out. The shop was next to the garage. His eye fell appreciatively on Mr

Smith's 2300. My, the very newest model. Charlotta, still fifty yards behind, halted in terror.

Alan, like a sleepwalker, moved towards the car. The mechanic was fetching another spanner. The door stood open. Alan got in. The key was in. He switched on. He got into gear. Charlotta screamed.

Bob, well along Chapel Street, heard Lotta scream, and rushed to come to her help.

He reached the end of the street. The car, swinging round to enter Chapel Street, knocked him flying.

In a moment, the Greek tragedy had reached its climax. The car was in a garden wall, and Bob's body lay lifeless on the pavement, a little girl huddled beside it trying to cradle the head.

Alan had finished his time 'outside'.

Chapter Thirteen

Chapel Street reacted to the tragedy with astonishment and shock. A little crowd of onlookers collected, first of all with the pleased anticipation of finding a fire or a fight or even a motor crash, or whatever it was. Their anticipation turned to a horrified silence, as they found out what had happened. They stood there, doing nothing, getting in the way of the usual efficient services.

The ambulance was the first on the scene. The attendants sprang out, only to lay a blanket right over Bob's figure. They reverently covered the face, and a little murmur went round... . 'He's dead.'

The police car came next, siren blaring. Alan, as he saw it, felt the sudden instinct to jump out of the mangled car and run, but withheld as he saw the unmoving figure of Charlotta. She still knelt beside the body. Dimly, Alan realised that it would be worse for Charlotta and the family if he did try to cut and run. He got out, not badly hurt, and ranged himself awkwardly beside Charlotta.

Mum appeared, being led up the street by Mrs Green. Tommy Tompkins, young Jerry, and the younger Patsy appeared, grouping themselves round Mum. Mrs Green came forward and made to put an arm round Charlotta.

The ambulance and the police conferred.

The mechanic came hurrying round from the garage, ready to lay violent hands on that young devil Alan Stiggins. But the intense grief of Charlotta had reached Alan, who stood nearly as quiet as she was. The mechanic turned with a frustrated gesture to the police and explained where the owner of the car could be found.

The driver of the police car radioed for a doctor, and the constable prudently slipped the handcuffs on to the unresisting Alan.

A doctor arrived, and confirmed that there was nothing more to be done but to lift Bob's body into the ambulance. Someone was supporting Mrs Stiggins, and the ambulance driver turned to check up on her. Was there someone who would take Mrs Stiggins home and look after her? For once, Chapel Street was ready actually to do something. There was a neighbour to take Mrs Stiggins home, and another to take Patsy and Jerry off and give them their tea. No one, and this was unusual in a street so ready with recriminations, was blaming Mr Alfred Smith for having the car, or indeed for leaving the car. And no one was blaming Alan. Charlotta's grief was moving the street almost as much as Bob's death.

She maintained her place beside Bob's body. She was holding his hand now. As the attendants lifted the body on to a stretcher and into the ambulance, she moved too. The ambulance men were nonplussed. Little girls do not get taken along as passengers to mortuaries. But equally, you do not use physical force on little girls suffering from shock. The suggestion that she should let them 'take him along with us, dear' had fallen upon deaf ears. Unseeing almost, and apparently unhearing, Charlotta had moved along beside the body, and now crouched next to it on the floor of the ambulance, still holding Bob's hand. What could they do?

It was Mr Alfred Smith who solved the problem (and it very often was). He had of course been summoned. The mechanic's garage would pick up the damaged 2300. Then they would provide a suitable car that Mr and Mrs Alfred Smith could have for getting home. So Mr Smith made the sensible suggestion that the ambulance, still bearing Charlotta, should proceed to the mortuary. He and his wife would follow in the loaned car, and probably by then the shock would have worn off and he would bring the little girl back. He would see to this first, before going along to report the whole matter to the police superintendent. Perhaps someone would make certain that his sister-in-law was all right? She too was in the crowd, and she should be escorted home.

The street, even in its new neighbourliness, was at once uneasy. Look after Mrs Letitia Smith? That really was asking a bit much. 'Funny old geezer' or 'fucking old bastard' – whichever she was, she was a lady, and not one of them. There was a rather awkward pause. Then it appeared that Mrs Green was ready to help. She, Mrs Green, would go along with Mr Smith, so that Mrs Alfred Smith could escort the old geezer back to her own house. This unwanted offer of help brought the scene to a close. The ambulance drove off. Mr Smith followed. The onlookers began to move away, in ones and twos and little groups.

At the mortuary, the scene was not unlike most mortuary scenes, except for the figure of the little girl motionless beside the body. Someone had given the child a cup of coffee, arid she was sitting there, the coffee untouched, the cup still held in her free hand.

Mrs Green approached her. 'Charlotta,' she said, in a voice that was not as comforting or authoritative as she would have liked, 'Charlotta, we have come to take you home.' There was a long pause. Charlotta appeared not to have heard, and indeed was hearing only her own voice once more as she had cried out when Alan got into the car.

It was not for nothing that Mrs Green had spent long years in dealing with those whose wits were astray. She took the cup firmly from Charlotta's hand. 'I'm going now,' she said, possessing herself of Charlotta's free hand, 'and you can come along with me.' She spoke as if there had never been any argument about it. To her relief, and the surprise of the ambulance personnel, Charlotta meekly got up and went with Mrs Green. They were escorted out of the mortuary, Charlotta's hand disengaged from her brother's and clinging, automatically it seemed, to Mrs Green's. They got into the car and were driven away by Mr Smith, leaving the ambulance staff to comment.

'What a tragedy, what a tragedy... . One of the best of the kids in the whole street, that young Bob.' They commented harshly on Alan. 'That older brother... Alan... quite out of hand... pretty useless... and now, what sort of a future?'

Most of all, they worried over Charlotta and her unnatural quietness. 'That sister of his. She's taking it hard. Too hard to do herself any good. There's going to be trouble there, real trouble if she goes on long like this. Poor little soul.'

Chapter Fourteen

The pattern continued. Charlotta went about her duties like a little ghost, uncomplaining, unweeping, in a different world from those around her. Mrs Stiggins wept, as much over Alan's departure as Bob's death. Alan had been her favourite and dimly she wondered if she had contributed to his downfall. Probation too was wondering this. Would there ever be enough support from the family to keep Alan straight? Mum continued to wonder if she ought to have had the cigarettes ready for him. However, there were still the little ones to look after, and her husband was good to her, and they had had a lot of sympathy from his mates at work. By 'the little ones' she meant Terry and Patsy. Charlotta was not a little one. Charlotta had now become frighteningly adult, and you really didn't know whether you ought to treat her as a child or as an equal.

As well as the funeral to prepare for, there were the seemingly endless questionings by authority. Charlotta, grey-faced, helped Pa and Ma through the questions. Though all that the questions revealed was the stark simplicity of the tragedy. Mr Alfred Smith had left his car at the garage, as he normally did. The mechanic had been making a minor adjustment. He had stepped over from the car to the counter to pick up a special spanner. Alan had been passing at that moment.

Seeing the car open, he had got in. Having got in, he had driven off. Whether he had got in with the intention of driving off or only of having a look was uncertain. Charlotta had screamed. Bob had rushed up – possibly to rescue his sister? The car, swinging round into Chapel Street, had hit the pavement and Bob. That was all. Questioning revealed nothing more. Mr A Smith had left the car, and the mechanic had been making an adjustment, and Alan had got in and driven off. Charlotta repeated her statements in a low clear voice. She had screamed. And the next thing had been the car with its bonnet in the wall and Bob lying dead beside it. No, she didn't know how Bob had arrived so quickly. Yes, Alan had taken cars before.

Help of course came for the family. The new social worker was alerted by the police to keep an eye on them. What she or anyone else could do for Charlotta was uncertain.

The sports master came from the school to tell Mr Stiggins what a fine footballer the school had lost in Bob. 'Not only his own performance,' explained sir, 'promising though that was. But his influence on the rest of the team.' He stopped himself in time from adding, 'So different from that blasted older brother of his.'

Probation came and conferred. They were so very sorry. They had really had great hopes. It was a pity. Taking cars. What a pity. They nearly said that they were glad to hear how well Bob, the next boy, was doing at school and stopped in time.

The police came. They explained, briefly and succinctly, what was going to happen to Alan. The police were angry. The police were exasperated at the whole chain of accidents. They felt it would have been better if more of the street had been demolished... and among themselves they used the same adjective about the street as did the inhabitants. They looked with silent respect at Charlotta, and brought her the biggest box of chocolates she had ever handled in her young life.

Chapel Street itself might not have known how to behave in the past. It might not know again in the future. But this week, with poor Bob's funeral yet to take place, it pulled together.

Take, just as one example, the question of the wreath. Or to put it more exactly, the question of collecting the money for the wreath. The street now knew what to do. Mrs Green would do the collecting. And as Mrs Green did not want to be responsible for keeping the surprising amount that did come in, the money would be held by the landlord. In the street's views he was the one who knew about counting money, and you could trust him about this. The actual ordering of the wreath would be entrusted to Mr Alfred Smith, through his contacts with business in the town.

The funeral would be held at the parish church, St Michael and All Angels. The vicar would conduct it. Then the family party would follow the hearse to the cemetery. The whole street would go to the parish church and just the family party would go to the cemetery.

There was some initial dissent in the family about what would constitute the family party. If Alan came, and after all he was family, he would have to be accompanied by the probation officer. It was probably lucky for Terry that no one heard him explaining to Patsy the reason for this: it was obvious to Terry that this measure was to prevent Alan nicking the bloody 'earse. If probation were coming, argued Mr Stiggins, that nice sports master from the school should be invited. Charlotta, appealed to, did not disagree. She thought that it would be difficult to get a message reliably to a master in another school, but then the new social worker came to the aid of the family. That mysterious network of communications, usually acting against the streets, was now working to help them. Yes, sir would come, would be honoured to come and represent the school.

This invitation gave Charlotta another thought. She pondered long. She knew that among the floral tributes was one coming 'With great sympathy' from 'Mr and Mrs Radford and Eileen'. That was all right. Eileen was a sort of honorary widow at the moment. In that case, oughtn't Mum to invite her to the funeral? Charlotta struggled with the intricacies of behaviour in an adult world. She knew that none of the others minded about Bob as she had done. As for his alliance with Eileen Radford, that had been, well, sort of political and ceremonial rather than passionate. These were not the words Charlotta used to herself, but they expressed her ideas: just because the alliance had been ceremonial, Eileen had the right to be at the funeral and the family had the duty of inviting her. Waves of sadness overcame Charlotta at every fresh reminder of what Bob was – of what Bob had been. She still had not wept and the educational psychologist would have told Mrs Stiggins that the child would be heading for trouble if she went on much longer being so quiet and restrained.

Charlotta approached her mother. 'Ma, about the funeral.' She paused. 'I think you ought to invite Eileen Radford.'

Ma for once was aghast. How could Charlotta even *think* such a thing? Invite Eileen Radford indeed! She, Ma, had heard tales about what went on in remote corners after school was over and even if Bob had been indulging in that sort of thing, she, Ma, saw no reason for inviting 'that girl' to the funeral. That girl indeed! Ma's tone as she said it would have done justice to any stage portrayal of outraged propriety. Ma had forgotten how recently others had been saying 'that girl' about the oldest Stiggins girl, and with more justification than about Eileen Radford. It was useless for Charlotta to say that it had not been 'like that', and that Eileen Radford was not 'that sort of a girl'. Ma for once felt herself on sure ground. She even brought in Pa as a reinforcement, and he concurred.

So Eileen was not invited to the funeral, but all Chapel Street was there, and Mr and Mrs Alfred Smith, and the probation, and the social workers and the sports master, together with a fair sprinkling of football enthusiasts and well-wishers.

The funeral passed off uneventfully. In the folklore of Chapel Street, Bob's funeral was to rank high. Nothing went wrong. It was as decorous as a funeral from any of the Closes and Crescents at the western end of the town. The flowers were lovely and none lovelier than the wreath from Chapel Street. There was a nice one from the Smiths. The vicar conducted the service with a sad sincerity. He could not sound personally involved with a family he had last seen at Ma and Pa's wedding, but the whole circumstances gave such cause for grief. Poor Bob, so young and promising, according to everyone who had known him. And poor Alan too, chief mourner after Mum and Dad, incongruously marching up the aisle with the probation officer as his partner.

It was not entirely clear who was to go to the cemetery, so almost everyone went. The exceptions included Mavis, in her advanced state of pregnancy, and Letitia Smith, in the old-fashioned and elegant 'funeral outfit' that had first been worn on some bygone civic occasion.

There was wide sympathy for the family. Many a funeral had taken place at St Michael and All Angels with more pomp and less sincerity.

The funeral was a definite event to be remembered, a day when everyone had behaved well, and everyone had given a little mild help to the bereaved Stiggins family. It was a day when 'all of them' – police, welfare, probation, usually referred to as 'the whole fucking lot' but today as 'all of them' – had been at one with Chapel Street. Ma and Pa felt comforted, and the two little ones rather enjoyed the excitement. Terry was a bit disappointed that Alan hadn't got up to any 'larks'.

Charlotta was untouched.

Chapter Fifteen

T he following week, Charlotta finally made up her mind that she would have to go and see Eileen Radford. Everything else had been done properly. Bob's funeral had been, rightly, a public occasion. Now you were left with doing what you could to help Ma and Pa, and the little 'uns. The school football team would go on. Yes, everything would go on, except for her. No more walks home across the cut with Bob. No one else to show you hope, or share a bit of pride in the street. But you'd better do your duty and go and see Eileen Radford.

She plodded dully up the street in the November twilight. She turned the fateful corner into Bond Street, where the garage was, then turned in the other direction and round to Jubilee Street. At the corner of Jubilee Street she halted. She did not know the Radfords' number, and she had hoped there would be children about. There were always children about in Chapel Street. She ventured a little way in, and was rewarded by seeing girls from her own school. Did they know which was Eileen Radford's house?

'Oh yes.' One of them gave a loud call. 'E-i-i-i-leen, you're wanted.'

Eileen Radford, dressed in a fashionable brown jumper and neat brown trousers, appeared. 'Okay, Bess, what is it?'

There was a momentary pause as the girl called Bess explained, and they both looked at Charlotta.

Then Eileen came forward. Eileen was from a well run and orderly household. Eileen's mother did not borrow frying pans or run out of tea. Mr Radford did not hit his wife. When he had been away, he returned at the time previously arranged, or else telephoned. Eileen was brought up to behave properly. Mr and Mrs Radford had not greatly approved of their daughter's alliance with Bob Stiggins, but they were sensible enough to know that school fashions had changed. They had been disappointed, and a shade nonplussed, at Bob's refusal of their invitation to come out with them. But in any case, Eileen usually knew how to behave, and they were wise enough to trust to that.

Eileen had not expected to be confronted with Bob's sister. She, Eileen, had grieved over Bob's death, and was doing something practical by way of rallying his football team. She and the other members of their netball team had made a point of going to watch the under-fifteen football match, already arranged when Bob died. There had been talk of cancelling it, and Eileen had been one to tell Bloxey, the vice captain, that he owed it to Bob *not* to cancel. Eileen was a thoroughly nice good girl, who could be relied on.

She was also intelligent enough to know that her own rather public friendship with Bob Stiggins had not had

244

the emotional intensity of his alliance with that quiet little sister of his.

Eileen was making up her mind about what she ought to do. It was something of an effort to go up to Charlotta. What should she say? Would Charlotta be crying? She told Bess to go away, and approached Charlotta.

Charlotta too was unsure of her ground. Would Eileen feel that she was being cheeky? But she knew what she had to say, and, out of respect for Bob, went on.

'Eileen,' she said, 'we wanted to say thank you to you for the wreath you and your parents sent. And also... well, I'd have invited you to come to the funeral. I asked Ma to, and she ought to have. But she didn't understand.'

Eileen reached out a hand. 'That's all right. But thank you for coming. I'd probably have cried if I had come.' Eileen looked at the frozen unweeping countenance in front of her, and felt for what might be a crumb of comfort. 'And in a way it wouldn't have been right, because Bob didn't, well didn't really mind about me so much. You were the one who mattered to him.' Eileen paused. 'It was jolly good of you to come round and say that. You can come in with me and meet Mummy if you like.'

Charlotta shook her head. She knew that this was a kind well meant invitation, but Jubilee Street was not her street or her scene. She shook her head. 'No, thank you very much, but I've got to get back to the kids.'

'I don't know if you heard,' said Eileen, 'but we all went to the football match. I think Bob's team will get on still. He's got...' she corrected herself... 'he had a jolly good vice captain. Would you like to come and watch next time?'

Again Charlotta shook her head. It was nice to be asked,

but she did not really like football, and she felt that her attendance would be... well, sort of phony. She liked football only when it meant... when it meant something for Bob. So she thanked Eileen and again said no.

Eileen still held Charlotte's hand. She had given, had she but known it, the one crumb of comfort that she could, in assuring Charlotta of Bob's feeling for her. Eileen, being practical, pressed on. 'You'll be coming up to our school next year, won't you? You needn't worry about it at all. I'll see you're looked after.'

Charlotta thanked her mechanically. That far ahead....

On a sudden impulse, Eileen threw her arms round Charlotta and kissed her, and the two girls separated, Eileen running nimbly back to her own well lit home, Charlotta dragging herself back to Chapel Street.

It was nice to hear that Bob had minded about her, and it was nice that Eileen didn't feel too bad. There were not many adjectives in use in Chapel Street, particularly to express approbation. Charlotta felt dully that it was nice of Eileen to have invited her in. And nice that Bob's beloved team was going on all right. A little gleam of brightness had sprung up at the mention of Bob's affection for her.

The little gleam wavered and went out as she turned into the dinginess of Chapel Street to go home. Home. Home. What was the use of going home? Or what was the point of anything anymore? Bob wasn't there.

Chapter Sixteen

Every day Charlotta took the little 'uns to school, and every day brought them back. That young Terry was getting to be a proper handful. His speed and antics were no longer signs of prowess to be shared with your older brother. They had become *problems*, and there was no one who would talk to you about them. Supposing he was showing signs that he might develop into a good athlete, or a good footballer, or a good anything else, what on earth did it matter?

Dimly, Charlotta tried to do some of the things she might have done with Bob. Watching his football team she did not do. This was not due to any laziness on her part... it simply did not occur to her that anyone would care if she watched or not. Bob had seen her as an ally, as someone worthwhile. There wasn't anyone now. So you trudged to school with the little 'uns, and you trudged home afterwards. Teachers somehow didn't bother you anymore, and you never got reprimanded for anything. Not that it mattered. Bob wasn't there. There wasn't anyone.

You tried to help Ma of course, especially with the kids.

And on that particular evening, Ma was in a proper state. Tea was late (as usual). Pa was out, at some union meeting or something, and Ma was properly upset; it was about Terry, it turned out. Terry had been lent a football, and the football had got to go back to the boy who owned it, and the football had got to go back that night. The boy who owned it lived on the council estate on the far side of the school. It was out of the question for Terry to go across the cut in the dark. Even Pa was never keen on doing that, and in any case Pa was out.

Charlotta, grey-faced and despondent, noticed the name stencilled on the football. A boy from a rough family. Not a boy she knew, but someone that Bob had hoped would make it as reserve for his team. If Bob had been there....

Mrs Stiggins was worried. She was worried about what might happen to Terry if he didn't return the football the night he said he must. It was a neighbourhood where little boys did well to carry out the commands of bigger boys. Or else... . She was also, in her vague sort of way, afraid that Terry might be found guilty of stealing, and she was anxious to avoid more trouble and possible involvement with the police. Then, to do her justice, she had never actually crossed the cut at night, and she was trying to convince herself that it would be quite all right. It was only seven o'clock and it wouldn't take long. So would Charlotta go? After all, you almost thought of her as a grown-up now.

Charlotta took the ball and went.

Setting out on the journey wasn't too bad. You could see the schools, stuck out as they were in the middle of emptiness. Some lights were still on, as the cleaners finished going through the classrooms. Several of the cleaners were actually leaving as she passed the entrance, and two of them called out goodnight to her. 'Goodnight, love.' 'Goodnight, Lottie, be careful.'

Everyone knew Charlotta now. The cleaners followed more slowly, on their way back to their homes on the council estate. They commented on Charlotta's presence 'away from her own street'. The children from the council estate and Chapel Street mixed at school, but no one cared much about crossing the cut at night, and the cleaners speculated on the reasons for Charlotta's presence. ''Er ma shouldn't have let her come out on 'er own,' said one, and another hinted darkly that, 'That girl can't be up to any good, and so soon after her poor brother's death.'

Charlotta neither heard, nor, if she had heard, would she have minded. The emptiness of life without her brother had blotted out everything else. She hurried on. She reached the houses. The estate was bigger than she had thought. It was a cold night, and most of the children were indoors watching the telly. She had counted on finding someone who knew where the owner of the football lived. And indeed, finally she did discover what the address was. It then took a long time to find out where it was. Everyone she found to ask knew of course, but most of the directions given ('left at Mrs Larkin's, and mind the dog') were intelligible only to someone who already knew the estate. After much questioning and knocking, she arrived at the address. There was a light on, and the noise of the telly. This did not mean that anyone was in. But presently, with the help of yet one more household and a man on his way to the pub, she found the rightful owner, and was escorted back to deposit the football.

She would have been surprised if she had known the stir her arrival had caused. Bob's sister, Lottie. Come across the cut to bring back the football that little bugger Terry had borrowed. All by herself. On a night like this. Charlotta was quite unconscious of the number of people who had become aware of her arrival. She would have been even more surprised if she had known of their concern.

She had some difficulty in refusing the invitation of the footballer's mum to come in and get warm. The footballer's mum said that it was good of her to come, as next morning would have done just as well. Neighbours passed by and called out that it was misty across the cut.

Charlotta enquired what the time was, and found that it was much later than she had expected. The whole expedition had taken quite a time, and now all she wanted was to get back home.

As she turned to face the journey back, she could hardly help a little shiver of apprehension.

Chapter Seventeen

The moon had come up. Between the council estate and Chapel Street was a blanket of dense white mist. The schools were completely hidden. The moonlight served only to give an eerie glow to the whole. It was not a place to attract the most intrepid. Even Charlotta, frozen in her misery, began to feel afraid. If... if anyone....

It was no use allowing oneself thoughts like that. She must concentrate on keeping to the path. She took the way that would lead past the schools and plunged into the mist. Her feet found the path. She reached the entrance to the junior school. She passed that. She came to the back entrance to the big school where Bob had so often met them. Then, the schools behind her, she approached the place where a broken seat stood. She was almost far enough to see the street light at the end of Chapel Street. Her heart beat a bit faster as she realised how near safety she was.

And then it happened. It was what she had feared. Two figures, boys or men, rose in front of her. There was the sound of another behind her. For a fleeting, fleeting moment she thought she might scream for help. Or run? Or... or what? What use? For a moment only she halted. Then, terrified, knees atremble, she tried to walk on.

The next hour was one that all four were to remember, in different ways, for the rest of their lives.

'Lotta,' (Lotta? What Bob had always called her), 'Lotta, it's all right,' said a boy's voice. 'Lotta, we've been trying to see you, without all the school knowing. We've got something for you.'

The relief was too great. She recognised the voice. It was Bloxey, Bob's vice captain. Then everything she had been through, the death, the funeral, going back to school, the anxiety of the venture tonight, the final crashing fear – and then – safety. She did not faint. She burst into a flood of tears. She would have fallen over if Bob's friend had not flung his arm round her and held her up. She cried and cried. The boys drew her on to the seat, and there was a babble of voices as they explained. They were overwhelmed at having given her a fright. Idiots that they were. They were three of Bob's friends – Bloxey and Bob two and Jacko. They had heard that she was coming back across the cut on her own. They didn't like the idea of her coming back alone. The mother of one of them was a cleaner at the school, and she had told them about it. And they had lost track of her on the council estate and decided to come on and make sure she was all right. Oh, idiots that they had been. 'Lotta, can you forgive us?'

The oldest boy had sat down on the seat next to Charlotta. This was Bloxey. He put his arm comfortingly round her as she wept. Lotta, what idiots we were. Bob two and Jacko crowded round.

The mist had closed them in. They were in a world of their own. In the light, it would have been different. A vice captain of the under-fifteens would have felt silly comforting a weeping girl and mopping up her tears, and the other two would have said... but never mind. Charlotta wept and wept. Some wisdom beyond their years must have given them the realisation that this was helping her. Other people interfered with you too much. They stood or sat, quite quietly, while Charlotta wept.

Presently she grew calmer. The oldest boy introduced himself. 'You know me?' Yes, she knew him. This was Bloxey, one of Bob's friends. He went on, 'I am – I mean I *was* his vice captain.' There was a sudden huskiness in his voice. Charlotta suddenly felt that she wanted to help *him*. She knew what he was feeling. She was only surprised at someone else feeling so sad, as she did. Poor Bloxey.

It was all a scene that would have been utterly bewildering to any of their teachers or the world around them. The restrained Charlotta crying and crying. Bloxey, the determined vice captain of his football team, on the verge of tears himself. Bob two and that little runt Jacko standing sympathetically by. The darkness round them and the affection they had all shared for Bob had taken them into a world apart. It was a world where you were no longer governed by the conventions of everyday, or the fear of ridicule. You were all just yourselves. It was like what you read in stories, about being converted, or something like that. You liked the people you were with, and, too, you knew that they liked you.

The boys started talking. They had a box of chocolates for Lotta. Of course it couldn't make up for Bob, but they wanted to do something for her. It wasn't as smashing as the box she had from the police, which had already earned a place in legend. But it was a good kind. Would Lotta please take it? She did, feeling wonder at their kindness. How had they known that she liked this sort? Oh well, Bob had said that that was what he would get if he had the money, and it was the sort he'd bought Eileen when they went to the school concert.

Bloxey brought up the question that concerned them. How did Lotta feel? Did she feel that Bob was dead, or did she feel that he was still sort of *there*? They had all dreamt about him. Had she dreamt about him?

Charlotta sniffed and tried to answer. She wasn't sure. Yes, she had dreamt about him, but she meant she wasn't sure how much he was still there. He was dead, only... . Then she remembered that Bloxey's much loved gran had died the year before (and it was a sign of recovery that Charlotta could think of anyone outside Pa and Ma and the little 'uns) and it was therefore right to ask Bloxey how he felt. Well, said Bloxey, he had felt bad of course, being Gran's favourite, but in a funny sort of way it made you grow up, and... he sought for the words. The council estate where he lived was not very articulate, though he knew what he meant. 'It makes you *see* more. It was a bit like that being with Bob. If you like someone, really like them, then you can see other people's thoughts. Even in football,' he concluded seriously.

Charlotta wiped her eyes. Yes, she thought, Bloxey was right. You did feel like that. She turned to the other two. Had they liked anyone a lot and then had them die?

The bigger boy, Bob two, considered this. Yes, he had,

only it wasn't a person. 'It was our old dog. One ear stuck up and one didn't. He used to meet me after school. And I always think of him when I get to that corner. No,' he added, with the honesty he felt the situation demanded, 'I *used* to think of him, and I still do sometimes. I'd understand anyone else who had a dog they liked. Like they said in history, when that Mary Queen of Scotland had her head cut off, and the little dog had been hidden under her dress and wouldn't go away. I think they were rotten.' He finished with vehemence, adding himself to the long list of admirers of that dead queen.

They turned to the little boy, Jacko. Everyone knew about poor illegitimate little Jacko, pushed not unkindly but with indifference from one place to another, and now living with a slattern called Auntie, who might have been a real biological sister to his long vanished biological mother. No daddy of course had ever appeared, biological or otherwise.

Jacko spoke. It sounded as if he was frowning. No, he hadn't lost anyone. Not exactly hadn't lost anyone, but he had never had anyone long enough to mind, if he did lose them. 'I believe my mum went away, and then I was with Auntie, and then in a sort of home, no, two homes, and then I came to live with this auntie. It's...' he tried to explain. 'I get something to eat, most evenings, and she only hits me when I've been bad. It's all right. We don't like each other very much, but we don't have much to do with each other. She's out a lot. And she doesn't hit me every time I've done something bad, because she doesn't always know.' He paused, and then added, 'I'd like more to eat.'

Time passed. The four children went on talking. This was what life was meant to be somehow, when you could be yourself without having to push someone else out first. They pondered on the inner mysteries. What was worse, not having enough to eat, or not having anyone who minded about you? Or, thought Charlotta, not having anyone that you loved?

Presently this reminded her of her duties, and Ma and Pa and Terry and Patsy, and what Terry might have been up to. She must go home.

Bloxey had another question. 'Lotta, I don't know what to do. You know I'm going to be the captain of the football team?' Lotta knew. Bloxey went on. 'It was pretty difficult at first, when Bob was killed, and some of them wanted to put off matches. One of the people who made me go on was Bob's girl, Eileen. She was jolly good. Well, now I'm going to be captain, I ought to have a girl to sit next to at the end-of-term carol service. I wanted to ask you if you'd mind if I asked Eileen.'

Charlotta considered this. How nice it was to talk to people who understood the meaning of these things, not people like her mother, who hadn't any idea. Like a mediaeval ruler, she considered the matter. This was a dynastic alliance demanded by school fashion, and possibly affecting the standing of the football team. 'Yes,' she opined, 'Eileen is a good sport, and this would be a good thing.'

'I wanted to ask you,' said Bloxey, 'because Bob minded more about what you thought than he did about anyone else.'

New life was creeping into Charlotta. To hear that she had meant so much to Bob, from two people now, gave her fresh warmth. And the talk, and the consideration of the mysteries of life and death, had brought her out of herself.

Time had gone on. The mist was becoming less dense. It seemed as if there were people about in Chapel Street. It would be nice to go home.

They got up. The three boys escorted her, like courteous gentle knights, to the end of Chapel Street. There they turned, waved, and with raucous twentieth-century cries plunged into the thinning mists round the cut. Charlotta suddenly smiled as she remembered the old conversation with Bob... fancy, she *was* glad to be coming back into Chapel Street.

Chapter Eighteen

Chapel Street was its usual dilapidated self. To Charlotta, after her fright of an hour ago, it was a vision of beauty, unequalled in any glossy *Homes and Gardens* publication. Not only that, but the last hour had given her – what? Not a forgetfulness of Bob, but the feeling that there were still things to live for. She thought about Bob's beloved football team going ahead. She wondered if Eileen would go out with Bloxey. It would be nice to go up to the new school with the feeling that you had someone there to look out for you. She reflected on Jacko, poor Jacko. She recollected the feel of the bony hand. She must get Mum to find some old pullover or something and pass on. And Eileen and Bloxey would keep Bob's wonderful football team going. She wiped her eyes again as she thought of Bob and his talks about his team.

She noted an agitated figure ahead. Chapel Street not uncommonly had agitated figures. This one was outside The Rising Sun, and appeared to be trying to look into the window of the 's oon' bar. This was not a very hopeful procedure when you came to think of the murkiness of the window, or indeed of the murkiness of the scene likely to be revealed inside.

The agitated figure stopped jumping up and down and turned in relief as Charlotta approached. It was Tommy Tompkins.

Tommy was not a boy you particularly liked or feared. Normally you tried to avoid getting involved in his footling escapades. Tonight, with its feeling of compassion, friendliness, call it what you will, still on her, Charlotta stopped.

'Wot yer jumping about like that for?' she enquired.

Tommy explained. The little bleeder (Mrs Green's little boy) had got out and gone down one of the gardens and he was in there, down there, behind the bloody pub, and 'e wouldn't fucking well come out and his ma wouldn't 'arf be in a state.

Charlotta interpreted this, rightly, as an unexpected act of kindness on the part of Tommy. It would have been more in character if he had simply sloped off and gone indoors. Perhaps even Tommy could think of other people sometimes and take trouble. Why the little bleeder had been out in the street and/or in the care of Tommy was just one of those things without any obvious explanation.

'All right,' said Charlotta, 'I'll go and get him.' It was the tragedy that had turned Charlotta into a special person in Chapel Street, but perhaps the effects of the Jubilee still lingered and even Chapel Street was showing neighbourliness. Mavis was away in the maternity unit. Perhaps Mrs Green had felt sorry for Tommy left on his own. Perhaps this had prompted her to let him take her son out. In any case, something had to be done about the little boy, that was for certain, if you didn't want the whole street in an uproar, and 'them' alerted, 'them' being the whole apparatus of the welfare state, with its ambulances and sirens and police and doctors.

So Charlotta, her chocolates clasped firmly in one hand, went into The Rising Sun. It was a Thursday, and the drunks were wearing their fairly clean jackets, in honour of Mrs Smith. The landlord, surprised as he was to see Charlotta, would never again be as shocked as he had been at the initial visit of Mrs Letitia Smith. He rallied himself. Then he heard himself saying, quite casually, as if it were an everyday occurrence to have a visit from a little girl, 'What is it, my dear?'

Charlotta explained.

'Oh, we'll go and get the – the little kid out,' he answered. 'This way.'

He put a hand out and took hold of Charlotta's free hand. Hand in hand, the unlikely pair went out to 'the back' where indeed they found the wanted boy. Charlotta thanked the landlord and led the child back into the street. She told Tommy to take him home, and watched while he did so. Tommy handed the boy over to his mother, and apparently received something (sweets?) in return. He then came back and hurried indoors.

Charlotta became aware of another agitated figure. This was Mrs Smith, calling for 'Pussums'. Mrs Smith's cats, possibly because they were fed regularly, had longer lives than most of the Chapel Street cats. Charlotta assured her that Pussums couldn't be far away, and went on up the street.

Mrs Hoggins appeared at her front door. Now that folk

hero Hoggins was 'away', Mrs H had more opportunity to take part in anything that was going on in Chapel Street. She looked at Charlotta. ''Allo, dearie,' she said by way of greeting, and added thoughtfully, 'you're looking a bit rough.' True, Charlotta was looking unkempt, and her face was bleared and smeary. All the same, the tragic quietness had gone. Mrs Hoggins suddenly said, ''Ere, 'arf a mo.' She dashed indoors and reappeared holding a nearly full packet of biscuits. ''Ere you are, dear; if you don't want 'em, your ma'll be glad of 'em.'

Charlotta thanked her. Coo – that 'orrible 'Oggins lot giving you something. She gave a little chuckle.

She then thought of the lonely Tommy and decided to go in and see what he was up to. She knocked, not that it was really necessary. Her knock was answered by a carefree if somewhat mumbly voice saying, 'Come in.' She went in. Tommy and Pussums were sitting on the settee together, sharing sardines, crisps, biscuits, sweets and pop. Tommy, for once, was enjoying himself. 'You nicked them things,' observed Charlotta. This was not said in any minatory tone, but in the tone with which in politer streets inhabitants commented on the weather. 'It's colder today.' 'You nicked them'. Tommy, his mouth being too full for speech, nodded. He indicated that Charlotta was welcome to join the party, but she refused.

She made for home. Bob's things, she was thinking, would be a bit big for Jacko, but Ma had better let her take that sweater Bob had had last year. Fancy Tommy Tompkins looking after that little boy, and giving a party to Pussums. She almost giggled. And Eileen Radford and Bloxey would look out for you when you went up to big

261

school. That was a relief. And Pa might be home now – yes, there was his bike. And somehow the mysterious processes of 'the welfare' (aided, unknown to the Stiggins family, by Mr Alfred Smith) had once more provided a telly and the licence. There would be a nice programme on, and a hot drink to look forward to.

Charlotta found that she was looking at the street with new eyes. It didn't look so bad when you thought about it. Mavis's new curtains were smashing. Of course, it wasn't like Jubilee Street, and you bet that people like Mr and Mrs Alfred Smith had posh houses too, and probably the probation officer and the social worker, though they couldn't have had much time at home as they were always in Chapel Street.

Chapel Street wasn't all that bad. Even if you didn't always feel sort of *exalted*, and above everything, like tonight, you'd remember how you'd felt.

'Coo-ee, Mum, coo-ee, Dad. I'm back.'

Number 49

There are three chapters in this book, and the chapter headings are all significant, all meaning something in lives

Chapter One   Prehistoric

Chapter Two   Contemporary

Chapter Three   Eternal

Chapter One

Prehistoric

T hree of us there were – High Street and the Cornhill and me, Chapel St, all near the centre of the town.

Near the centre of town? We *were* the centre of the town.

I can date this period by telling you it was when that vet, up the other end of the street, was still going to work with a horse and trap. He treated motors as if they were a sort of bastard horse and if he stopped to speak to some passer-by, he naturally expected what was behind him to pull up and wait. The people living here were two in number. This is just the right number to be the hero and heroine, which I know a story has to have. I will call him Bertie Foster. He had a really fine voice and if you were doing something for charity, he never charged you anything! Just for the good of your cause. He would tell you that during the war (the First World War) he'd been in charge of Russian POWs and how they could sing! Almost a choir

265

by themselves. (I wonder what happened to them afterwards.)

Bertie finished the war in hospital, gassed, and came out with the hospital matron as his housekeeper. His housekeeper the heroine of this story? Not at all. Just his housekeeper and a very good one at that, as retired hospital matrons often are. It was a large house; twelve rooms, and she efficiently shut off the seven rooms they didn't use. Bertie taught music in that lovely room, on the left as you go in, with the fireplace and marble mantelpiece. They had a large bedroom each on the first floor, and what had started as a little dressing room that a later generation would make into a kitchen. She sometimes wondered whether to put servants up in the third floor. You can understand exactly that kindly respectable well endowed household; a card that turned up later addressed to Bertie, 'from your musical Chinese niece'.

Some readers may understand what I described in what I call... prehistoric.

Chapter Two

Contemporary

T he time passes, and both Bertie and his housekeeper die. By then there are servants on the top floor. Some people still alive may remember this.

However, there are Bertie's executors (solicitors still working in the town) faced with the sale of a large house, twelve rooms, four staircases, two toilets and one bathroom. Furthermore I am 'listed'.

I was interested in a conversation I had with the High Street, one, you may remember of us three streets. As it has some of the banks, it hears things that the other two of us don't. I knew a man seriously interested in buying number 49. He was a builder, a carpenter by trade. I shall call him Charles Turner, not a bad name for a carpenter. I liked him – he was very straightforward, though it was a long time before I met his wife. She worked in an office at the other end of the street, possibly in health or education or somewhere where you organised other people's lives (or tried to), a bit like Bertie Foster's housekeeper. But it's Charles Turner that my colleague in the High Street told me about. Charles, as well as being a good carpenter, always kept his bank manager up to date, so he seeks an interview with his bank manager. This takes place. It's difficult to identify the actual bank manager as they all act the same. I will refer to him as Mr Graham, which might even be his name. 'Oh, yes, Mr Turner,' says Mr Graham. 'It's very unfortunate that the government has just clamped down on overdrafts. Very unfortunate, I can see the place has potential.' (Bank managers have professional elocution lessons, on how to say things regrettably, especially the word 'potential'.) Charles sensibly says nothing. Mr Graham then asks, as if he didn't already know the answer, where Mr Turner's wife's account is, which leads to the conclusion that a transfer of a new account to Mr Graham's bank might mean that Mr Graham might be able to authorise an overdraft. Just a small one. Readers will hardly be surprised to know that this is an initial miracle. The next miracle occurs at the auction. The auctioneer stresses that I am 'listed' and most of the buyers depart. Charles makes a modest bid. The auctioneer knows Charles well enough to know that his modest bid will be honoured, and I am immediately knocked down (metaphysically) to Mr and Mrs Turner. This looked very promising. Our friend the High Street told us all about the man. There was that interview with Mr Graham, when Robert was granted an overdraft. We reckon Mr Graham was surprised when he had to honour his promise. No one would have dreamed of selling such a slice of property for so little. (Talk about jam on it.) So I was ready for Robert.

The other end of the street told me about Robert's' wife. A good hard-working soul, extremely intelligent; surprising how many things seemed to have people going to her office. What with her intelligence and his ability, and his commonsense, I thought and most of the street agreed with me that these were going to be the hero and the heroine. Particularly when they celebrated one of those multi-year weddings. They are called all sorts of things, and this, for no observable reason apart from custom, was silver.

Angela is the name of Robert's wife, one of the things Angela does is in one of the local chapels, which is where the Turners go. So this, I am told by the other end of the street, was quite an occasion. Nice as Angela is, there are some of the chapels who think a lot of themselves. The son of one of them had managed to come home from boarding school, and Robert had given him sandwiches for the journey back and taken him to the station.

I am making a lot of something trivial, but something trivial may turn into something significant. It's not always easy to spot what is significant. So there we are. Either Robert or Angela, or both, will attract people to come. The end of the 'do' at the chapel saw the last stray waiting for transport. Typical.

As I said, there we are. Robert had plenty to do. He was faced with a bathroom and a separate WC, a small kitchen, two diminutive sculleries and a palace. The first thing was a reasonable kitchen, while Angela did her office job.

Interesting people like the retired admiral came in. Some who drifted in were on their way to worthwhile efforts. The woman who worked for Something International? The headmaster of Something School? The single parent who would bring her son up so devotedly? The foreign girl who didn't realise that au pairs were expected to work? If you want an icon for that period it was a large green settee given to Angela by a member of her congregation. People stayed for one night or two, or a really long period of four days. There were also financial developments as Charles finished turning some of the twelve rooms into flats. Flats that each had a toilet and a bathroom! The leases were gradually sorted out.

And the garden developed. The pears were all scooped out – that was by the squirrels. And cats came, including Pussy (dear Pussy) who somehow crossed the dual carriageway at the back, probably in the night hours. Flats had tenants, and some of them became part of the household, some with their own cats and children. A home with twelve rooms and only two residents attracts newcomers. The first to get instated we will refer to as Anatole, a seventeen-year-old, ex-beatnik, ex-public school. He looked at the home with admiration – with admiration not unmixed with his own idea of what he would get these friendly people to turn it into. He was the one who turned up at our wedding.

Have I told you that my owners are also 'riparian owners'. There is a stream way beyond our garden. Charles let some enterprising chap do a dig. Didn't find much that you could sell. But it showed how much had accumulated – general rubbish – over the years since our stream had been the house's drinking water. And next door, number 51, used to be The Rising Sun. How much water from the stream...? Or was it The Seven Stars? To get back to my story, a story as I have already mentioned has to have a hero and a heroine. (Charles Turner, good, solid, kind-hearted Charles and his wife, good, kind-hearted, organising wife?) But the hero and the heroine need to have some close background. And why was she always up so late, talking to the ex-beatnik and the others who followed him? I could tell you the story of the green settee and the people who would be found who had turned up in the night. And how often was Angela out after midnight, taking people to the 2.30 a.m. train or taking them to where the town ended and you were out on the road to get a lift to wherever? And my friend, East Street (not quite like the three of us, but later in history) told me about the way that... . Oh well, East Street is a chatty little street. It had its time when the railway came here, and you still get little bits of information, though it's not quite like us three. A place gets a character, doesn't it? I like to think St Mary's Street has been used for helping people – lepers, or friars or something. And that back extension when the Turners came had been a home for fallen women, operating as a laundry. There was a row of metal stands where they put the irons. The window bars, oddly, had been straight up and down, and narrow enough to keep the inmates in. A friend of Angela's, who did a lot of good work in the town, said that her grandmother had been there, but being slight was able to get out.

Anatole the ex-beatnik... to introduce the childless Turners to a whole lot of people. Perhaps some of their children are still consulting the Turners about their problems? But back to the ex-beatnik. Anatole carefully considered the new situation. He would address Mr Turner in respectful but comradely fashion, by his forename Charles. He looked appraisingly at good hard-working Angela. She seemed to be the organiser in any situation. 'Angela,' he said. 'Oh no, Angel.' Perhaps he had done some Roman history. 'Angel,' he repeated. He combined this with calling her, in private, a bastard. Good hard-working Angela Turner had not been addressed like this for many years. Angel? You bastard? Anyway, she rather fell for it. The young followed the ex-beatnik's example, and soon the whole town was addressing her as Angel; after all she did a lot of good.

The ex-beatnik period was when a lot of people passed through a lot who stayed two days? Twelve months? Anatole's girlfriend. She had not been expelled from her school, just asked not to come back. The boy who had been expelled along with Anatole. The one who hadn't been expelled, only been demoted from prefect.

There was a large green settee in the kitchen, seemed to be a token for 'anyone welcome here'. Anatole felt that he had a vision – on the road so to speak. Were some people finding a view of what they might become? Or like the au pair, realising with surprise that people expected you to work?

Chapter Three

Eternal

Now I will tell you about the ones who became the real hero and heroine. Yes, they're here. Already here, and we've never noticed them? The tenants of one of the flats that are being occupied while Charles finishes them. A mother and son. Mr and Mrs Stone. A mother and her son as hero and heroine.

He has been a cook in the navy. In fact, serving a rather important military establishment in Paris in 1945. But known because he was admitted to the very exclusive nightclub (as he explains to me, those girls, tall as they were, were hungry – that's how I got in). His mother is in her third marriage. Her naval husband, Harry's father, was killed in the war, and the second. Her present one, a plain responsible night caretaker of one of those factories on the Bristol Road. And Mrs Stone, the kind of woman that keeps her political parties going. Sales of work, canvassing for the council, believing it all. There she is in the party photographs, in an unfashionable hat, but wearing gloves. One evening while the little crowd is waiting outside the Town Hall for the results, a young man says her party won't work. So she clouts him with her handbag and that ignorant young man calls a policeman. Ignorant young man – lucky not to get *himself* arrested. Our police know who is who.

The time comes when she will have to end her life with a few days in hospital. I sit with her for a couple of hours while we wait for the ambulance. And all those two hours she rambles on without a single unpleasant word for anyone!! Had all her life really been spent in such pleasant waters? With such good-natured colleagues?

The son, the ex-cook for top military, has a range of – well, colleagues, as they all become, Charles and Angela, and the ex-beatniks, and the university students. And when Angela's aging father comes, it is this son who is obviously ready to help out. Get coffee, as you are both out? Get dinner for all of us? Father on his own – we'll have a game of cribbage. We learnt that in that navy.

So there you are. The real hero and heroine. Mrs Stone and her son, the ex-cook from the navy.

The next century dawns. The real values that persisted? The squirrels? The cats? The elderly, like Bertie and his housekeeper and father? The hard-working, middle-aged, like Angela and Charles? The young and visionary? Like Anatole and his girlfriend?

Perhaps Harry and his mother were the real hero and heroine because they listened and did not repeat.

Other people live here now. One I rather have hopes of.